Secrets will Link

Secrets will Link

A Chattertowne Mystery

K.B. Jackson

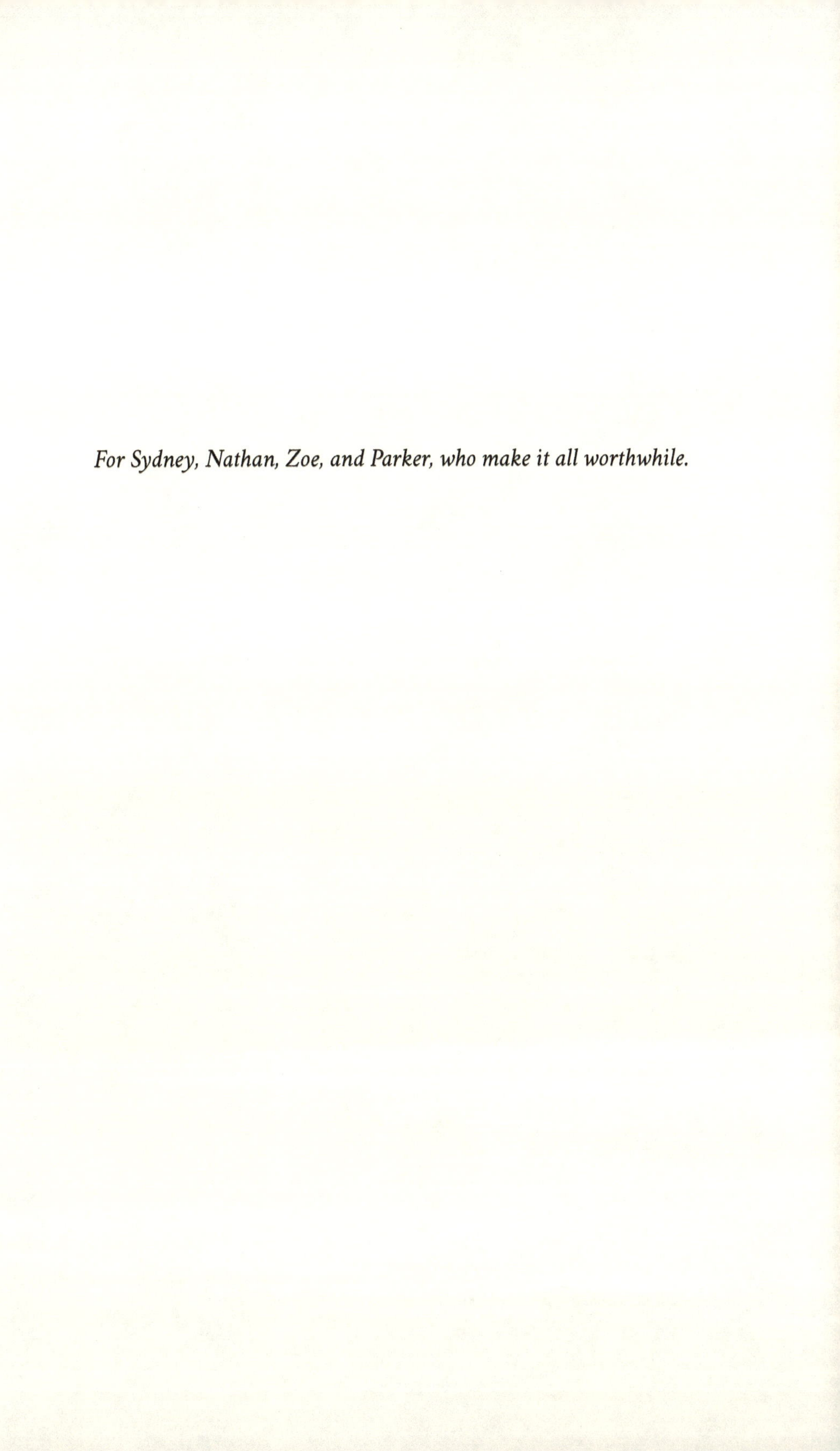

For Sydney, Nathan, Zoe, and Parker, who make it all worthwhile.

Praise for Secrets Will Link

"The mystery was executed with all that I enjoy in a whodunit with visually descriptive narrative, engaging dialogue, an eclectic cast of characters, a small-town atmosphere and a body or two that kept me both intrigued and in suspense as the multi-plot story unfolded."—Dru Ann Love, Dru's Book Musing

You are cordially invited
To the wedding of
Vivienne O'Connell
And
Lacey Kimball
Sunday, April 13
4pm
Chattertowne Golf & Country Club
Semi-formal attire
(Green preferred)
RSVP ASAP
(Sorry for the late notice)

Chapter One

It was a well-established fact that murder ruined weddings. A real vibe killer, so to speak.

That's why I took a deep breath and silently vowed *not* to murder my sister—one of the brides—despite her egregious choice for my Maid of Honor dress.

I gaped at my reflection. The dress she'd selected was the kind of hideous that signified deeply rooted resentments and grudges, borne out in offensive oodles of chartreuse tulle and taffeta that gave my body the shape of a loofah and drained all signs of life from my complexion.

"Is this payback for something I did to you when we were kids?"

"What do you mean? I think it's pretty."

I narrowed my gaze at her through the display mirror in the middle of Kayla's Bridal Boutique. It was like one of those multipaned funhouse mirrors: there was no escaping the horrific sight, no matter which direction I turned.

I glanced at Kayla, owner of Chattertowne's sole bridal shop, who held up her hands in mock surrender. She'd joked earlier about how many bridezillas she'd encountered in the five years she'd owned the shop, and how she'd learned when not to get involved in sticky situations like arguing with the bride about her selection of bridesmaid dresses.

"It's too late anyway." Vivienne pushed out her lower lip and twisted her platinum blonde hair the way she'd always done since she was little. "The wedding is days away. There's not enough time to get another dress."

"Mom, help me out, here," I pleaded.

My mother, Claudine O'Connell, was the most refined dresser I knew, so I figured she must have approved the purchase sight unseen. She flared her nostrils like she smelled something putrid. Unsurprising, considering I looked like I'd been dunked in a vat of radioactive toxic waste.

"Vivienne, I know you want this wedding to feel very springlike, but this dress does make Audrey look like something you might find scattered across an alfalfa pasture."

"She means I look like cow poop."

Vivienne emitted a gasp of either exasperation or offense. "You do not! You look like lime meringue."

"Not helping your case. I've seen the other bridesmaid dresses you chose. They're not terrible. Why can't I wear what they're wearing?"

It was bad enough that Vivienne and her fiancée, Lacey Kimball, had given us only six weeks to pull together a golf-themed wedding. The monstrosity of a dress she'd selected for me to wear made me want to shove my head in the hole on the 18th green at the Chattertowne Golf and Country Club where, according to the evites—another aspect of the rushed nuptials my mother found distasteful and tacky—the loving couple would be "eternally linked on the links."

Add to that the fact they'd chosen a Nickelback song for their first dance as a married couple, well, it was all par for the course.

Pun intended.

"You know how important this is to Lacey." Vivienne's lower lip trembled like she was about to cry. "And to me. You're my maid of honor. I don't want you looking like all the other bridesmaids. You're my only sister."

Ugh. She was playing me like the back nine at Augusta National, and I was defenseless against her tactics. I'd spent my whole life, from the time she was born, in protector mode. That was exacerbated by her near drowning as a toddler on my watch. Whatever Vivienne wanted or needed, I'd always felt a responsibility to make it happen.

Especially when she looked up at me with those big golden eyes, which was most of the time since she was a petite 5'2" and barely more than a hundred pounds, and I was a good four inches taller.

I closed my eyes and reopened just one, in a partial squint. Still atrocious.

"Is this really the one you want?" It was her day, after all.

"It reminds me of those old Southern dresses."

"Viv, those old Southern dresses are considered in poor taste. They romanticize antebellum plantation culture."

Her mouth formed an O. "I certainly don't want to do that. I was just thinking since the Masters tournament is in Georgia, and when I think of Georgia, I think of *Gone with the Wind*, a floofy dress fits the vibe. But I guess when you think about it, *Gone with the Wind* also romanticizes that era. Well, shoot."

A spark of hope flickered. "So we can look for another dress?"

Her shoulders slumped. "Kayla, do you have anything else in green that would work? I know we're pretty much out of time. Maybe something in the back?"

"I still don't understand why it must be green," muttered our mother. "How about a nice rose or lilac?"

Vivienne clucked her tongue. "Because the Masters golf tournament is all about the quest for the green jacket!"

"You don't even golf!" I said.

"I do now. Lacey's teaching me. Couples who play together stay together."

"I'll be sure to cross-stitch that on a pillow as a wedding gift."

My mother shot me a look. Like the hundreds of other times she'd given the same silent warning, I shut my trap.

Kayla tapped her mouth with her perfectly manicured finger. "I have a couple ideas. Let me work on it, and I'll give you a call later today."

"Thanks, Kay. You're the best." Vivienne stood and swung her purse over her shoulder.

On an average day, I was a good four inches taller and at least thirty pounds heavier than Viv's five-foot-two-inch petite frame, but standing on the platform in three-inch heels, looking like a head of iceberg lettuce, I felt even more cumbersome next to her than usual.

My instincts must have been spot on, because our mother scanned me up and down, wearing a pinched expression. "Audrey, are you coming with us to the country club? We have a meeting with the caterer in twenty minutes."

"I'll have to meet you there. I need to stop by the office and grab a few things."

Vivienne clutched me tightly, giving my upper arm a painful squeeze in the process. "Hurry," she whispered in my ear. "I need backup, or she'll take over the whole thing."

I rubbed my arm as the two of them hustled out the door.

I wasn't worried about Vivienne. She could hold her own.

Our mother hadn't been raised in high society—Chattertowne didn't really have one—but she'd always played the part and wanted us to do the same. Unfortunately, Vivienne and I were a constant source of disappointment in this respect. Me, most of all, despite the fact I'd spent my entire life trying to toe the line, follow the rules, and chase the gold star.

Viv, on the other hand, didn't bother. She was a signal left, turn right kind of person.

The wedding, despite the fact one of the brides had recently been released from the Washington Corrections Center for Women—or, as Vivienne called it, lady jail—was my mother's best hope for making a splash on the pages of my employer, the *Chattertowne Coastal Current* newspaper, where I was the head investigative reporter. Technically, I was the only investigative reporter. Times were lean in the newspaper world.

Not that a blurb in a local paper with a circulation of fifteen thousand or so was going to make anyone famous, but Vivienne's wedding had a Very Important Person on the guest list that could possibly get the event on the pages of the *Seattle Times*, the *Los Angeles Times*, and TMZ.

Chattertowne's own Onyx Carpenter had been featured in *TIME* magazine's 100 most Influential People (twice), had her own TV talk show, a popular skin care line, and had written a bestselling memoir titled *Between a Rock and a Hard Rock Place* about her rise from girl next door to model to wife of Bonzerkind's lead singer Meacham Fields and titan of her own business empire.

Onyx had been a Chattertowne High cheerleader with both Vivienne and me. She was on the squad with me when I was a senior, and she was a junior.

Onyx was elected co-captain for her senior year, while Vivienne was one of only two girls who'd been selected to join as freshmen that year.

Onyx had left for L.A. at the end of her graduation summer and never looked back. She did still occasionally keep in touch with her friends back home, including her old cheer pals, the O'Connell sisters. It was merely luck that Vivienne's wedding coincided with Onyx's planned visit to Chattertowne for her induction into the Chattertowne High Hall of Fame.

Rumor had it that Meacham might also accompany her on the trip, since Bonzerkind was about to have a brief tour hiatus, and if there was one thing Chattertowne excelled at, it was churning gossip through the rumor mill.

All the more reason to nix wearing a dress that made me look like both of Cinderella's stepsisters rolled into one. If a photo of me wearing that ensemble ended up on every tabloid website in the world, I might actually kill her.

* * *

I drove through downtown to the *Chattertowne Coastal Current* offices, housed in an old brick building overlooking the Jeanetta River. About twenty miles inland from Puget Sound, Chattertowne was nestled in a valley at the foothills of the spectacular Cascade Mountain Range north of Seattle. Because the Jeanetta was an important shipping route, the town also had a marina near the city hall building, but I tried to avoid that area if at all possible.

Spring was attempting to arrive, despite the groundhog's warning that it might be delayed by six weeks. Actually, in Chattertowne, we had a ground*frog*, not a groundhog. Every February second, the mayor hosted a giant jumping frog (was there any kind of frog other than a jumping frog?) named—what else—Kermit and announced what the supposedly prescient amphibian has declared about the weather forecast. Kermit's accuracy rate was somewhere between a fortune cookie and an animatronic fortune teller.

When I got to my office, I had a visitor waiting for me.

"I thought I locked my door."

"Maybe you did, maybe you didn't."

I set my purse on my desk. "Is breaking and entering no longer illegal?"

Chattertowne police chief Cole Loveland leaned back in the chair and plopped his cowboy boots up on my desk. My instinct was to knock them off, but if he was in my office, there was a good chance he had a story for me. News had been slow, and I couldn't afford to miss an opportunity. As it was, circulation was down 20% and sinking like a tee shot off the 12th at Augusta…aka to the bottom of the Raes Creek water trap.

"I didn't break in. Anderson was passing by, and he has a master key."

Nicholas Anderson, head editor of the *Current*, had been my advisor on the Chattertowne High weekly paper and still taught English part-time at the school, my alma mater.

Because the newspaper was in an old brick building, built back when open concept wasn't popular, we all had our own offices. My office was originally one large space, but it had been subdivided with a thin wall of sheetrock. The other side of the shared wall was Keith, our sports reporter.

If it were up to Anderson, I wouldn't even have an office that locked. He often waxed poetic about the good old days when the newsroom was buzzing and reporters fed off each other's energy.

My colleagues consisted mostly of seasonally depressed decaf soy latte drinking man-bun wearing millennials (Viv likes to say I'm a millennial by birth but a boomer by personality), overly-cologned IT engineers, and Keith, who poured Zipfizz drink powder straight down his throat like it was a Pixie Stix three times a day.

I preferred privacy and quiet over matching that energy, thank you very much.

"So, tell me, do you have a story for me? A lead?"

He tipped back his cowboy hat and scratched his head, further mussing his dark blond hair. "I was hoping *you* could help *me* out for a change."

He ignored my indignant scoff.

"On two things, actually."

"That's not how this works. You tell me about the thing, I write about the thing. It's a symbiotic relationship."

His left brow shot up, presumably at my use of the word *relationship.* "Symbiotic or parasitic?"

This time, he allowed himself a satisfied smirk in response to my indignant cry.

"As I'm sure you're aware, Onyx Carpenter is coming to town, and word on the street is that Meacham Fields is joining her."

"By *the street,*" I made air quotes, "do you mean my sister?"

Vivienne was Cole's administrative assistant.

"I don't have the manpower for dealing with the horde that a celebrity might bring, much less two celebrities of their magnitude."

"I still don't get what you want from me."

"Vivienne is off for the next couple weeks for the wedding and honeymoon, and she's already informed me she's blocked my number until the day she's due back at work. I need someone to let me know when Onyx hits town, so I can stay on top of things. At least as much as I can."

It was Tuesday, and the wedding was scheduled for Sunday afternoon at 4 p.m., or whenever the Masters champ had finished slipping on their green jacket.

On Monday morning, Vivienne and her new wife, Lacey, were scheduled to leave for a camping trip near Leavenworth. Washington, not Kansas. One was a Bavarian-themed town in the Cascade Mountains, the other was home to a penitentiary, and Lacey had spent more than enough time at one of those. Also, the conditions of her parole required her to remain in the state, so Hawaii or Cancun were off the table, honeymoon-wise.

"I'm headed to the golf club after this, so I'll see what I can find out from Vivienne. What else?"

He blinked at me. "What else, what?"

"You said you needed my help for two things."

"Oh!" He removed his boots from my desk and planted them on the floor. "I've been asked to give a talk to a bunch of high school kids tonight—"

"Hard pass."

"You haven't even heard what I was going to say."

"I'm washing my hair."

He tilted his head. "Looks clean enough to me."

"I think I'm allergic to anyone under the age of eighteen. I was an awkward teenager, and it wasn't fun to hang around other teens back then. Why would I choose to do it now?"

He gave me a skeptical look. "What do you mean, you were an awkward teenager? Vivienne said you both were cheerleaders with Onyx."

"I was only a cheerleader because I like football. I barely made the squad my senior year. You've seen how klutzy I am."

"I have. I assumed that was a more recent development. A diminishment of your sense of balance as you've aged."

"Nope."

He waved his hands dismissively. "No matter. I need you."

I stifled the *Austin Powers* quote about turntables turning that Vivienne and I used against each other often. "What is this talk you're doing, and why do you need me?"

"Wylie Barrett has asked me to talk to his 3F kids about the dangers of drugs and alcohol."

In addition to being one of Lacey's groomsmen (bridesmen?) Wylie was the Chattertowne High golf coach and also the head of the local chapter of 3F, an organization created to provide a safe, engaging environment for kids to socialize while learning to set goals for their futures. The three Fs were fun-forward-focus.

One of Vivienne's wedding activities was a best ball scramble golf tournament—bridal party vs bridal party—on Friday, leading up to the rehearsal dinner that evening. I'd decided I could use some pointers from Wylie, who was undisputedly the best golfer around. He'd even briefly made it onto the tour.

Calling me a novice golfer would be a generous description since the extent of my experience was hitting balls at Top Golf while downing a pitcher of margaritas, but Holden Villalobos was Lacey's Best Man, and I really, *really* wanted to beat him—ahem—them.

"Count me in."

Cole's left eyebrow shot up. "Really?"

"Sure, why not?"

"All the reasons you initially gave? Allergies to children and whatnot."

"Pssh. I'll take a Benadryl. It'll be fine."

"I've never done one of these talks. Back in Jackson Hole, we had a designated officer who did stuff like this. I need you for moral support."

Likely story. "And?"

"And…I could use some good press."

Bingo. "What's the issue? You haven't been getting any bad press that I've seen. As a matter of fact, I wrote an article last week about the county council giving you that award next month."

He shifted in his seat.

I narrowed my gaze. "What?"

"Nothing."

"Well, you won't look at me, so I don't believe you."

"Off the record?"

"Sure."

"I'm…I'm thinking of running for County Sheriff."

I sprang to my feet. "What? Since when?"

His gaze widened as he took in my reaction. "I've been thinking about it for a while."

I pursed my lips. "Let me guess. You've been thinking about it almost as long as you've been dating Miranda."

The pink that crept up his neck to his ears was answer enough. "We aren't dating, we're seeing each other."

"Same thing."

"It's not. And that's not why I'm running."

"So you *are* running."

"I don't know." He threw his hands in the air. "Maybe."

"And Miranda has *nothing* to do with this." Cynicism dripped from my tongue.

He shrugged. I took that as an admission of guilt.

I'd never say it to Cole, but Miranda Gadling Dodd was a social climber of the highest order. As a junior, she'd been co-captain of the cheer squad with Onyx the year I'd been on it, and she'd made my life a living hell under the guise of hazing.

All through high school, she'd dated a guy named Hank Dodd, who was the captain of the football team. She'd been obsessed with Hank and their status as Chattertowne High's "it" couple, but he'd broken up with her so he could be single on his graduation trip to Cancun.

They reunited at a Fourth of July party, but Hank broke up with Miranda again when she left for college at San Diego State University. It must have been one heck of a goodbye party, because she showed up on Hank's doorstep the following May—Mother's Day to be exact—holding his son. They were married a month later.

The marriage fizzled when Miranda realized Hank wasn't going anywhere in life…well, nowhere she wanted to go, anyway. He was content drinking beer at Louden's Tavern and living his blue-collar life. Miranda preferred mimosas and Pilates, even before Pilates had become the preferred exercise for the country club set. Along with pickleball, of course.

Miranda was one of Vivienne's bridesmaids, which meant I'd been spending a lot more time with her of late, and I hadn't particularly enjoyed it. She had a penchant for backwards compliments but feigned ignorance when called out on it.

Cole huffed and got to his feet. "I'll come by and pick you up around six-thirty. Does that work?"

"Won't Miranda be jealous?"

He said nothing as he walked out of my office, slowly shaking his head.

* * *

On my way to the club restaurant to meet my mother and Viv, I popped into the pro shop.

A guy in his early to mid-twenties greeted me from behind the counter. "Afternoon. You look like you could use some gear. We've got a sale on our FJ Bel Airs. Today only. Ten percent off. They never go on sale."

"I have no idea what that is."

He pointed at the wall of shoes. "FootJoy. Bel Air is one of our most popular styles."

I picked up the shoe and turned it over. One hundred and ninety dollars. I was no math whiz, but even I could figure out that one ninety minus ten percent was one seventy-one. "They may give my feet joy, but my wallet will be screaming for mercy."

"Don't come crying to me when you realize you let a smoking deal slip through your fingers."

I walked to the counter. He was about five foot seven, and I was pretty sure I weighed more than him. His bushy hair hit just above the collar of his polo shirt and was the same ashy blond color as his wimpy attempt at a mustache. He had a slight gap between his front two teeth. On his chest was a silver nametag that read *Ike*.

I slapped my hands on the counter. "Ike. May I call you Ike?"

"That's my name."

"Ike. I'm looking for Wylie Barrett. Seen him?"

Ike blanched. "Are you police?"

"What? No. Why would you ask that?"

He shrugged. "No reason. Uh, he's out with one of his students."

"Any idea when he might be back?"

Ike tugged at his collar. His neck was pink. "Uh, not really."

I considered myself subpar when it came to reading body language, but I could read Ike like a neon sign. He was lying. Or something. Maybe not lying, but he was definitely uncomfortable with my line of questioning.

I put that in my mental back pocket for later.

"If you see him, tell him Audrey O'Connell was looking for him. I have a question for him, but I'll see him tonight at 3F."

"Will do."

Something was off with the dude. I didn't have time to process the strange interaction, however, because I was headed back into the lion's den, aka wedding planning central.

* * *

Cole and I arrived at Chattertowne Methodist at 6:45. The event was scheduled to begin at 7 p.m., but the multipurpose room of the church, which was used for everything from pickup basketball games to children's musicals to funeral receptions, was already buzzing with activity.

I glanced at Cole, whose eyes were wide open and unblinking. A bead of sweat trickled down the side of his face. He'd always been cool as a cucumber. Who knew his greatest fear was talking to a bunch of hormonal adolescents?

"You okay?"

He swiped his forehead with the back of his hand. "Mm hmm."

I scanned the room. "I don't miss this at all."

Several boys were shooting hoops while a gaggle of girls stood to the side watching. Their appreciative stares were interrupted only by whispers and giggles. Another circle of boys and girls sat crisscrossed on the floor, textbooks open in front of them. Nine out of the ten wore glasses.

One of the bespectacled boys from the study circle gazed longingly toward the corner where a girl was doing some sort of dance or exercise routine, kicking her long legs to the beat of whatever music was playing in her earbuds.

I didn't blame him. She was beautiful, with her long brown hair and medium olive complexion that offset her greenish-blue hooded eyes. She had high cheekbones, a prominent forehead, full lips, and the kind of upturned pixie nose I'd envied so much as a kid, I once tried to fasten my own nose into that position with Scotch tape.

One of the boys standing near the basketball hoop made a right-handed bank shot, to the delight of onlookers. He waved and called to the girl doing the exercise routine. "Lee, did you see that?" He was tall—at least six feet—and had wavy brown hair that flopped in front of his blue eyes.

She continued her routine without response.

"Laveda!"

Once again, no response.

He jogged in the girl's direction, stopping to fist-bump a brown haired boy with Down Syndrome. "My man! So glad you're here!"

The boy smiled. "Jack, are you going to win the state championship this year?"

"I'm gonna try my best."

"I know you can do it! I believe in you."

"Thanks, man."

"I'll save you a seat, okay, Jack?"

"You do that! I'll be right back." As he jogged past us, he threw a strained smile at Cole and flipped his hair. "How's it going?"

Cole gave him a head nod. "Good to see you, Jack."

"Who was that?"

He blew out a long breath. "That's Jack Dodd."

"Jack D—" I paused. "Wait, is that Miranda's son?"

"Yep."

"What's he like?"

"Good kid. Stays out of trouble. Gets good grades. Captain of the golf team. He's got some pretty impressive scholarship prospects if this season goes well. I worry about the pressure he's under, though… from Miranda, from his dad, from Wylie, but especially himself. I keep telling Miranda she needs to ease up. The kid is hard enough on himself. She's got really high hopes for him to make it onto the PGA tour, though."

"And how does he feel about you *seeing* his mother?" I made air quotes.

"I haven't asked. I can tell you he's always been respectful. Actually, I met Miranda because of Jack. He started a chapter of Safety First at Chattertowne High and invited me to one of their events."

"What's Safety First? Some sort of sex ed program?"

"No. It's a program that encourages abstinence from drugs, while also providing information for harm reduction to prevent addiction and or death in the case a student does choose to use."

"I like that approach."

"Yeah. He also volunteers at Sunrise Peak once a month."

Sunrise Peak was an assisted living facility at the north end of town.

"Wow. Sounds like he really does have a lot on his shoulders."

I turned back to look at Jack, who had joined the pretty girl in the corner. He brushed a hair out of her face and tucked it behind her ear. Her brows were knitted with worry, and her mouth was turned down. She leaned toward him to whisper in his ear, and then pulled away to look at his face. He gave her an earnest nod. She gave him a relieved smile and hugged him. I glanced at the studying boy who'd been watching her. His shoulders slumped.

"What's the story there?" I nodded toward the couple.

"That's Jack's girlfriend, Laveda Volkova. Her family immigrated from Ukraine about four years ago. She's also on the golf team. She's reigning district champion in the girls' division. Wylie's their coach."

As if on cue, a harried Wylie Barrett rushed through the double doors with arms full of pink pastry boxes from Abigail's bakery.

"Donuts have arrived!" His voice echoed through the room.

The kids stampeded toward the table where he'd placed the boxes.

Wylie was handsome in high school, but now, in his thirties, he was even more so. He was about 6'2", fit, tan, and had sun-streaked highlights in his curly brown hair.

No wonder he'd snagged Onyx Carpenter before she was famous. No one ever knew why they broke up—a rarity for Chattertowne. Usually, the true story surfaced in the gossip mill eventually. One day toward the end of the summer she just left town—leaving Wylie behind too—and headed to Los Angeles.

Wylie caught sight of Cole and made his way toward us, hand outstretched. "Chief Loveland. Thank you so much for taking the time."

They shook hands.

"Cole, please. And it's my pleasure. You know Audrey O'Connell?"

"Of course. Not only did we go to school together—she was a year ahead of me—I'm a groomsman in her sister's wedding. Wait, I guess I'm not a groomsman, since it's two brides. But that doesn't make me a bridesmaid, does it?"

"I don't think so."

"Well, whatever I am, it's gonna be fun. Great to see you, Audrey."

"You too, Wylie."

"And thanks for coming. Oh, Ike at the pro shop told me you came in this afternoon looking for me. Are you here in an official capacity? You writing an article about 3F?"

If I told him I was writing an article to boost Cole's chances at getting elected sheriff, that wouldn't be a good look—for either of us. It also didn't seem like a good time to beg him for a free golf lesson, especially in light of the fact we'd be competing against each other in the scramble.

"We can talk later about why I stopped by. Tonight I'm just here for moral support."

Wylie got a twinkle in his eye and winked. "I think you're going to be glad you came. You'll get the scoop!" He turned away and headed toward the stage.

"Scoop? What scoop?" I called after him, but he just waved his hand in the air.

He jumped onto the stage and grabbed the mic. "Hello, hello, hello! I'm gonna need everyone to take a seat on the floor in front of me."

It took a few minutes, but soon everyone was settled. Cole and I stood in the back.

"Welcome to 3F, where we are all about having fun, learning to set goals, and looking toward the future. Repeat after me. Fun!" He pumped his fist in the air.

"Fun!" yelled the crowd.

"Forward!" Another fist pump.

"Forward!"

"Focus!"

"Focus!"

I leaned toward Cole and whispered in his ear. "Is it just me, or does this feel a little cult-y?"

He gave me a half-chuckle/half-shush.

"I have a few announcements about upcoming events, but I'll save them for the end. Tonight we have a very special guest."

I sensed Cole straightening beside me.

"Put your hands together for…"

Cole leaned forward like he was about to take a step.

"Onyx Carpenter!"

Onyx appeared from behind the curtain, waving both hands like a toddler saying *bye-bye*.

Chaos broke out. Pure mayhem. Kids were screaming and cheering, girls were crying, even the parent chaperones were jumping up and down.

Cole stood rooted to his spot, still leaning forward like the Tower of Pisa. I grabbed his hand and pulled him back.

"Hey, Cole?"

"Hm."

"Onyx Carpenter's in town."

His mouth was set firm, as was his grip, which tightened further.

I looked down at our clasped hands. He followed my gaze and did a double-take before releasing me.

Wylie handed Onyx the mic.

"Hello Chattertowne!" She gave a beaming smile.

Onyx was the kind of beautiful typically reserved for the covers of magazines. In fact, her first cover was the *Sports Illustrated* Swimsuit Edition. Her mother was Filipino, and her father had been born in Ireland. She had her mother's tan skin and thick, dark hair, and her father's bright green eyes. Her perfect smile was the result of two years in braces, including headgear she had to wear at night. I'd discovered that during one of our squad sleepovers.

She spotted me and waved enthusiastically. "Oh, look, it's my old friend Audrey O'Connell."

All the kids turned to look at me with awe. I sheepishly waved back.

She pointed at Cole. "Unless you're married now and have a different last name?"

He grunted.

I held up my ringless left hand. "Nope."

A few of the kids said, "Aww."

"It's fine, really," I mumbled. Not that anyone cared.

"I'm just so excited to be here with you all." Onyx giggled. "I do believe, as Whitney sang, the children are our future. I'm so grateful to Wylie, I mean

Mr. Barrett, for allowing me to surprise you all tonight. We've been good friends for a long time, haven't we?" She shot him an even broader smile that hinted at a shared secret.

His entire face and neck turned the color of a radish.

"Now, you guys, I must ask that you keep my visit on the down-low." She held her finger to her mouth. "You know how the press can be. Relentless."

I scoffed with offense at her characterization of the press, even though there was no way she meant a small-town reporter like me.

Shoot. I'd turned off my reporter brain. I needed to be taking photos. I pulled out my phone and grabbed a few discreet shots. I hadn't yet decided when and how I would use them, but I'd need them eventually.

Onyx made a few more generic remarks about working hard, being good kids, and studying in school so they could get into good colleges and be successful adults. It was a tough argument to make, considering her path to success was paved by things like toothpaste commercials—the orthodontia had been exceedingly effective—and reality show stints, not college.

Not to say she hadn't earned her way to superstardom. Some argued she'd ridden her husband's coattails to fame, but she'd worked very hard to attain her level of success all on her own. It just wasn't anything like the path she was advocating to the kids.

Poor Cole had to follow Onyx's talk with his Nancy Reagan *just say no to drugs and alcohol* speech. It was a tough gig even under ideal circumstances, but, following Onyx, any speech was destined to be a dud.

I recorded it for posterity, but it wasn't likely to procure him many votes, if any. He had a certain charisma, but if he planned to be a politician, he was going to have to polish up on his public speaking.

After the closing remarks by Wylie, many of the kids surrounded Onyx. She signed autographs and took selfies.

"You ready to go?" Cole asked.

He looked so defeated, I wanted to hug him.

I refrained. "Yeah, but first I need to use the ladies' room."

I rounded the corner just as Laveda broke away from what appeared to be an intense conversation with Wylie. Her expression was troubled as she strode in my direction down the dimly lit hallway. Wylie ducked into the men's room.

I stopped and turned to watch Laveda leave. Jack was waiting for her near the door. He gave her a pointed look, but she shook her head. He handed her a blue Gatorade bottle and possessively flung his arm around her as they walked outside together.

* * *

Twenty minutes later, Cole pulled his car in front of my house and put it in park. The windshield wipers squeaked back and forth across the damp glass.

"That was not how I thought tonight would go."

"I know you're disappointed, Cole, but no one could have topped Onyx showing up. Frankly, I'm even more surprised about her appearance at Wylie's event, considering she broke his heart when she left town. I guess he's gotten over that."

Just as Cole was about to respond, his radio beeped, followed by static and then a woman's voice.

"Dispatch to all available units. We've just received a call about an off-road vehicle crash into a tree 14500 block of Harley Road. Devil's Elbow. Outskirts of Chattertowne. Two people reported injured, one unresponsive."

Cole picked up his radio and pressed the button. "Loveland here. Headed that way. Probably ten minutes out. Any other details?"

I reached for the door handle and mouthed, "I should go."

He held up his hand for me to wait.

The radio squawked. "Caller says they heard the crash from their nearby home and ran down to the location. Vehicle is light blue, seems to be a classic car. Two teens. One male. One female."

Cole and I exchanged horrified glances.

More static.

"Caller says driver is Jack Dodd, eighteen. Passenger is Laveda Volkova, sixteen."

Chapter Two

Cole didn't bother asking if I wanted to come with him to the crash site. He put his car in gear, turned on his lights and siren, and started driving.

"Seatbelt."

I clicked my buckle. "Do you even know where you're going?"

"I was hoping you could tell me. I know the general area, but what's Devil's Elbow?"

I pointed. "Turn right up here. Devil's Elbow is out by Coyote Lake. It's a notoriously sharp turn in an area without any streetlights. The city council's been debating for years what to do about that road. Every time there's a crash, they talk about trying to make it safer, but some have argued it's a waste of taxpayer funds since most of the wrecks are the result of reckless driving. Like when Mickey McQuaid crashed his motorcycle, racing his buddies around that curve at over a hundred miles an hour."

"I take it he didn't survive."

"I'll spare you the gory details, but no. And they aren't necessarily wrong about most of the crashes being from taking the turn too fast, I mean. Including the accident I was in, back in high school."

He jerked his head to look at me, but quickly returned his attention to the road. "What happened? Were you hurt?"

"Thankfully, no. It was after a football game. We were all going to Gabby Baylor's house to spend the night. Oh, and Miranda was there too. I'm surprised she hasn't mentioned it to you. It was pretty traumatic. Although, you haven't been dating that long, sooo…"

Cole's jaw clenched. "What happened?"

"Gabby always drove like a bat out of hell. She went flying around the corner and didn't quite make it. Not sure streetlamps would have done any good. We slid off the embankment. Skidded is probably a more accurate word. You should have seen the tire marks that little Mazda 3 left behind on the road leading up to the edge. I think she put down a tire's worth of rubber. It was one of the most surreal experiences I've ever had. One minute we were singing along to the radio, and the next we were flying through the air, almost in slow motion. We're lucky we didn't hit a tree. When we landed, I remember one of the girls asked if we were dead."

Cole stared, unblinking, into the darkness as he drove out of town, past the trailhead, and into what us townies called "the boonies." I'd known him long enough to recognize his *processing* face.

"Do you think we should call Miranda?" I asked.

"Not yet. I want to see what we're dealing with first."

We approached the dangerous curve where two firetrucks, an aid car, and a police car had beaten us to the scene. Sergeant Tony Bianchi's imposing form was illuminated in the glow of headlights.

"Bianchi's here."

Cole said nothing. I'd never seen him so solemn. I could only guess the thoughts racing through his head. What if Jack was dead? How would Miranda handle that?

He stopped the car behind Bianchi's police SUV, its lights flashing red and blue against the pine trees. He'd barely turned off the engine before jumping out. I quickly unbuckled and scrambled out of the car, trying not to twist an ankle in the ditch.

"Chief." Bianchi greeted him. He glanced at me. "Audrey."

"What's the status?" Cole strained to look over Bianchi's shoulder.

The back end of a silvery blue car with three circular red taillights on each side was barely visible above the berm. The license plate said UNDRPRR. Under par. Cute. It also had what looked to be a vintage Mt. St. Helens sticker on the bumper—pre-eruption.

I snapped a quick shot with the camera on my phone. Cole seemed too preoccupied to notice.

Bianchi read from his notebook. "Looks to me to be an early sixties Chevy Impala hardtop. We'll know more once we can get the registration from the glove box. Witness says she heard a crash about nine fifteen or so. She lives up there." He pointed at a house set back from the road up a steep driveway. "Came down to the scene where she saw the vehicle had gone off the road and hit a tree. Called emergency services. While on the phone, one of the kids in the car, the driver, was conscious enough to give their names. Jack Dodd and Laveda Volkova. The passenger is in pretty bad shape. Ejected."

"It's definitely Jack's car." Cole rubbed the back of his neck. "I can't believe this happened. I was just with them."

"What do you mean?"

"Audrey and I—" he anemically gestured toward me. "We were at the 3F meeting. They left just a few minutes before us."

Bianchi looked over his shoulder. "Looks like one of 'em is being brought up now."

Cole brushed past him, and I followed close behind. I figured he must have been distracted by worry because, typically, he would have ordered me to stay back with Bianchi.

The patient on the gurney wore an oxygen mask, but I could see the wavy brown hair of Jack Dodd. I could also see an abrasion and blood on his left cheek. His left arm was scraped and bleeding as well.

Cole rushed up to him. "Jack. It's Cole Loveland. Can you hear me?"

Jack nodded.

"Can you tell me what happened?"

"Steer—" He gasped. "Steering. Went. Out. Maybe brakes, too. Lee...I couldn't find her. She wasn't in the car. Where is she? Where did she go?"

One of the paramedics said, "We need to get him to the hospital, sir."

Cole nodded. "I'll call your mom, have her meet you there. It's gonna be okay, son." He patted Jack on the shoulder.

Jack's gaze stayed focused on Cole as he was hoisted into the ambulance. He was still looking at Cole, and then he looked at me for a brief moment. What appeared to be a spark of recognition flickered just as the doors shut.

Cole walked over to Fire Chief Norvald. "What about the passenger? The girl."

"Not looking good. Unresponsive. Head injury. Probably internal injuries. Went through the windshield. Looks like she might not have been wearing her seatbelt. Not that it woulda helped much. They only have lap belts in those old cars. Why do they want those tin cans? They've got no safety features at all. Dumb kids."

His words were harsh, but the tone alluded to angry grief over an unnecessary risk that might prove fatal.

Just as the ambulance began to pull away, with lights flashing and sirens blaring, Cole's phone rang. He pulled it out of his pocket and stared at the screen. "Dammit. It's Miranda." He blew out a deep sigh before answering the call. "Hey there." If he was attempting casual, he failed. His voice was shaky. "I was just about to call you."

He wandered away from me and the crowd of first responders. All the flashing lights caused the normally pitch black intersection to look like a scene from *Close Encounters of the Third Kind.*

I watched Cole rub the back of his neck again as he broke the news. His chin dropped to his chest, and his shoulders slumped.

This wasn't his first time relaying difficult or heartbreaking information to a family member, but I doubted he'd ever had to do so with someone he was dating. Seeing. Whatever.

When he returned, he said, "She's headed to Everett General Hospital. I told her I'd get there as soon as I could."

One of the paramedics approached Bianchi, holding a piece of paper.

Bianchi took it and looked it over. "'64 Chevy Impala registered to Hank Dodd." He glanced up at Cole. "That Jack's dad?"

He nodded. "Yep."

A flurry of activity down in the ravine was followed by the emergence of another gurney. Nausea punched my gut when I saw that the figure was completely shrouded. The firefighters and paramedics wore grim expressions.

One of them addressed Bianchi, who was running the scene. "Victim's name, according to her identification, is indeed Laveda Volkova."

A cry rang out from behind us.

I whipped around to find Wylie Barrett. His face was as white as the sheet covering his star golfer.

Chapter Three

"It can't be," Wylie wailed. "Tell me it can't be!" His gaze was frantic, darting all around like a pinball.

I touched his shoulder. "I'm so sorry."

"What…what happened?" He covered his mouth with both hands and dragged his fingers to his chin.

Bianchi cleared his throat. "We're trying to determine that. Driver says his steering wasn't working. I know these kids were just at one of your meetings. Could they have been drinking? Drugs?"

Wylie whipped his head to meet Tony's gaze. "Not a chance. These are good kids with good grades. They're scholarship-level athletes."

Cole, who normally had plenty to say, stood silent.

Bianchi glanced at Cole and then back at Wylie. "Even elite athletes make bad choices sometimes."

Wylie shook his head. "Not these kids. They know they've got too much on the line."

I thought back to the end of the evening, when I'd spotted Laveda and Wylie talking in the dark hallway. "Did she say anything to you tonight? Laveda, I mean."

His gaze cut to me. "What do you mean?"

He knew what I meant. The subtle shift in his jaw and intensity of his demeanor said as much.

I shrugged, unwilling to tip my hand just yet. "Just wondering."

Had he not seen me in the hallway where I'd seen him talking to Laveda? Or was he simply unwilling to admit the conversation had even taken place?

If so, why?

"I don't see how any of that matters, especially now." Wylie scanned the area. "Where's Jack? Is he still in the car?"

"No, they took him in the ambulance," I said.

"When?"

"A few minutes ago."

"Where are they taking him? Harborview?"

Finally, Cole found his voice. "He's on his way to Everett General." He squinted at Wylie. "You should have passed the ambulance on the way."

"I've gotta go." Wylie turned on his heel and hustled toward his car, which he'd parked behind Cole's.

"I'm gonna need to ask you some more questions," Bianchi called after him.

Wylie merely waved in response.

The dark form of someone sitting in the passenger seat of his luxury SUV was highlighted by the flashing lights of the aid car.

Within two minutes, the car made a U-turn and raced back down Harley Road, away from the accident scene.

* * *

A line of mostly teenagers had formed outside the hospital's ER entrance, winding all the way from the double doors to the parking garage.

"What's going on here?" Cole asked the two girls huddled together at the back of the line.

The short blonde girl turned around. She had mascara smudged beneath her eyes like she'd been crying. "Our friend Jack was in a car accident. We want to see him, but the security guard up front isn't letting anyone in."

The taller girl's light brown bob haircut bounced as she nodded. "It's because Onyx Carpenter's in there. Someone said she showed up with Coach Barrett. It's all over social media." She scowled. "Most of the people here don't even know Jack. They just want to spot a celebrity."

Cole moved toward the front of the line. I stuck as close to the back of him as possible. He smelled like musky leather and sweat.

The beleaguered security guard held up a hand. "Sir, we're only allowing staff and emergency patients inside at this time. There was an incident over at the children's theater, so the waiting room is quite full. Also, there are a lot of Onyx Carpenter fans trying to get in because word got out she's here." He exhaled. "Letting her and her friend inside was a big mistake."

Cole held up his badge. "Cole Loveland. Chattertowne's chief of police. I'm investigating an accident that took place tonight on the outskirts of town, and I need to speak with the young man they just brought in by aid car."

The guard shifted his gaze side to side. "I, uh, I guess that would be okay." He spotted me lurking over Cole's shoulder. "She with you, or is she another celebrity stalker?"

Cole crooked his head and startled at the sight of me hovering so close to him. "Uh, yeah, no, not a stalker. Of Onyx Carpenter, at least. She's with me."

The guard stepped aside, to the howls and complaints of the crowd behind us. "He's a cop! And if you all don't settle down, I'll have him arrest you all for disturbing the peace."

The melee quieted to a dull roar.

"Don't tell them that," Cole said. "This isn't even my jurisdiction."

The guard shrugged as he held the door open. "They don't need to know that."

The emergency room waiting area looked like a combination circus tent and battlefield triage tent. I spotted at least five clowns—actual clowns— huddled in the corner nursing various injuries. One was a big guy who was well over six feet and at least three hundred pounds, wearing a blue and green striped romper, a green wig, and a halo of blood-soaked gauze. Another could only be described as an off-brand Ronald McDonald. His red one-piece costume was paired with oversized gold shoes. His wig was burnt orange. At least, I assumed it was a wig. I'd never seen ringlets like that on a grown man. He held an ice pack to his forearm.

There was no sign of Wylie or Onyx.

Cole approached the reception desk and flashed his badge. "I'm hoping to speak with Jack Dodd."

The woman blinked at him with her eyes barely open. When she opened her mouth, there was a 50-50 chance she'd either cuss him out or yawn.

It would remain a mystery, though, since at that moment Miranda peeked her head through the doorway.

"Cole." His eyes were red-rimmed.

He was at her side in an instant, pulling her into his arms. He didn't even glance back at me before leaving the waiting room with her.

I stood awkwardly, unsure what to do. The receptionist gave me a look of pity. I quashed the urge to explain it wasn't like that between him and me.

I scanned the room in search of a place to sit. It was quite a sight; a literal three-ring circus of sick and wounded.

One open seat was next to a mom and her screaming, red-faced baby with green snot draining from his flared nostrils.

There were two spots on each side of a shirtless man who didn't appear to have showered in quite some time and was arguing with either himself or someone only he could see.

The last spot was clown adjacent.

I didn't consider myself a fearful person in general. I was a rule follower because I'd always believed rules were there for a reason, so I was cautious, yes, but not fearful. (The main exception being a pretty severe case of aquaphobia I'd battled since Vivienne's near-drowning accident. Why a six-year-old was put in charge of a toddler near water was a question for my mother.) Other than that, though, I had no other phobias…even of clowns, which was a fairly common one for a lot of people.

But a posse of them in their full clown regalia, sporting gashes, bruises, and blood oozing down their smeared face paint, caused a jolt of panic to shoot through me.

The shirtless man began chanting, "Welcome to Seattle, where ballers ball and players play. Gang-gang-gang. Welcome to Seattle, where ballers ball and players play. Gang-gang-gang…" On his last gang-gang-gang, he pretended to be a robot powering down. Then his head shot up and he started all over again. "Welcome to Seattle—"

It sounded vaguely like the lyrics to a rap song, but not one I could readily place.

The baby didn't like the performance and kicked his screams up a notch. His poor mother was also crying at this point.

"Clowns it is," I muttered under my breath.

As I approached the empty seat, a petite lady with yarn for hair and a plastic red bulb on her nose gave me a welcoming smile. No, that wasn't quite right. As I got closer, I realized the smile was actually painted on her otherwise placid face.

"Have a seat." Her voice was surprisingly deep for her diminutive size.

"Thanks."

"You here to visit a patient?" She primly folded her white-gloved hands and set them in her lap.

"Sort of. There was a car accident on the outskirts of Chattertowne. Two kids. One of them was brought here."

"Oh, dear. Why only one of them?"

I gave her a grimace in return.

"Oh. Oh, no. That's so sad."

"What about you guys?" I nodded toward the other clowns.

"We were fifteen minutes into our opening night performance when it all came crashing down."

"What did?"

"All of it. Clarence over there—" she jerked her thumb toward discount Ronald. "He had the bright idea to use guys he'd rounded up in the hardware store parking lot to build our sets. Thought he'd save a couple bucks by going non-union. Now he's gonna have to refund all those tickets *and* pay for therapy for about fifty kids."

"That's...I don't even know what to say."

She gave a somber nod. "What can you say?"

"Audrey." Cole waved to me from the door and then gestured for me to come toward him.

I turned to the lady clown next to me. "Good luck. Hope you feel better."

She held up her right hand, which was swollen and covered in purple bruises. "Thanks."

"Making friends, I see," Cole said as he ushered me through the doorway and into the emergency department.

Machines beeped and buzzed from every direction, and personnel rushed from room to room.

"Wherever I go. How's Jack?"

"He's okay. A little banged up, according to Miranda, but not bad considering Laveda..."

"What's he saying?"

We passed a room where the glass door was open, but the curtain was drawn. Through a tiny sliver, I saw a woman writhe back and forth on the bed, wailing at the top of her lungs. She looked strung out, likely going through drug withdrawals.

"I haven't questioned him yet. I wanted to get the lay of the land first. And I thought you should be there when I did."

This was a significant about-face. Since he'd arrived in Chattertowne, Cole had done his best to keep on-duty journalist Audrey at arm's length. He'd pretty much kept off-duty Audrey at arm's length as well.

Cole pulled back the curtain of the room at the end of the hall. Jack was lying on the bed with a thin sheet draped over his legs. He had a decent gash just above his left eyebrow that looked to have been glued, and his left undereye area was beginning to develop purple undertones. He had an IV in his arm and various monitors attached to his smooth, bare chest, which was quite tan for the time of year. Miranda had posted pictures on social media of his trip to Cabo with buddies for spring break.

She glanced up at me when I stepped into the room. "Hey, Audrey."

"Miranda. How are you?"

She feebly gestured at her son, a tremor in her voice. "I've been better."

"Yeah." I pulled the curtain closed behind me, but left the sliding glass door open.

Cole grabbed a stool and rolled up next to Jack. "I know you've been through a lot tonight. I've found that the mind does a bang-up job, uh, sorry, poor choice of words." He cleared his throat. "The mind is a powerful thing when it comes to trauma. It goes into self-protection mode. It has a way of anesthetizing itself by dulling details that might create stress or anxiety. That's why it's really important I get as much information from you about what happened while it's fresh and before that sets in."

Jack's mouth pulled at both corners. "I can't believe she's gone." His voice was barely above a whisper.

Miranda awkwardly jumped from her chair and raced to his side. She gripped his hand. "Oh, honey, I know."

"Ouch. Mom, you're hurting my IV." He rubbed his arm. His left elbow was scraped and bleeding, and his bicep was covered in abrasions.

She dropped his hand. "Oh, sorry." She remained next to the bed, hovering but not touching.

"Can you tell me what you remember about the accident?" Cole asked.

Jack stared up at the acoustical ceiling tiles with a bemused expression. I followed his gaze. There was a brown water stain in the corner of the tile directly above him. The stain resembled male genitalia, but it seemed like an inappropriate time to comment on it.

"Jack?"

Jack looked at Cole. "Oh, uh, we were talking about prom." He paused. "I don't think I was going over the speed limit. It's just so dark out there; it was wet from the rain, and as I was listening to her talking about what color dress she wanted to get, we came up to Devil's Elbow. I slowed down to turn, but it was like my steering wheel was made of cement. I cranked it, but it was too late. I couldn't turn, and I couldn't stop. We just went over. It was…" He seemed to struggle to find the word.

"Surreal," I whispered. I hadn't meant to say it out loud.

He looked at me. "Yeah. Like, you're outside of space and time. I could hear Lee screaming, only it was like she was far away. Or under water. After we landed, it was dead quiet other than the music that was still playing." He grunted. "Ironically, the song was *Lose Control* by Teddy Swims."

Cole leaned forward, his clasped hands hanging between his legs. "Let's go back to the steering issues. Have you been having trouble with the car? I know you've been working on it quite a bit."

"Not at all. It's been running great. In fact, I just did a thirty-point inspection two days ago. Power steering fluid level was exactly what it should be. Brakes were good. Rotors and pads were good."

"Something must have happened to cause your steering to fail. I guess that's the thing about classic cars."

Jack's expression clouded. "You don't think…"

"What, honey?" Miranda rubbed his arm.

"You don't think anyone could have…messed with it. Do you?"

Cole's gaze narrowed. "What are you trying to say? You think it wasn't an accident?"

"Why would someone do that?" Miranda's voice rose an octave. "Why would someone purposely hurt you?"

Jack shrugged. "Maybe it was a prank gone wrong. I dunno."

Cole wrinkled his brow.

"Why? Who would be so stupid as to risk your life for a prank, Jack?" Miranda jerked her head to look at Cole. "If this was an intentional act, your investigation will show that, won't it?"

"It should. You know, Jack, if someone tampered with your vehicle, that's not a prank. It's a felony. Laveda is…well, it's manslaughter at the very least."

Miranda started to cry. "Who would want to hurt my baby boy?"

The curtain was pulled back, and I turned to see Wylie standing in the doorway to the exam room. Onyx peered over his shoulder. Her expression was inscrutable.

"Hey, buddy. How are you feeling?" Wylie stepped into the room.

Jack blinked at him. "Did you mess with my car? Did you kill Lee because you wanted to get me out of the picture?"

Chapter Four

Wylie froze in the doorway of the examination room. "What do you mean, Jack? Mess with your car? Out of what picture?"

Miranda looked between Jack and Wylie. "Honey, what are you saying? Why would your coach want to hurt you?"

Jack ignored his mother, his attention laser-focused on Wylie. "I know what's been going on with you and Lee. Maybe you wanted me permanently silenced so I wouldn't tell."

Wylie's face drained of color. "What are you talking about?"

I glanced at Cole, who looked as confused as I felt about the insinuation that hung heavy in the air. Was he accusing Wylie of inappropriate involvement with one of his students?

Cole stood and put a hand on Wylie's arm. "Let's step outside for a minute."

Wylie resisted, still staring at Jack. "What are you doing, Jack? Why are you saying these things? This makes no sense."

Jack's gaze never wavered from Wylie's face.

Cole used more force when attempting to escort Wylie out of the room a second time. "Come on, let's go have a chat."

Onyx stood in the hallway, wringing her hands. She glanced into the room once more, and Miranda spotted her. Miranda tilted her head and gave Onyx a look that was a cross between curious and concerned. Onyx furrowed her brow and frowned. Miranda gave her a quick head nod of acknowledgment, and Onyx did the same. They held eye contact for what felt like an awkwardly long moment until Miranda finally looked away.

An entire conversation without a single word exchanged.

A nurse swept in to take Jack's vitals and slid the door closed, blocking us from any of the sights or sounds in the room.

"What do I do, Audrey?" Onyx's voice wobbled.

"I don't know." It was the most honest answer I could give, considering I wasn't even sure I understood what she was referring to. The most reasonable explanation was she didn't know whether or not to follow after Wylie.

I wanted to hear what Wylie had to say about the allegations, but there was a chance Cole would prevent us from listening in on their conversation.

I also wanted to stay and see if I could hear from Jack about why he believed Wylie would tamper with his car. It made no sense, but there had to be a reason he'd said it.

Still, with the examination room door shut for the time being, we'd likely have better luck with Cole.

"Let's go."

I hustled down the hallway in the direction Cole had taken Wylie with Onyx right on my heels. We weaved our way into another part of the hospital. No one stopped us to make sure we were where we were supposed to be, and I made a mental note to write a story about hospital security.

"I had no idea you were in town yet," I said over my shoulder.

"I came in early to surprise the 3F kids. Wylie reached out to me when he heard I was coming for the induction ceremony and asked if I'd make an appearance."

"I didn't realize you guys kept in touch."

"We don't. We haven't. He reached out to me via Instagram DM, and my P.A. passed along the message."

"You have a personal assistant?"

Her laugh was bitter. "I have a whole team. How else do you think I keep all these balls in the air?"

She had a point. I struggled to manage my own simple life, and I didn't even have a pet. Unless you counted the raccoon family that lived under my house last fall.

We rounded the corner to a small waiting area outside the radiology department, which was closed since it was after hours. Cole and Wylie were sitting in two of the six chairs.

Cole glanced up and gave an exasperated sigh. "I said I wanted to speak to him alone."

"No, you said you wanted to chat with him. You never said alone."

"It's okay," said Wylie. "I have nothing to hide."

I eased into the chair next to him while Onyx sat next to Wylie, who gave her a sad but grateful smile. She squeezed his knee. Her hands were still trembling as she folded them in her lap.

"Why would Jack think you might have tampered with his vehicle?" asked Cole.

"I have no idea."

"What did he mean about something going on with Laveda?"

Wylie shook his head. "No clue about that either."

Cole leaned back in the chair and folded his arms across his chest. "How about you tell me what you do know?"

Wylie quickly glanced at Onyx, who gave him a tentative but encouraging smile.

"I've coached Laveda for three years. First at the club, and then eventually at the school as well. I've worked with Jack even longer. Miranda had him in lessons from the time he was eight. Wanted him to be the next Tiger. In fact, she tried getting everyone to call him Jaguar, but the nickname never stuck."

I bit the inside of my cheek to keep from laughing. Cole shifted in his seat. I didn't dare look at him.

"Laveda was a natural-born golfer, if there is such a thing. She was so adaptable. I'd watch her swing, give her feedback, and by the next swing she'd have completely corrected herself."

"So, you're saying she was malleable, and you had tremendous influence over her?"

I jerked my head to look at Cole. What was he doing?

"That's not what I said," Wylie protested.

Onyx pursed her mouth. "You're twisting his words! That's an unfair characterization."

I had to agree with them, but part of me wondered if he was employing some sort of interrogation tactic, and I didn't want to interfere.

"Jack's accusations were quite serious. I need to ask. Was there anything inappropriate going on between you and Laveda Volkova?"

Cole's question hit Wylie right between the eyes. He could have at least called *Fore!* before launching that shot.

Wylie reared back in shock and horror. "No! Of course not. How could you even ask such a thing?"

"It's been known to happen. Jack is certainly implying that lines may have been crossed."

Onyx placed her hand on Wylie's arm just as he opened his mouth to protest. "You know, this is starting to feel like a situation where Wylie might need legal counsel." She stood. "Let's go. We can call my lawyer on the way back to town. He'd tear up this place right now if he knew this kind of police questioning was happening without representation."

Wylie got to his feet, shellshocked. "I would never—"

Onyx put one siren red fingernail to his mouth and shushed him. "Not one word. Trust me."

She led him out of the radiology waiting room and around the corner. A minute later, a door slammed shut.

Cole and I sat in silence. Not my strong suit, but the energy pouring off of him was so charged it felt like I might get zapped if I said anything. It took everything I had to keep quiet.

Cole, on the other hand, could have been a monk or a mime in another life. He'd mastered the art of silence, especially when he sensed I wanted to get information from him. Sometimes he seemed to relish it. The look of distress on his face told me that this time. that wasn't it.

"Something's not right." He furrowed his brow, causing deep lines to appear on his forehead.

"Of course not. A young girl is dead. But you don't really think this was more than an accident, do you? Jack's upset, understandably so. He probably has a concussion, too."

"I don't know. My gut is screaming something's not right here. Something's off. I just don't know what." He pushed himself up out of the chair. "I need to talk to the kid."

"Jack."

He grunted his response. I tailed him back to Jack's room, but the glass door was still shut.

We hovered in the hallway for about ten minutes until Miranda finally slid the door open.

"Oh, I didn't know you were back." She looked like she'd been crying again.

"Yeah." Cole tipped his chin toward the room. "He up for a chat?"

She slid the door shut behind her. "I don't think so."

He stared at her. When she didn't add anything to her rejection, he frowned. "Okay. When do you think he'll be available?"

"I don't know. The doctor says he will probably release him soon. They want to do a scan of his abdomen. Make sure he doesn't have any internal injuries."

"He made some pretty serious accusations. I don't take these things lightly. I need to speak with him."

She clenched her jaw. "He needs his rest."

When it came to police officer stubbornness vs. mama bear protecting her cub, I'd put my money on mama bear every time.

I looped my arm through Cole's. "I'm sure Jack will be up for talking after he's had a good night's sleep. Let's take off. You can talk to him in the morning."

I felt him resist my pull toward the exit. Miranda narrowed her gaze at our linked arms but said nothing.

"Call me if you need me," he grumbled, touching the brim of his hat.

"Will do," she replied. "See you tomorrow morning for brunch, Audrey."

"Oh, will you be there? I figured you'd want to skip it."

"My best friend is getting married. I'm not missing her bridal brunch."

I swallowed my annoyance at her description of herself as Vivienne's best friend. Out of all the people in Viv's life, I didn't think Miranda would even make the top ten. She'd made her a bridesmaid, though, so maybe they were closer than I'd realized.

That, or Miranda had heard the rumors about Onyx coming to the wedding and saw it as her opportunity to get famous. Her encounter with Onyx at the ER had been odd, though. Perhaps they'd had a falling out. I'd have to ask Vivienne when I got the chance.

By the time Cole pulled his car in front of my house for the second time that night, it was nearly midnight. I tried to stifle my yawn.

If he noticed, he didn't say so.

"You look like you've got a lot on your mind."

He stared out the windshield as if the answers to his questions might appear in the night sky. "Like I said back at the hospital. There's something bothering me, but I can't quite put my finger on it."

"I'm sure you'll figure it out. You always do. Miranda will get Jack home, and you'll be able to interview him about the accident tomorrow."

He bounced the palm of his right hand against the steering wheel. "Why didn't he see the ambulance?"

"Who?"

"Wylie. He didn't see the first ambulance."

"So?"

"So, where was he?"

"I'm not sure what you're getting at."

He increased the pace of his thumping. "Does he live nearby?"

"Uh, kind of, I guess. Near Lake Pilchuck. But I don't think he was going home."

"Why do you say that?"

"Because I'm pretty sure I saw Onyx in the passenger seat of his car. I don't think he picked her up from the Bed and Breakfast where she's staying on the way to the hospital. I think she was already with him. So, unless he was taking her to his house, he wasn't going home."

"I can't imagine Meacham Fields would be thrilled to know his wife was skulking around the dark backroads of Chattertowne with her high school sweetheart."

"I suspect not. But let's get back to what you said about him not seeing the ambulance."

He shook his head. "I don't know. It's bugging me, that's all. Maybe it's nothing."

Maybe it was nothing. Or maybe it was a whole lot of something.

Chapter Five

I was a hot mess when I stumbled into the French Bistro for brunch the next morning. It was difficult to sleep with visions of that terrible accident flashing in my mind. Around two, I got up and took an Advil PM. I was paying the price now, because I felt like I was walking around in a haze.

"Finally!" Vivienne waved me over to the long table set up near the window overlooking Lake Camora.

It was a man-made lake, more like a pond. When we were kids, it iced over at least once every winter, and some years it froze solid enough to ice skate.

"Audrey, you know you're supposed to sleep in the bed, not under it, right?" Lacey mussed my hair. "I know you hate it when I do that, but in this case, it's actually an improvement."

Said the woman who shaved most of her hair off rather than have to deal with it.

"Hardy har har."

"Hey, we're family now. This is what families do, we rib each other."

Vivienne was beaming, so I suppressed any snippy retort directed at my future sister-in-law.

"Where should I sit?" I scanned the length of the table. There were two open seats. One was next to my mother, whose current expression held disgust at my disheveled appearance. The other was at the end of the table next to Holden. I cursed under my breath. Sophie's choice.

"Audrey, come sit by me," Holden taunted.

I wanted to wipe his smug grin off his face. He knew me well enough to know when it came to choosing between my mother's running commentary on how I forgot to run a brush through my hair and other ways in which my life was a disappointment to her or enduring a meal's worth of Holden's antics, he held a very slight advantage. A razor-thin margin, but in his favor, nonetheless.

Vivienne gave me a sympathetic smile. "Sorry. I should have saved you a seat next to me."

"It's fine."

It wasn't that I didn't like Holden. I mean, what was there not to like? The man was gorgeous, like Cristiano Reynaldo plus twenty extra pounds of bicep. And he was smart. And funny. And had rescued me more times than I cared to count.

In fact, it was probably more that I liked Holden *too* much, but I tried not to think about that.

My ex-boyfriend—Marcus—and Holden had been good friends growing up, so I'd spent a decent amount of time with him as a teen. When I'd returned to Chattertowne from Portland a couple years ago, Holden and I had rekindled our friendship. Beneath the surface, though, there had been something more than just friendship. Unfortunately for everyone involved, he'd been engaged at the time, and while no lines had technically been crossed, they'd gotten a little blurry.

Once he and his fiancée had ended their engagement and she'd moved to Spokane, I'd flirted with the possibility of pursuing something more, but at the moment, things were still platonic. Mostly. It was complicated.

As was often the case with situations like ours, we mitigated our repressed chemistry by bickering. Any time one of us sensed the other might be wavering toward romance, the other was sure to douse the heat with a big bucket of icy snark.

We were currently in a heavy snark phase. All the wedding activities meant proximity to each other. When it came to Holden and me, proximity was fuel for a fire neither of us were sure we wanted to inflame, so the bickering and bantering were at an all-time high.

I slid in next to him and tried not to make eye contact.

"Good morning, Ms. O'Connell. How are you?"

"I'm fine."

The woman sitting across the table from me thrust out her hand. "Hi, you must be Audrey." Her booming voice was husky, as was her body type. Her neck, what there was of it, was thick. I'd always wondered what the idiom *built like a sparkplug* might look like in real life, and this woman was the closest I'd encountered.

"I am." I offered my hand, and she shook it like she was testing to see how well my wrist was attached to my arm. When she released it, I squeezed to make sure it was indeed still intact. "You must be Lacey's cousin. I'm sorry, I don't recall your name."

"Yellin."

"Helen?"

"Yellin."

Holden squinted at her. "Did you say Yellin? Not Ellen?"

"Birth certificate says Ellen, but I had colic as a baby, and my dad, well, he called me Yellin' Ellen. It stuck."

I hoped the horror I felt didn't show, but considering I was well known to have a terrible poker face, I didn't have high hopes.

Thankfully, the server arrived with a tray of mimosas to grab everyone's attention.

I scanned the table. "No, Wylie, I see. Understandable. He was pretty shaken up last night."

"Yeah, he texted me and said he had a massive migraine," Holden said.

"So, Audrey, I hear you're a reporter or something." Yellin took a swig of orange juice and champagne.

"Something like that," Holden mumbled under his breath.

I kicked him under the table, but instead of wincing, he just smiled.

"I write for the *Coastal Current* newspaper."

"So, do you know what's going on with that car crash last night?" Yellin bellowed. "I heard a girl died."

"Yellin!" Lacey called down the table. "That's not pleasant brunch talk."

Yellin got a sheepish look on her face, and her cheeks flushed. "Sorry."

"We published a story first thing this morning about it. You can find it on the website. I haven't heard anything new since last night." I didn't mention that much of what I learned the night before hadn't made it into the article.

"I read the article. Found it confusing, though. Left me with a lot of unanswered questions." Yellin swigged her mimosa.

"Miranda might know more. She said she'd be here, despite her son being in the hospital last night."

"Speak of the devil." Holden nodded toward the entrance.

Miranda sashayed into the room. "So sorry I'm late. I didn't get to sleep until two in the morning."

Vivienne jumped up to hug her. "I'm so glad you made it. How is Jack?"

Miranda's dismissive wave held a slight tremor. "He's fine. Physically, at least. But let's not talk about that. This is your day."

Yellin leaned forward and attempted a whisper that sounded like Snoqualmie Falls after a heavy rainstorm. "You know what I don't get?"

"What's that?" I swigged my own mimosa.

"Power steering went out, right?"

"That's the word."

"I know that car the kid was driving. I saw it at Cruisin' Colby in Everett last summer. I talked to the guy who must've sold it to the kid, and I'm pretty sure he said he replaced a whole bunch of stuff on it, including the power steering pump."

"Hmm. You into cars?"

"My daddy wanted a boy. I tried to be the next best thing. Handing him wrenches while he worked on his vehicles, going to classic car shows with him. Cruisin' Colby is a great one. You ever been?"

I shook my head. "No, but I've been to the Chattertowne classic car show while covering the Kupit Festival."

"Wait." Holden tapped the table. "Let's go back to what you just said. Are you sure it's the same car?"

"Oh, yeah. The paper had a photo of the back of the car, and I recognized the Mt St. Helens sticker on the bumper."

My photo, accompanying my recap of the accident. "You should let Chief Loveland know what you just told us."

Yellin's gaze widened. "Do you think it's significant?"

"Jack Dodd believes it wasn't an accident," I said. "Your information may prove him correct."

* * *

After brunch, cornered me near my car. "I saw your article."

"Okay."

"You called it an accident."

"As far as I know, it was an accident."

She folded her arms, swaying a bit as she did so. "You don't know that. No one knows that. Jack seems pretty convinced someone messed with his car."

"Someone like Wylie? You can't possibly believe that. Wylie loves Jack."

Her blue eyes glinted in a dangerous way. "I believe my son."

"Look, unless and until I'm given official word that it wasn't an accident, that's the story we'll be running."

Miranda flicked her long hair over her shoulder. She was naturally a brunette, but she had blonde highlights throughout. Her roots were darker and more obvious than she normally kept them, and her acrylic nails were grown out. For someone who took meticulous care of her appearance, it was unusual. Perhaps she hadn't had time for self-care recently.

"Has Cole had a chance to speak to Jack yet today?" I asked.

She sniffed and scrunched her nose. "He was sleeping. I'll take him down to the station when he's up for it."

Holden jogged over to where we were standing. "Did you hear the news?"

"What news?"

"I was just on the phone with Tony Bianchi, and get this. He says Cole brought Wylie Barrett in for questioning."

Miranda gasped and then turned on me, jabbing her overgrown fingernail into my shoulder. "I told you!"

"Why would he do that?" I rubbed the spot on my shoulder she'd poked.

"What changed since last night?"

Holden shrugged. "Bianchi says after Jack made those comments about it not being an accident, Cole requested the car get a thorough examination. Got it towed to the Washington State Patrol forensics lab first thing this morning. Their guy got under the hood and found the power steering lines didn't fail or break. They were intentionally cut, clean through. Fluid was completely drained."

"What does that mean?" I asked.

"It means the police no longer believe it was an accident. It was murder."

Chapter Six

I debated about whether to go to the police station to talk to Cole about Wylie being questioned or go straight to the office to write up the story. Since we were now predominantly an online newspaper with a limited print run for subscribers still wishing to have the full inky-finger experience, breaking news no longer had to wait until the morning edition to be disseminated.

Off to the *Coastal Current* I went.

I passed Tasha at the front desk. She was on the phone, so she mouthed something I couldn't understand and enthusiastically and dramatically waved at me with her left hand. Light reflected off her diamond wedding ring. Having recently gotten married to Sandros, our IT guy, she did that a lot these days, the showing off her ring unnecessarily thing.

When I passed Keith's office, his door was open, but he wasn't at his desk. Instead, his big laugh boomed from…wait, was that coming from my office? My office, which should have been locked?

Sure enough, Keith was perched on the corner of my desk. In the chair opposite him sat Onyx. Judging by her expression and fake laugh, she was placating him.

"What's happening? Why is my office open, and what are you doing in here, Keith?"

He jumped off the desk, knocking over my *Rockford Files* Detective Agency mug where I kept my pens. "Audrey! I saw Onyx, uh, Ms. Carpenter here, waiting outside your door. I grabbed the master key from Tasha, so she didn't have to stand in the hallway like a bum."

"I'd rather you didn't do that from now on. Also, when you get back to your office, pull up that list I made for you about terms to avoid using in our current millennium. Add bum."

He scrunched his face. "What if I'm referring to this?" He slapped his backside and then left the room laughing without waiting for my response.

"Sorry about him." I hung my purse on the hook behind my desk. "What's up?"

She wrung her hands. She'd been doing that a lot in the past twenty-four hours. "Wylie's been brought in for questioning."

"I heard that." I eased into my chair. "Were you…were you with him when it happened?"

She shook her head, causing her thick ponytail to swish. "No. He called me on his way downtown."

By downtown, she meant the Chattertowne Police station, which was on the first floor of City Hall building on Main Street, situated on the banks of the Jeanetta River, overlooking the marina. Technically, it *was* down the hill from First Street if you came via Oakwood, but the term *downtown* was a bit of a hyperbole.

"Audrey, I'm worried they might arrest him."

"I heard the car was inspected, and it appears the power steering lines were cut. That does lend credence to the idea this wasn't just an accident."

"That may be true, but I don't believe Wylie is responsible."

"Why accuse Wylie? Has he said anything to explain why Jack is pointing the finger at him?"

She tucked a stray brown strand behind her ear. "I asked him if he could think of anything he'd said or done that would incriminate him. He broke down in tears and said he'd devoted his life to teaching these kids."

In my experience, dramatic denials were often a telltale sign someone was hiding something. Same with the Mother Theresa routine. Anyone who came across as straight an arrow as Wylie did was typically the most bent. It was cynical, but true.

"I can understand how upsetting it might be for him to be accused, especially if he's truly innocent."

"He is! I know it. I know him." Tears welled in her eyes.

The question was, how well did we know anyone, much less someone we'd known as a kid? "I guess what I'm wondering, Onyx, is, why are you here?"

She wiped a stray tear. "You have to help him, Audrey. If not for Wylie, for Lacey and Viv's wedding. If he gets arrested, it will ruin their special day."

"Help him? How? What can I do?"

"I've been reading your articles. I know you helped solve both Marcus Washburn's murder and who set all those fires and sprayed the graffiti. I still subscribe to the *Current*. The digital version, of course. It helps me feel connected to Chattertowne. Connected to what's pure and authentic when the world I live in feels so plastic that I'm afraid everything and everyone around me might melt when the Santa Ana winds start to blow."

"If you've been reading my articles, then you should know that Chattertowne has a façade just like L.A. does. It's human nature for people to lie to protect themselves, to present themselves one way, while behaving completely differently behind closed doors."

She sniffed. "I understand that. I still believe that at the heart of this town and its people is a desire to do the right thing."

If believing the fairy tale about her hometown kept her feeling grounded, who was I to rob her of that?

"I'm still not sure what you think I can do to help Wylie."

"Investigate it!" She reached out to grip my hand like she might blow away if she let go. "Your job is to find out what happened. So do that. I don't trust this new police chief, Cade Loverboy—"

"Cole Loveland."

She waved a dismissive hand. "Whatever. He doesn't know Wylie, and he doesn't know Chattertowne. Not really. Your sister's getting married on Sunday. The last thing Viv and Lacey need on their special day is this dark cloud hanging over the wedding."

She had a point, even if it was furthering her own specific agenda, the least of which was my sister's happiness.

For me, however, Vivienne's happily ever after was much deserved and long overdue, and I would do anything to make sure she got it.

"I'll see what I can find out. I can't promise anything. If Wylie's a creep under that nice guy image…or worse, a murderer, well, there's not a lot I can do about it."

She jumped up from her chair and raced around the desk to give me an awkward hug. Well, she probably looked beautiful and graceful as always. I was sure I looked awkward, though.

"So what's your plan?" she asked.

"I'm starting with writing up this article that I need to get posted by noon, and then I'll head to the police station to see if Cole will tell me anything. What about you?"

She pouted. "Come to think of it, I don't want to sit around all day at the bed and breakfast. The lady who owns it keeps trying to talk to me about religion. Like, come on, lady. I'm a spiritual person, but I picked your place to stay because you have great cinnamon rolls and hypoallergenic pillows, not to have your missionary friends come save my soul."

Somewhere in her rant, I got a sinking feeling she wanted to tag along. "Onyx, I work alone."

"Come on, Audrey, it'll be fun!"

"How exactly am I supposed to keep a low profile if I've got last year's *Sports Illustrated* Swimsuit Edition cover model in tow?"

"Maybe people will be more willing to talk to you if I'm there."

Willing, maybe. Distracted, definitely.

* * *

Charlotte Murphy was filling in for Vivienne at the police station while she was off schedule for the wedding. I wasn't Charlotte's favorite person. Besides the fact I'd outed her husband, Kyle as part of a criminal conspiracy—for which he got eighteen months' probation—she also found out I had a less than flattering nickname for him: the weasel. She was especially tender about it because everyone told her their son looked just like his father.

"He's busy."

"I haven't even—"

"He's busy," she repeated, her mouth set in a firm line.

Onyx popped out from behind me. "Hi there!"

In a flash, Charlotte's face went from sour to delighted. "Oh my gosh! Onyx Carpenter!"

Onyx glanced at the nameplate on the other side of the glass. "Charlotte, is it?"

Charlotte nodded. "My friends call me Charlie."

They did? I supposed that meant she didn't count me among her friends.

"Charlie. What a beautiful name. I understand Chief Loveless—"

"Loveland," I muttered.

"Right. Chief Love*land* is busy with this car accident thing. I was just hoping—"

I cleared my throat.

"*We* were just hoping to speak with him for one teeny tiny moment."

Suddenly, Charlotte morphed into Emily Post, the hostess with the mostest. "Oh, of course! I'll see what I can do!" She picked up the phone and urgently whispered into it, her hand covering the receiver. She hung up and gave Onyx a broad smile. "He says he has a few minutes to spare."

"Oh, thank you, Charlie. You're the best!"

Charlotte beamed as she pressed the button to unlock the door. Her smile fell when she glanced at me.

I led Onyx down the hall to Cole's office and tapped on his door.

"Come in."

That in and of itself was unusual. Typically, he ignored my knock, assuming I would barge my way into his office whether he greeted me or not.

He was sitting at his desk writing on a yellow legal notepad. He glanced up at us with a broad smile. "Hello, ladies. How can I help you?"

What in the H-E-double hockey sticks were these shenanigans all about? Was Cole not as immune to Onyx's fame and charms as he'd always claimed?

Onyx floated into his office and lowered herself into a chair. I followed, but my seating was much less demure. More like a plopping than an easing.

"Sheriff—"

He held up a hand. "Let me stop you, Ms. Carpenter. I'm not with the county sheriff's office. I'm the Chattertowne chief of police."

"Chief—"

"Call me Cole, please."

"Oh, for the love of—" I mumbled.

"Cole. I fear we may have gotten off on the wrong foot last night."

"Boot," I said.

She turned to me. "Pardon?"

My face warmed. Had I said that out loud? "You, uh, you said you got off on the wrong foot. But Cole wears cowboy boots."

He shook his head.

Onyx tittered. "Oh! Hah. Audrey made a funny."

Instead of laughing with her, I wanted to cry in the corner. The whole situation had me out of sorts. Cole wasn't acting like himself; I wasn't acting like myself. Even Charlotte was acting strangely.

"Big fan of your work, by the way."

She brightened. "My talk show?"

"Do you have a talk show? I wasn't aware. I meant your toothpaste commercials. They used to come on during the Mariners games."

I leaned toward her. "Don't take it personally. He's not a big fan of technology. Hates social media. Rarely watches TV, except for sports."

Onyx grimaced and gave a forced laugh.

"Sorry, didn't mean to offend. How can I help you?" He directed his statement to Onyx.

I couldn't recall a time he'd ever uttered those words to me. Not without sarcasm, at least.

She pursed her lips, but inevitably chose not to address his lack of awareness of just how famous she was. "I heard you brought Wylie Barrett in for questioning."

"I cannot speak about the status of an ongoing investigation."

I leaned forward. "But you're saying there is an ongoing investigation. That must mean you don't believe it was an accident. Is it because of the cut power steering lines?"

Cole leaned back and crossed his arms. "Who told you that?"

"I have my sources."

"Better not have been one of my officers."

"I did not get the information from one of your officers. I promise." I crossed my heart without fear of repercussion. My statement was technically one hundred percent truthful. I got the information from Holden. He's the one who got it from Bianchi.

Cole," Onyx began, batting her lashes. "I know you're new to Chattertowne—"

"Not really. I've been here for nearly two years."

"In a small town, that's the blink of an eye. I know families that have been here for two generations who are just now shaking off the newbie label."

I nodded my agreement. "She's right. Just look at the mayor. She's been here well over a decade and they're still acting like she's an outsider."

"I'm aware."

Onyx crossed her long, tan legs. Cole's gaze flicked toward them but immediately returned to her face.

"All I'm trying to say is Wylie's family has been here forever. I've known him since we were in kindergarten together. He's not capable of hurting anyone, much less two kids."

"If that's the case, the investigation will bear it out."

He was being tighter-lipped than usual. Perhaps Onyx's belief that her presence would make him more willing to reveal all was misguided. Perhaps she was having the opposite effect. I felt a blip of satisfaction at the thought.

"Onyx, Charlotte at the front desk is a key player in the Chattertowne gossip tree. Maybe you can rattle the branches a bit, see if anything shakes out."

"Good idea! I'll be right back." She hopped up and scuttled out of Cole's office.

He gave me a wry smile. "Nice metaphor."

"Thanks."

"You got rid of her on purpose."

"I just sent her on an errand."

His smile broadened. "You know that Charlotte's information is suspect. The woman didn't even know what her own husband was up to."

"I just thought her presence might be a distraction to you."

"Jealous?"

I scoffed. "Of what? Of Onyx? Look, she's famous and beautiful and rich and successful. Good for her. I remember her covered in zit cream, wearing headgear. I know she snores like a chainsaw, or at least she did before she had her nose job."

"Definitely jealous." He popped his boots onto his desk.

"I'm not! I just thought maybe, since you and I have established a rapport of trust, you might be more willing to share information with me if she wasn't around. It's obvious she's biased in favor of Wylie."

He observed me for a moment, chewing on his lower lip. He'd shaved his entire face, other than a tiny tuft of hair on his chin just below his mouth. "You two are working together, though, right? You and Onyx. A little *Cagney & Lacey* action? *Rizzoli & Isles*? I'd watch it. Ooh, maybe throw in that cop Garcia from Lynnwood PD. The one who got suspended for having an OnlyFans account where she posted videos of her wearing nothing but her holster and badge. It would be a hit."

I'd promised my mother I'd stop rolling my eyes, but he was definitely weakening my resolve. "So, you're saying you're not going to give me anything?"

"Off the record?"

"Fine."

He rubbed his chin. "Here's what I can tell you. I'm still waiting on Jack's official statement. I spoke with Wylie, and he reiterated that he had nothing to do with the accident. Someone from the Washington State Patrol's felony collision division retrieved the vehicle, following a preliminary investigation by our team that indicates the power steering lines were cut."

"Can you be more specific?"

He sighed and turned to his computer screen. "According to this report, there were two types of power steering pumps on Impalas from 1961-'64, and two different gearboxes. Both used a hydraulic ram to push the tie rod to assist in steering, but they used different ways of controlling the hydraulic circuit. It's a complex system, but I guess the guy examining the car is an expert on Corvettes and other Chevy vehicles from that era. He gave me a long and detailed description of both systems, the Eaton and the Saginaw box, if you'd like me to read it to you."

"I don't even understand half of what you're saying."

"Doesn't really matter. The gist is the car oscillates when the power steering fails, and in this case, the lines show a very clean cut. They will continue to examine the car and submit a full report, but he says the cause of the failure is not in doubt."

"Okay, so the lines were cut. That doesn't mean Wylie did it."

"I haven't charged him. I just brought him in for a chat."

"Hah. Right. Did he bring an attorney with him for the interview?"

"Nope. He came alone."

"That's got to speak to his innocence, right? He didn't feel the need to shield himself."

"I've seen it both ways. Just because someone's dumb enough not to bring their attorney with them while being questioned doesn't mean they're innocent."

"Fair enough."

"It's also possible he just didn't have time to hire one yet. He said something about Onyx trying to get in touch with her attorney in Los Angeles."

"Did he have any idea why Jack would accuse him of causing the accident?"

"Suspects typically don't provide us their possible motives."

"I can tell you exactly why I accused him," said a male voice behind me.

I whipped my head around. Jack was standing in the doorway with Miranda flaring her nostrils behind him.

"I accused him of causing the accident because he wants me dead."

"That's a lie!" Onyx's voice squeaked from the hallway. "Why are you saying that? It's not true, Jack! You have to know he would never do that."

Jack's gaze narrowed. "Coach wanted me out of the way so he could have Lee all to himself."

Miranda nodded. "He is a grade-A creep and pervert. He nearly killed my son, and as it is, his training will be interrupted at a crucial time. Wylie Barrett should be locked up. Cole, if you care about me and Jack at all, you'll arrest him. Now!"

Chapter Seven

All hell broke loose in Cole's office after Miranda declared Wylie a pervert and demanded Cole arrest him. Onyx lunged for her, but Miranda grabbed her purse and clotheslined Onyx. Jack tried to step in between them, but Miranda held him at bay.

Onyx pleaded to Jack to recant, all the way trying to swipe at Miranda.

Cole hopped up from behind his desk like he'd sat on a spur and jumped between the two women, but not before Miranda got hold of a chunk of Onyx's hair. I sat in stunned awe watching the entire thing unfold. I was never one for conflict, but this was a car crash—ooh, poor choice of words—a *melee* from which I couldn't avert my eyes.

Tony Bianchi arrived on the scene, and Cole directed him to take Miranda and Jack to the conference room. He gave Onyx a stern warning about her attempted assault and banished us from his office and the police station.

Outside of City Hall, Onyx straightened her blouse and silk shorts. "That woman. I should sue her."

"Who, Miranda? Onyx, you tried to tackle her."

"She's spewing lies that could ruin a man's life!"

A family walking passed us stopped in their tracks at her outburst. A glimmer of recognition crossed each of their faces one by one.

I grabbed Onyx's arm. "Come on, we need to get you out of here before your presence causes a riot."

"Where are we going?"

"Just follow me."

I took her down the steps toward the marina.

"Audrey, what about your fear of water?"

"I've been working through it. Now, stick close to me and keep your head down." I gripped her arm tighter within mine. This was more for me than for her, but I'd have denied it if called out on it.

By *working through it*, I meant that my therapist had taught me some techniques to keep me from going into full-blown panic attacks every time I had to go near the river for a story.

"Mmm hmm hmm hmm hmm hmm hmm," I hummed.

"What…what is that?"

"What?"

"What you're humming. It sounds familiar."

"Hmm? Uh, I don't know." We'd made it to the gangplank to dock B, and as dread began to rise within me, my humming became more insistent. "Hmm Hmm Hmm Hmm Hmm Hmm hmm hmm hmm hmm."

"I'm sure I know the song."

My breathing started to constrict, which made the humming more difficult. "Hmm-gasp-hmm hmm-hmm." I coughed.

"You're swaying. You're not gonna pass out on me, are you?"

"Maybe."

"Tell me where we're going."

"Sailboat. Down there." I pointed and hummed.

Onyx was now propping me upright as my head swirled from the immense air I was expelling while humming.

"This one?"

I nodded vigorously. She climbed down onto the boat and guided me down as well.

Once we got inside, I could pretend I wasn't near the water, despite the gentle rocking of the boat.

"Are we allowed to be here?" Onyx asked.

I pulled a key from my purse and, with fumbling fingers, unlocked the door. "It's Lacey and Viv's boat. They live here. Well, Lacey does, and Viv does most of the time. She's moving in full-time after the wedding."

When I'd returned to Chattertowne from Portland, Vivienne and I had shared her drab apartment. I'd recently moved into my dead ex-boyfriend's home that he'd shared with his wife and kids after she'd relocated the family to Canada—a long, convoluted story—while Vivienne had stayed in the apartment. Her lease was up at the end of the month, and she was transitioning to full-time boating life in addition to married life.

Once Onyx and I were sitting on the couch, the stars started to clear from my vision, and my breathing began to regulate.

She scanned the living room and kitchen. "Nice digs. I thought Lacey worked construction."

"She does. Well, technically, she and Holden are running Fred Harper's old company. The one Fred had before—" I slashed my thumb across my throat with added sound effects.

"His throat was slit?" She grimaced.

"Uh, no. Rat poison." Another long, convoluted story. "Anyway, Lacey used to be assistant police chief. She got caught up in the City Hall scandal, and, well, a murder, but they didn't seize the boat, which was likely paid for with bribes. I mean, I assume it was. I didn't ask."

"You're a reporter."

"I know, but as it was, Viv was devastated by Lacey's arrest, and there was a plea deal in place. I didn't want to make things worse. She did her time."

"If she was involved with a murder, I'm not sure she did."

"Hello?" a voice called from outside. "Is somebody in there?"

"It's me, Viv. Onyx is with me."

Vivienne walked into the living room clutching her chest. "Geez, you guys gave me a heart attack. I thought I was interrupting a burglary."

"Nope, just a run-of-the-mill home invasion."

"Your boat is beautiful, Viv," said Onyx.

"Thanks, we like it. When Lacey's off probation, we want to take it up to Alaska." Vivienne gave a quick wave. "Not to be rude, but what *are* you guys doing here?"

"Escaping Onyx's fans."

Onyx laughed. "It was a suburban family of four. They were harmless."

My sister narrowed her gaze at me. "You hate coming down here."

"She did some weird humming thing the whole way."

"Humming?" Vivienne asked.

I shrugged.

"What do you mean, humming?"

Onyx held up her hands. "I think it's something her therapist talked her into doing. Seemed like all it did was make her hyperventilate. The song sounded familiar, but I can't place it." Onyx hummed the tune.

Vivienne burst out laughing. "*Safety Dance*? You were humming *Safety Dance* by Men Without Hats?"

I shrugged again. "My therapist told me to pick something that would make me feel safe. Seemed a reasonable choice."

"I knew I recognized it!" Onyx slapped her leg.

"But let's go back. Why were you down at the marina in the first place?" asked Vivienne.

"We were at City Hall talking to Cole, trying to get information. Then Miranda showed up and things went sideways." I said.

"Sideways?"

Onyx looked sheepish. "In my defense, she was saying awful things about Wylie."

Vivienne's gaze widened. "What happened?"

"Jack's claiming Wylie was either involved or *wanted* to be involved with Laveda Volkova," I said.

"Which is preposterous." Onyx flailed her arms. "And Miranda called him a pervert and a creep."

"It wouldn't be the first time a coach or teacher crossed a line," said Vivienne.

"Come on, Viv. You know Wylie. He's not like that," said Onyx.

Vivienne sighed. "I've come to realize people are rarely who they appear to be on the surface."

She was speaking from experience, and it was a concept I'd also learned a lot about over the past few years.

"What about Jack?" I asked Vivienne. "You and Miranda are friends. What's your take on him? Would he lie about something like that just to get

Wylie in trouble?"

"Everything I've seen indicates he's a good kid. If you ask Miranda, he's perfect." Vivienne's expression softened. "Onyx, I know Wylie means a lot to you. And I know you have a lot of guilt about how things ended between the two of you. But I can't imagine Meacham is going to be thrilled that you're spending so much energy trying to help your ex-boyfriend. I mean, you've said in the past he can be a bit…jealous."

"What am I supposed to do? Let Wylie get railroaded for a crime he didn't commit? He *couldn't* have committed, I might add."

"How can you know that?" Vivienne's voice was quiet, but firm.

"I know that because I was with him all evening."

Chapter Eight

Onyx's confession that she'd been with Wylie the entire evening of the accident landed with a thud. Could it be trusted, considering she was trying to exonerate him? What better way to help him than by giving him an alibi?

It was pretty shocking, the lengths she seemed to be willing to go for a man she hadn't been in a relationship with for more than a decade.

Not to mention that she was married to one of the biggest rock stars on the planet, a notoriously jealous man who was expected to arrive in town within a day or two and was no doubt bringing with him a horde of paparazzi. Onyx was taking a pretty big risk, but that made it even more likely she was telling the truth. She'd been at the 3F meeting with Wylie, and I was pretty sure she was the figure I'd spotted in his car at the accident scene. Not long after that, they'd arrived together at the hospital.

"Onyx, what's going on between you and Wylie?" asked Vivienne.

"Nothing. We're just friends. We were talking, that's all. Like you said, I've never stopped feeling guilty for how I just took off after graduation, breaking his heart in the process. I felt I owed him an explanation."

I studied her for a moment. "Where were you talking?"

She jerked her chin to look at me. Her green eyes blazed. Then she dropped her gaze to her hands in her lap. She toyed with her fingernails. "At the same place where the 3F meeting was held. The church, or whatever."

She was lying. The reason *why* she was lying, I had no clue, but she was definitely lying.

"I'm surprised you guys didn't see the ambulance on your way to the scene."

She returned her gaze to mine. "We did. Of course, we did."

"Wylie said you hadn't."

She waved a dismissive hand. "We were in the middle of a conversation. He was distracted."

Vivienne scrunched her brows together. "Too distracted to notice an ambulance flying by with lights and sirens on a dark two-lane road?"

Onyx sucked in her cheeks. "Apparently."

So, she was doubling down. It was an interesting—and telling—choice. It'd be a shame if it came back to bite her in the rear.

"If we're done with the interrogation, I'd like to head back to my B and B for a quick nap. Audrey?"

"Oh, do you have to go too?" Vivienne asked me. "I wanted to talk to you about dressing up Rachel's wheelchair with flowers and ribbons."

Rachel was our cousin on our dad's side. She'd been born nine weeks premature and was diagnosed with cerebral palsy shortly after birth. By far the most successful person in our family, Rachel was not only an attorney, but she was also an alternate for the US women's Parapan American Games' wheelchair basketball team a few years back. That athletic gene certainly hadn't made its way to me.

"Why wasn't she at brunch this morning?"

"She was meeting with the Washington State Attorney General's office about some potential ADA noncompliance issues in the proposed transit station plans."

"Do you have to talk about that now? Audrey's my ride." Onyx crossed her arms.

It was only about a mile to her B&B so technically she could walk, but a mile in public for Onyx was likely to cause a ruckus.

"I'll FaceTime you later, Viv. We can talk about it then."

With Onyx on my heels, I slid open the back door of the sailboat and was temporarily blinded by a ray of sunlight beaming through the clouds.

"Onyx!" "Onyx!" "Over here!" The shouts were instantaneous and aggressive.

I shielded my eyes from the sun. A half dozen frenzied men holding various types of cameras stared back at me from the docks above.

"That's not Onyx," one of them shouted.

I glanced over my shoulder. She'd crouched down behind me.

"What are you doing?" I hissed.

"I'm hiding. What does it look like?"

"She's behind her!" someone squealed.

"Apparently not very well," I said.

She sighed and got to her feet. "Hello, boys. Nice to see you again…not."

"What's this we hear about you being involved with a murder?" This came from the big dude in back who looked a bit like Uncle Fester from *the Addams Family*.

She skirted around me. "Help me up and I'll give you a statement."

Onyx stepped onto the ladder and grabbed hold of a higher rung with her left hand. She reached up her right hand, and they all clambered to offer theirs to her.

One dude got knocked over in the mayhem. "Hey!" They ignored him.

After she was helped onto the dock, I started to climb the ladder, but no one even acknowledged me, much less offered to give me a hand. I threw my leg up onto the dock in my standard, less-than-graceful manner, and if even one of them had been paying any attention to me at all, I would have been mortified. In her presence, I was invisible. Normally, that would be a huge blow to my ego, but in this case, all I felt was relief. I scrambled to my feet and brushed myself off.

"So, what's the scoop?" Uncle Fester bellowed. "About the murder, I mean."

She flashed a brilliant smile tinged with condescension. "There is no murder, just a very unfortunate accident. Two kids were driving on a dark and winding road, and they missed a turn. Nothing more than that. I met them earlier in the evening at a youth event where I was trying to inspire a roomful of teens to imagine a life beyond Chattertowne, like I did. Great kids. So much lost potential. Poor girl. A real tragedy."

The man who had been pushed to the ground wrinkled his forehead. "If that's true, that it was an accident, why was your high school sweetheart just arrested for murder?"

Her smile faltered. "You must be mistaken. Wylie Barrett went to the station this morning for an interview, but that's all. He's their golf coach and also an inspirational speaker. Like me."

"No." It was Fester again. He shook his head. "Not this morning. Just now. We heard you'd been spotted at City Hall, so we hightailed it over here. Right as we arrived, we ran into a family who claimed they saw you headed this way. Next thing we knew, the dude was perp-walked past us in custody. Handcuffed behind his back and everything!"

The color drained from her face. She whipped around and began running down the docks toward the exit. After a split-second hesitation, the rest of us chased after her. It was like a scene from *Scooby-Doo, Where Are You?* Someone even yelled, "after her!" and I could have sworn I heard the cartoon's theme song playing overhead.

Traveling in a pack of paparazzi was not on my bingo card for this lifetime.

On the plus side, I was in the middle of the herd, so I felt protected from possibly falling in the water. Unless we all went in, which, while horrifying, would also have been a fitting end to the scene.

We made our way to street level and rounded the corner of City Hall. An officer stationed at the front door had stopped Onyx in her tracks. I was pretty sure he was the kid who used to eat paste in my kindergarten class.

"Do you have any idea who I am?" Onyx actually stomped her foot.

"Ma'am, I don't care if you're the Queen of Sheba. If you don't take a step back out of my face, you will be spending the night in jail."

I rushed up and pulled her back. "Hi, uh, Billy, isn't it?"

He gave me a wary look. "I go by William now, and I know who you are, Audrey. And who you work for."

"Oh, but you don't know me?" Onyx squealed.

"Of course, I do. You're the woman who was just screaming in my face." He wiped his nose and mouth in a dramatic gesture. "And spitting."

The paparazzi crew howled with laughter.

I held up my hands in a *calm-down* gesture. "Billy. Bill. Billiam? Come on, now. Let's be reasonable."

He scowled. "William."

"William. I apologize." I softened my tone, hoping to appease him. "Onyx didn't mean to invade your personal space." I jerked my head to give her an insistent glare. "Did you?"

She was about to respond when his gaze widened. "Onyx? Onyx Carpenter?" His voice rose two octaves. "That is you! Oh, wow!"

She preened. "So you *do* know who I am."

His face transitioned from jubilant to straight-faced, and he crossed his arms. It was a bait and switch, and she'd fallen for it. "Of course I do. Everyone in the world pretty much knows who you are. That doesn't give you the right to scream in my face."

"I just need to get in there to find out what's going on with Wylie!"

"Chief asked me to stand guard, keep the press out." He glanced at me. "I guess that includes you."

Heat began to rise from my chest to my ears. "You might want to double-check that."

He shrugged.

"I'm not press," Onyx said. "And I'm not really with her."

Throwing me under the bus. Nice.

"You and your entourage need to find someplace else to congregate. We have laws about these kinds of things."

"Yeah, it's called the First Amendment, and we have the right to peaceably assemble," I countered.

"And I have the right to disperse an unruly mob, which this is quickly becoming." He jerked his chin in the direction of those gathered behind me.

I turned and saw that not only were the paparazzi recording the entire thing, about twenty passersby had stopped and were recording with their phones.

I grabbed Onyx's arm. "We've got to get out of here. We're making a scene."

"What are we going to do, Audrey? This is such a mess!" She covered her face with her hands and began to make little mewling noises that sounded like a lost kitten. Whether an act or genuine, it was unclear.

"We'll figure something out. I'll get ahold of Cole and figure out what's happening."

She removed her hands, and her cheeks were indeed damp, red, and splotchy. "It's getting late in the day. People are going home soon, like lawyers and judges. What if Wylie has to sit in jail all night until he can get released?"

A car door slammed behind us. The paparazzi, the looky-loos, and I turned around. A black Lincoln Town Car idled at the curb.

Standing in front of it was none other than Meacham Fields, who was wearing a peculiar look on his face. "'Allo, love. Wanna explain to me why you're standin' on a street corner cryin' over your ex-boyfriend?"

Chapter Nine

The situation went from bad to worse. A van full of paparazzi pulled up on the scene outside City Hall just in time to witness the standoff between a teary Onyx and her rockstar husband, who was less than pleased that his wife was sobbing about the arrest of her ex-boyfriend.

Even though they were in competition with each other, the paparazzi tended to share resources. One of them told me they'd been following Meacham since his private plane had landed at the small local airfield called Paine Field. Someone had tipped them off that he wouldn't be landing at SeaTac International, so they'd been ready and waiting.

So much for his stealthy arrival.

In addition to the horde of photographers and tabloid journalists, the crowd of onlookers had grown exponentially.

Some of the original observers had gone live on social media, which had people all over Chattertowne dropping what they were doing to race to the area. Then, of course, was the infamous—some would say notorious—Chattertowne gossip mill. I wouldn't have been surprised if all the cell towers in the area blew from the spike in calls and texts among the locals.

We'd all been delusional, thinking this wedding would be anything other than a circus with these two involved...and that was *before* the possible murder investigation.

I gave Billy, uh, William, a pleading look. "We need to get them inside. I'll help you keep the rest of the crowd at bay, but things will only get more chaotic if they stay out here."

He eyed me up and down. "I highly doubt you'll be able to restrain the mob. Weren't you the one who cried every day at lunch?"

"I was six and homesick. Cut me some slack." Probably not a good idea to bring up his penchant for chugging Elmer's paste when I needed his help, but his disdain nearly pushed me over the edge.

"I just gotta ask." He sneered. "How's it feel to have a dirty cop marrying your sister?"

So that was it. He was mad about Lacey's past transgressions. "She served her time."

"Not even close."

"It's not like that!" Onyx whimpered from behind me.

I glanced over my shoulder. She wasn't speaking to Billy. She was arguing with her husband.

Meacham spoke low into her ear, probably so that no one could hear what he was saying, but his scowl was menacing.

I whipped back to Officer Unfriendly. "Please? I'm begging you."

He scanned the growing crowd, and then his eyes settled on Meacham and Onyx. "You two." He crooked two fingers. "Come here."

After a moment's hesitation, they did as he asked. He opened the door and ushered them inside, much to the vocal disappointment of the bystanders and the vultures.

"You should go inside, too," he said to me. "I've got this." He indicated the throng that was pressing closer to the door.

"Are you sure?"

"Go, before I change my mind."

"Thank you!"

He held open the door, and I ducked under his arm. Through the glass, I heard him shout, "Settle down now. I'm in the mood to cuff some people."

Charlotte spotted me from behind the glass. "He's busy."

"I know he's busy. I'm the one who sent Onyx and Meacham in here."

She pinched her mouth and made a face like I was a bug she wanted to squash. "Don't you ever get tired of it?"

Hoo boy. "Tired of what, Charlotte?"

"Of meddling. You're always inserting yourself into situations that don't concern you."

"I'm a reporter. It's kind of my job."

"Well, my job is to keep out the riffraff." She cocked an eyebrow.

Cole poked his head through the doorway. "Oh, good, you're here. I need you."

I gave Charlotte a victorious smirk as I flounced past her. Not mature by any means, but definitely satisfying.

"Billiam is quite the gatekeeper."

He shot a curious glance over his shoulder. "Billiam?"

"Billy boy. Apparently, he no longer likes to be called that, though. He prefers William. Does he still eat paste?"

Cole shook his head. "Every day I'm reminded how odd the citizens of Chattertowne are."

"Oh, come on. Every elementary school has a paste eater. Just like every school has the kid who cuts their own bangs during art and one who's mercilessly teased for the entire year because they fell in the mud at a particularly rainy recess and was forced to wear pants from the lost and found that smelled like old cheese and were ten years out of style."

He stopped halfway down the hall, and his shoulders shook silently.

"Are you crying?"

He shook his head but kept his back to me. He began emitting wheezy bursts of laughter.

I wheeled him to face me. Tears were streaming down his face.

"It…was—" He gasped. "It was you, wasn't it? With the pants, I mean." He wiped his cheek.

I set my mouth in a firm line. "You're missing the point. Billy was acting pretty high and mighty out there for someone who decoupaged their internal organs."

"I've heard it has a hint of mint."

"Cole Loveland! Were *you* the paste eater in your class?"

He wiped his eyes and chuckled. "I'll never tell."

Inside his office, Onyx and Meacham were sitting next to each other, but their body language indicated things were not copacetic between them.

Meacham kept pursing his lips, while Onyx picked at her cuticles.

I'd never seen Meacham in real life, only on TV, the cover of CDs, and in magazines. Up close, he had crow's feet around his gray eyes and dark circles underneath them. His weathered forehead showed signs of too much sun exposure. His forearms were covered with tattoos of everything from Onyx's name to Celtic crosses to a bottle of Crown Royal. And, surprisingly, he had flakes of dandruff in his hair.

The dandruff definitely made him less intimidating.

I offered my hand to him. "Audrey O'Connell. I'm an old friend of Onyx."

He warily shook my hand, but then his gaze widened. "O'Connell? Are you the one who's gettin' married?"

"No, that's my sister Vivienne."

"Oh, yeah, right. Right. Brilliant."

Cole sat on the corner of his desk. "So, as I was saying, we're on a tight window to get Wylie bailed out today. Snohomish County courthouse is twenty minutes away, and even if we could get him processed quickly, I doubt we can get him a hearing before the end of the day."

"And as *I* was saying, *that* is unacceptable." Onyx narrowed her eyes. "You created this predicament by arresting him. You should fix it."

I held up my hand. "Can someone catch me up to speed? Why *was* Wylie arrested?"

Cole crossed his arms. "Evidence has presented itself that indicates Jack's allegations have merit. Both the relationship between Wylie and Laveda, and of Wylie's motive to cut the break lines."

"What kind of evidence?"

He shook his head. "Can't disclose that at this time. Let's just say it's both digital and physical evidence."

"Digital. Like text messages?"

"As I said, I can't disclose that at this time. As a result, I have placed Wylie Barrett in custody. The D.A. is preparing charging papers."

Onyx huffed. "My attorney will have a lot to say about that."

Cole looked at me with eyebrows raised. I took that to mean he wanted me to manage her.

Before I could open my mouth, Meacham growled. "*Your* attorney? Why is *your*— meaning *our*—attorney gettin' involved? Where is *his* attorney?"

Onyx's phone rang in her hand. "This is him now." She pressed a button to connect. "Eugene, hi. Thanks for getting back to me so quickly."

The person on the other end of the phone heaved a weary sigh. "What's he done now?"

"You're on speaker phone," she sang through gritted teeth. "And it's not about Meacham this time."

"Yeah, Gene, *this time* it's not me. It's her ex-boyfriend. She's tryin' to get 'im off."

Unfortunate choice of words.

"Geez, I'm not trying to get him off. I'm trying to bail him out. The sheriff here…say hi, sheriff." She held the phone toward Cole.

He cleared his throat. "Uh, sir, this is Chattertowne Chief of Police Cole Loveland. I'm not the sheriff."

"Not yet, at least," I said under my breath.

Cole gave me a look of warning.

Sorry, I mouthed.

"Onyx, what in the world is going on up there?" said the attorney.

"Gene, an old friend of mine—"

Meacham interrupted her with a guffaw. "Friend. Right."

"An old *friend* of mine was arrested this afternoon, and the sheriff here seems to want to hold him overnight rather than letting me bail him out of jail."

Another deep sigh. "Onyx, I'm not licensed to practice law in the state of Washington. If your *friend* had been arrested in California, New York, Illinois, or Florida, I could help you. As it stands, you're gonna need to hire somebody else. Someone local."

"But we're running out of time! He can't spend the night in jail. He's not built for the big house."

Since I was fighting the urge to roll my eyes, I was certain Eugene the attorney was as well.

"I'm sure the good people of…what's the name of the county again?"

"Snohomish."

"Sno-what-ish?"

"Sno-ho-mish."

"Well, I'm sure the good people of Snohomish County will treat your friend just fine for one night. In the meantime, try to find someone local to help him."

"What do I pay you for?" she screamed into the phone before hanging up the call.

Not a good look.

"How about this?" said Cole. "I'll keep him here overnight. I'll transfer him tomorrow to Snohomish County Superior Court for his first appearance hearing. That way, he won't have to spend the night with the general population. You get someone to take his case, he should be bailed out before having to spend another night in custody."

Her lower lip quivered. "I suppose that's better than nothing. But how are we going to find an attorney at this late hour? Especially one who'd be willing to take a case on short notice?"

I smirked at Cole. "Oh, I happen to know someone. But he's a little bit of a drive away, down in Tacoma."

Cole slowly shook his head. "You can't be serious."

"Who?" Onyx perked up.

"Oh, I'm absolutely serious."

"Who are you talking about?"

Cole cocked his brow. "Don't you still have him on retainer?"

"Best dollar I ever spent."

Onyx jumped to her feet. "Would someone please explain to me who you're talking about?"

"Todd Wainwright. Come on. I'll fill you in as we head to his office."

"Tacoma. Isn't that far? We won't get there before five o'clock. Won't his office be closed?"

"Not Todd's office. He's used to clients who need him after hours."

"But he's good?"

"He's good." I refrained from adding, *for a lawyer who operates out of a strip mall between a liquor store and a tattoo parlor.*

Chapter Ten

Meacham insisted we take his Town Car, which had been parked in the loading zone for over an hour. If it weren't for Chattertowne PD having to deal with crowd control, it would have been ticketed and towed by the time we exited City Hall.

I gave the driver the address for Todd Wainwright's law office and sat back into the comfy leather seat for the long ride to Tacoma. What might have taken forty-five minutes in the middle of the day was likely to take at least twice that long in rush hour.

"So, how do you know this guy?" Onyx sat across from me.

"He was helpful in a recent case I was investigating for the paper. The spray painting arson case you mentioned, remember? Anyway, Todd's a little unorthodox, but under the circumstances, he's probably the best we are going to get."

"He's a defense attorney?"

"Not exactly."

"Well, what kind of attorney is he, *exactly?*"

"He specializes in civil rights cases, but he also takes on a lot of divorces."

"Wylie's civil rights are definitely being violated. He's being held against his will."

Meacham scoffed. "His rights aren't being violated, O. He's been arrested for murder. That's kind of how it works."

She flared her nostrils, but didn't respond to his jab. To me, she said, "Did you let him know we're coming?"

"I texted him and he said he'd be there until at least seven. We'll make it by about six-thirty, so it'll be close, but he'll wait for us. He knows it's you."

The air in the limo was charged. Onyx was stressed about Wylie's arrest, and Meacham was pissed that Onyx was more worried about her ex than his feelings.

"So, Meacham," I began. "How's the tour going?"

"It's fine. We played the United Center last night. Sold out crowd."

"I mean, it's no Soldier Field like Taylor got, but it's a decent venue." Judging by her sour expression and narrowed gaze, Onyx knew she was picking a fight.

Oh, goody. Nothing like being stuck in a car in traffic with feuding spouses. At least it was a nice car. I spotted a crystal decanter of what I assumed was whisky of some sort. That would come in handy.

"Well, if that venue's good enough for Madonna, it's good enough for us." He turned away from her so that his back was to her.

She did the same in the opposite direction.

Uncomfortable silence was preferable to arguing.

I pulled out my phone.

I had a text from Vivienne asking me to call asap, a text from my mother with a photo of a less ugly but still very green bridesmaid dress, and a gif from Holden featuring Happy Gilmore angrily yelling at a golf ball with the caption "**You.**"

I returned Holden's text with an emoji sticking out its tongue and then sent a thumbs up to the dress to my mother because it was less horrible than the original, and at that point, beggars couldn't be choosers.

I texted Viv a question mark. Immediately, my phone began to ring.

"Do you guys mind if I take this? It's my sister."

Onyx shrugged her shoulders. Meacham didn't even respond.

I swiped the phone to answer. "Hey."

Sniffling came through the phone.

"Viv, what's wrong?"

"Wylie's been arrested."

"I know."

"You know? How can you be so calm? My wedding is in four days. You don't have a dress, Miranda's son's girlfriend is dead, and now one of Lacey's groomsmen is in jail for murder!"

"First, mom seems to have located a dress that is less pond scum color and more sage. I don't hate it. Second, we're headed to see Todd Wainwright in Tacoma as we speak. He's going to help Wylie. At least I hope he is."

"Who's we?"

"I'm with Onyx and Meacham. We're in their limo."

"You're in a limo with Meacham Fields?" she squeaked. "Why didn't you invite me?"

"Technically, it's a Town Car," muttered Onyx.

"Because we left City Hall and headed straight here. In fact, we're about to get off the exit. We're going to do everything we can to get Wylie released first thing in the morning."

"This wedding is a disaster. Maybe we should call it off and just have Margarita marry us in the mayor's office."

"Don't you dare. Mom would kill you, and neither of us will ever hear the end of it. We're almost to the finish line. Just breathe. I'll update you when I know more."

"Fine." She paused. "Is he as hot in person?"

I glanced over at Meacham. "Ehh."

"Really! Okay. Call me when you get home."

"I will."

Onyx gave me a subdued pout. "What was all that about?"

"Viv is stressed about Wylie being in jail instead of at the wedding."

"No. I got that part. I mean, when you said, *Ehh*."

Lying wasn't my strong suit, and since my poker face was notoriously bad, panic rose within me.

Thankfully, the car pulled into the strip mall parking lot where Todd's office was located.

"Oh, we're here!"

Onyx and Meacham both looked out the window.

"Is this a joke?" he asked. "Are we being pranked?" He looked up at the roof of the car. "Is there a camera hidden inside? Ashton? You can come out now."

I opened the door. "Nope. No joke. But I promise you that Todd Wainwright is the best attorney based in a strip mall in the region."

Onyx's mouth was pinched into a pucker. "Audrey, I swear, if you dragged me all this way to meet with some sleazeball, I'm going to kill you."

I gave a forced laugh. "Ha ha. Poor choice of words." I gave Meacham a pleading look. "Right? Ha ha."

He was stone-faced.

"Come on. Trust me. He's a little rough around the edges, but he's good at his job." I clambered out the door.

The chauffeur rushed around to the other side of the car. He glared at me, probably because I hadn't waited for him to open the door. He stood by as Meacham exited, and then he held out his hand for Onyx.

Meacham gripped the driver's shoulder. "Keep it running, mate. I have a feeling this won't take long."

"On the plus side, there's barely anyone in the parking lot, so we'll be able to sneak in without being seen." I shuffled toward the entrance of the law office.

Meacham glanced at the Union Jack-emblazoned MINI Cooper parked in front of the office. He put his hand over his heart. "My people."

"That belongs to Todd's receptionist. Her name is Lottie."

I opened the front door, and a bell rang overhead.

Lottie looked up from behind her oak desk. "Oh, hey there, Audrey! How are you?" She was chewing gum, which smacked noisily as she talked. She wore her signature bright red lipstick, and her brown hair was as voluptuous as her breasts peeking out from the top of her black scoop-necked shirt. "Mr. Wainwright said to expect you. He's finishing up wit' a client, then he—" Her gaze widened, her mouth fell open, and her gum dropped on the counter in front of her. She silently pointed a bright red coffin nail toward the door.

I glanced over my shoulder. She was staring at Meacham.

"I guess he didn't tell you to expect *him*."

"You-you're M-Meacham F-Fields. I had your poster on my wall at university," she whispered.

Meacham, who'd had decades of this type of adoration, went into rockstar mode. "Hiya Chicken. Aren't you just a sight for sore eyes. That must be your car outside."

"Wait, you know each other?" I asked.

"No, no. I just mean meetin' a fellow Brit. Makes me homesick."

Onyx slumped into a chair. "Maybe you should move back there." She said it loud enough for me to hear it, but quiet enough that Lottie and Meacham couldn't.

Probably for the best. While Todd was a skilled divorce attorney, that wasn't the purpose of our visit.

While we waited, Onyx scrolled through all the comments on her latest social media post. Meacham leaned back in his seat and closed his eyes, as if unbothered by everything that had happened since he landed in Washington. It was a ruse, though, because every time Onyx made a coo or an affronted gasp, his left eye fluttered open just a smidge.

Occasionally, I caught Lottie sneaking furtive glances at Meacham.

"Honestly, do these people have nothing better to do?" Onyx thrust her phone into my face. "Just look at this."

Fatbottomgrl75 had commented, "**Onyx is showing her age. Get some Botox why don't you?**"

In response, OnyxStan posted, "**Why don't you crawl back under your rock.**"

PatriotEagle1776 said, "**I hear Onyx and Meacham drink each other's blood. Maybe that's why she's looking so old. 'Cause he's got old blood.**"

"Gross," I said.

Another comment caught my eye. "**She's protecting a murderer.**" The account name was User63452912788. The profile pic on the account was a default gray figure. I clicked on it and saw the account was private and had no followers. It followed two accounts, but since the settings were private, I couldn't see who they were.

I handed her back her phone. "Is your comment section always like this?"

"It's been worse. Remember when I came out with my skincare line, and someone claimed I stole their idea? You should have seen the nasty stuff that woman and her dumb friends said to me. Like, beyotch, you don't own the concept of naming products after cocktails, and just because you spilled your pina colada on your legs and it made them smell like a beach party doesn't mean you're the *only* person to think of making lotion from those scents. Take your kiwi mojito eye cream and shove it up your—"

"Audrey, Mr. Wainwright is ready for you." Lottie pointed toward the hallway.

"Thanks."

A small man wearing a wrinkled, oversized brown suit rounded the corner into the lobby. He saluted Lottie. "See you next week."

"Looking forward to it, Arthur!"

She smiled, watching him walk out the door, and then burst into tears.

Meacham's eyes flew open. "What's the kerfuffle about?"

"Sorry. It's just that poor man. Every week he comes here, and every week he's thinner and frailer, and then he leaves by saying he'll see me next week, but I know one day soon, he's not gonna come." She let out a wail.

"What's wrong with him?" asked Onyx.

She sniffed. "I can't tell you. Lawyer confidentiality an' all that."

I was pretty sure that didn't apply to a law office receptionist, but no point in arguing.

"He may not live to see the resolution of his case, which is against his former employer." She dipped her chin. "Chemical exposure," she whispered. "But you didn't hear it from me."

"So sad," I said.

"Bloody hell," muttered Meacham.

"That's just awful." Onyx nodded solemnly.

"Anyway." Lottie honked into a tissue and wiped her nose. "Like I said, he'll see you now."

I'd previously been referred to Todd Wainwright by Chattertowne Mayor Margarita Guzman. He was a classic case of *you shouldn't judge a book by its cover*. Although his office was housed in a portion of an old K-Mart, the furniture was sparse and utilitarian, and Todd himself looked like a lounge singer, he was actually pretty decent at his job.

"Audrey, good to see you." He rose from behind his cluttered oak desk and extended his hand. Two gold bracelets jangled from his wrist as we shook.

The smell of stale cigars and heavy cologne—Paco Rabanne if I had to guess—permeated the air. Todd's red hair was slicked back in his signature style, and his standard gold chains and tufts of chest hair peeked out from his mint green dress shirt, unbuttoned to the third button.

He gave Onyx a broad smile. "Onyx Carpenter. It's a pleasure to meet you."

She gave him a quick limp-wristed shake before withdrawing her hand. Probably, she was worried about smelling like him for the next three days.

A valid concern, to be sure.

Todd turned his attention to Meacham. He bowed slightly. "Sir, it's an honor."

Meacham made a fist and thumped it against his chest over his heart.

"He's not a sir yet," said Onyx. "The Queen liked him a lot more than her son the King does, and even she didn't knight him."

This comment seemed to catch Todd off guard, but he recovered quickly. "Please, have a seat." He gestured to the chairs opposite him. "Audrey says you're in a bit of a predicament?"

"Not me." Meacham jerked his thumb toward Onyx. "It's the wife's ex. Been arrested for murder and maybe some nasty stuff wit' a young girl. Somehow, and don't ask me, that's become *our* problem now."

Todd frowned. "I'm confused."

I looked at Onyx. "Shall I?"

She nodded, primly folding her hands in her lap.

"Okay, so, not sure if you heard, but last night there was an accident up in our neck of the woods. Literally. It was out on a dark wooded stretch north of town, a place called Devil's Elbow."

"Ominous." Todd tented his fingers. "I'm intrigued."

"Two kids were in the car. Boyfriend and girlfriend. The passenger died, but the driver survived. Both of them have been coached for a couple years by Wylie Barrett, who's the golf pro at Chattertowne Country Club and also coaches the golf team at Chattertowne High. After the accident, Jack Dodd, the driver, accused Wylie of an inappropriate relationship with the passenger, a young girl named Laveda Volkova. He also claimed that perhaps it wasn't an accident, and that Wylie was to blame. When the car was inspected by the state patrol, the power steering lines appeared to have been cut. Cole said the arrest was based on both digital and physical evidence substantiating Jack's claims."

Todd whistled. "Not looking good for the coach." He glanced at Onyx. "I take it this coach is the ex?"

She nodded. "He didn't do it."

Todd tilted his head in thought. "I didn't realize losing power steering could cause that kind of accident."

"It's a classic car," I said.

"Ah. That explains it. What it doesn't explain is why you drove all the way down here," he pulled at the blinds on his office window, "in a Lincoln Town Car, through rush hour traffic just to consult with little old me. There have to be plenty of qualified and capable Snohomish County attorneys you could meet with next week. High-powered guys who do their own commercials."

"That's just it." Onyx sat up in her chair. "This can't wait a week. As it is, Chief Loveland is letting him spend the night at the Chattertowne police department rather than at the Snohomish County jail, but we're hoping to get him out on bail by lunchtime tomorrow. I'm being inducted into the Chattertowne High School Hall of Fame tomorrow evening."

"Congratulations."

"Thanks."

"But lunchtime tomorrow? That's a tall order."

"He has to be out tomorrow! He's innocent. This whole thing is so unfair. Plus, Audrey's sister is getting married on Sunday and he's supposed to be in the wedding."

He glanced at me. "Mazel tov."

"Thanks," I said.

He shook his head slowly. "I'm just not sure I can be of much help."

"But Audrey said you were our best chance." Tears welled in her eyes.

"Please. I'll pay you double. Triple."

Todd's eyebrows shot up. He turned his attention to Meacham, who sat with his arms crossed and a sour expression on his face.

"I'm curious. How do you feel about your wife's efforts to exonerate her ex-boyfriend?"

"What O wants, O gets. Don't s'pose my feelings matter much in this case."

"That's not what I asked."

Meacham grunted. "The guy can rot in a jail cell or rot in hell, as far as I'm concerned."

Chapter Eleven

"I can't believe you said that." Onyx flung open the door of Wainwright and Associates Law Firm and stomped outside.

"He asked me. I told the truth." Meacham held the door open for me to pass through.

She turned on her heel. "You don't care if he rots in jail or in hell?" Her shrill voice echoed through the nearly empty parking lot.

Meacham scanned our surroundings. "Would you please keep your voice down? The last thing we need is TMZ getting hold of footage of us arguing in the parking lot of a seedy strip mall outside a sleazebag lawyer's office."

I swallowed my defense of Todd. While he was a decent attorney, and he'd been helpful to me in the past, I couldn't argue the seedy strip mall charge, and he definitely gave off sleazebag vibes.

We scuttled one by one into the waiting car.

"Besides," Meacham continued. "He said he'd take the case. You got your way. As usual."

Onyx's only response was a pouty silence for the entirety of the ride back to Chattertowne.

Todd had agreed to represent Wylie, and he'd rearranged his schedule to be at the courthouse first thing in the morning, trying to get him bonded out as quickly as possible.

My phone buzzed with a text from Vivienne. **Any luck? What did the lawyer say?**

I responded, **We're almost back to City Hall. I'll fill you in when I see you.**

A few moments later, my phone buzzed again. **I'll meet you there.**

As the car turned onto Main Street, the chauffeur rolled down the tinted privacy divider and made eye contact with me through the rearview mirror. "Ma'am, where should I drop you?"

"I left my car parked near City Hall."

He pulled alongside the curb. Vivienne was leaning against the building, wearing a Mariner's baseball hat and joggers. If I didn't know better, I'd have thought she'd been running. The only place Vivienne ran was from her car to Abigail's for her prizewinning cinnamon rolls. Not that Viv's figure tattled on her. We got two different versions of the metabolism gene. I gained three pounds just smelling the pastries.

"Thank you," I said to the driver. "Onyx, how about I pick you up first thing in the morning so we can head to the courthouse? I'd like to be there."

She pursed her lips. "Maybe I should stay with you tonight."

Meacham threw his hands in the air. "Oh, for the love of—"

"Seems to me the two of you need to talk."

"I don't think there's anything to talk about," she said.

The driver opened the door, but as I scooted across the seat to get out, Vivienne popped her head inside the car.

"Hey, guys!" She glanced at Meacham, and a small gasp escaped her. "Oh, hello."

His head bobbed. "Hello."

"I was just getting out." I widened my eyes and blinked twice in an attempt to telepathically warn Vivienne that the situation between Meacham and Onyx was tense.

She didn't catch my signal.

"Scootch." She bumped me with her hip and slid in next to me. "I have a problem." She blinked at us as we all waited for her to continue. "No one's going to ask what my problem is?"

"What's your problem, Viv?" I asked.

"First, how are things looking with getting Wylie bailed out in time for the wedding?"

"Todd thinks he should be able to get him out, as long as the DA doesn't charge him with first-degree murder or special circumstances."

"I don't know if that's good news or bad news. Miranda says she's going to pull out of the wedding if Wylie is included."

"Don't blame her," Meacham grumbled.

Onyx elbowed him. "Meach, how about you head back to the B and B? I'll meet you there in a bit."

"Sure. Fine."

Vivienne and I climbed out of the car. Meacham said something to Onyx that I couldn't hear. She gave him a long stare and a curt nod before exiting the car and slamming the door behind her.

Vivienne watched the car drive away. "Uh, everything good?"

"Yeah. Fine." Onyx gave a dismissive wave. "So, back to your problem that I don't see as a problem. To me, it's an easy choice. If Miranda is gonna behave that way when it comes to *your* wedding, let her go."

"I don't disagree. I'm not a fan of ultimatums. The problem is that leaves me one bridesmaid short." Blink. Blink.

"So what?" I asked. "There's no requirement that there be the same number of attendants on each side."

"Oh, really? Since when are you a wedding expert? The photos will be lopsided."

One of her fiancée's attendants was being accused of murder by one of her own bridesmaids, but Vivienne was worried about symmetry.

"If Wylie can't get out, you'll be off one way or another. It's just not that big of a deal," I said.

"It is to me. That's why I'm hoping that someone will volunteer to take her place." Vivienne fluttered her eyelashes at Onyx.

"Oh! Vivi, do you want me to be in your wedding?"

"I do." Vivienne laughed. "I do. Get it? Vows? I do. I do. It sounds so formal. I guess I should practice that phrase."

"I'd love to be in your wedding!" Onyx lunged past me to hug her. "Nobody ever wants me in their wedding because they don't want me stealing the attention."

I coughed. "So humble."

She swatted at me. "You know what I mean. Oh, I'll need to get a dress."

I groaned. "Hope you look good in toxic waste green."

"Honey, I look good in anything."

* * *

Kayla reopened the bridal shop for Onyx to try on dresses. It was sure to be a boon to her business to have her store listed in *People* magazine alongside a photo of Onyx Carpenter. Thankfully, she'd also located a dress for me that didn't make me look like a bowl of split pea soup. It was a dusty sage chiffon fabric tailored in a fit and flare style that hugged my curves in just the right way.

Onyx's chosen dress was a rich forest green satin A-line single shoulder gown with a leg slit that was likely to make our mother blush.

I had to hand it to Vivienne. Onyx was right. Unlike many brides, Viv wasn't afraid of her attendants looking good.

The dresses needed only minor alterations, and Kayla promised to have them ready for pickup before the rehearsal dinner Friday night.

"We should go get a drink to celebrate," Onyx said as we left the shop. "I missed your bridal shower and your bachelorette party."

"I didn't do a bachelorette party. We just went up to Leavenworth for the weekend and stayed at the Post Hotel. It's adults only, but it's the tamest adults-only hotel I've ever visited. They kept shushing us as we laughed and talked in the hot tub. I felt like I was in a convent."

"Do you really think going to a bar tonight is a good idea?" I asked. "I mean, aren't you trying to keep a low profile? Those paparazzi have to be lurking around somewhere."

Onyx snatched Viv's hat and placed it on her own head.

Vivienne squawked. "Hey! I put that on because my roots are grown out. I'm getting them done in the morning." She covered the crown of her platinum blonde head with her hands.

Onyx pulled down the brim. "I need to be incognito. How do I look?"

"Like a master of disguise." If she noticed my sarcasm, she didn't acknowledge it.

"Where did Onyx go, and who is this stranger in her place?" Vivienne gave a pouty smirk.

Onyx playfully stuck out her tongue. "Hardy-har. It's dark. No one will notice your roots, Viv. When I left town, I wasn't old enough to drink. Legally, at least. Where can we go that has dim lighting?"

"I'd say either Nautilus or Louden's Tavern."

Vivienne shook her head. "Not Nautilus. I don't want to see any of my co-workers."

In addition to her job at the police station, Vivienne had a weekend gig singing at Nautilus, an old bar that was renovated into a bougie jazz club a few years earlier.

"Louden's it is." Onyx marched down the street in the opposite direction from the bar.

"Wrong way!" Vivienne called.

She turned on her heel and marched past us. "I knew that. I was just testing you."

When we got to Louden's, a bouncer was standing outside checking ID. He verified Vivienne and I were over twenty-one. Then he looked at Onyx's license. His eyes grew wide, and his head jerked up to look at her face.

"Holy sh—"

"I'm trying to keep a low profile. Maybe you can keep this to yourself?" She placed her fingers on his forearm and batted her lashes at him.

"Sure. Sure. Of course."

There was no way this dude wasn't going to immediately text everyone he knew that he'd just carded Onyx Carpenter.

She sashayed through the bar, and if there was any question of whether we'd be able to stay under the radar, regardless of whether the guy at the front door spread the news or not, it was immediately dispelled by the reaction of the bar patrons. Onyx had always been beautiful and charismatic. She'd always turned heads, even as a teen. But a decade of living as a celebrity had fundamentally changed her aura. The energy pouring off her was palpable, and it created a magnetic current that drew all eyes to her presence.

By the time she slid into a back corner booth, the bar was abuzz with excitement and conversation about who'd just walked through the door.

"We're screwed," I said.

"What do you mean?" She lowered the brim of the hat a little more.

"I mean, every single person in this bar knows you're here."

"No, I kept my head down."

"You were as subtle as Caesar sweeping into Zela. All that was missing was a declaration of *Veni, Vidi, Vici.*"

Onyx turned to Vivienne. "Any idea what she's talking about?"

Vivienne shook her head. "She's a history nerd. The speaking Italian thing is new, though. Audrey, have you been playing Duolingo?"

"It's Latin."

Vivienne shrugged. "Same thing."

"It's not. You know, I came, I saw, I conquered? Ring a bell?"

"Was that from *Braveheart*? I loved that movie." Onyx raised the menu to cover her face. "Better?"

"Like the invisible man. Or woman." Vivienne grabbed her own menu.

"I loved that movie, too."

"Hey. Is that…Hank Dodd?" I nodded toward a man slumped over the bar. His sweatshirt hood was pulled up over the back of his head, but his profile was visible.

"It can't be," said Onyx. "Hank Dodd was hot. Captain of the football team. That guy looks twenty years older than us."

Vivienne slowly shook her head. "Oh, it's Hank Dodd all right. After he and Miranda split up, he went straight to the bottom of a bottle and hasn't found his way out yet."

"That's so sad." Onyx watched him for a moment. "What kind of father was he to Jack?"

"Not sure," I said. "Cole said he isn't really in Jack's life too much these days. Viv, do you know?"

"Uh, not a terrible dad, but not great, to hear Miranda tell it. Definitely worse since the divorce. She says he's a loser, but he seems to be trying to get his act together."

Onyx continued observing Hank.

A weathered woman with a tall, spiked, bleach blonde mullet slapped three napkins on the table to break Onyx out of her stupor. "I'm Lou, I'll be taking care of you ladies tonight. I gotta tell you, though, the minute things get out of hand, you need to leave."

"Out of hand?" I pulled the napkin toward me.

She bobbed her head in Onyx's direction, and the spikes waved like wheat in the wind. "I don't need a scene. We've got three dings against our liquor license for serving minors, and another drunken brawl may get us shut down for good."

Mental note: Write article on the possibility that Louden's Tavern has been serving minors.

"We aren't responsible for the behavior of your other customers, especially if you've overserved them." Vivienne gave Lou her best judgy expression.

I willed her not to mention that her job technically put her in law enforcement. Lou's attitude was already unfriendly.

"Lou. You're not the Lou in Louden's, are you?" I asked.

"Yep. It was always a dream of mine to have a place like this. Me and my old man Dennis opened this place in nineteen eighty-one. Get it? Lou-Den."

"I always thought it was pronounced *Loud*-ens, rhyming with cloud, not *Lou*-dens, rhyming with clue," Vivienne said.

Me too, but I didn't say it because Lou scowled.

"Well, you were wrong. Anyway, Denny's been gone six years now, and I'll be damned if I let some little twerps with fake IDs or a B-list celebrity—" she flared her nostrils at Onyx, "steal that dream." She wiped a tear from under her right eye.

"I'm so sorry for your loss," I said.

Vivienne nodded. "Me too."

"RIP."

Onyx made the sign of the cross, which was charitable since she'd just been called a B-list celebrity. It was also odd, considering she wasn't Catholic. We'd gone to the same Lutheran Sunday school.

Lou scrunched her nose. "Den's not dead. He just left me for some barfly.

Now let's get you those drinks so you can skedaddle."

Despite Lou's fears, we made it out of Louden's without incident. Mostly.

Hank had raised his head as we passed, and he and I made eye contact. His bloodshot gaze was unexpectedly sharp, and I felt a shiver. Perhaps he wasn't as out of it as I'd assumed.

We left Vivienne at the entrance to the marina, since she was staying the night with Lacey on the sailboat. Rather than getting in my car and driving to Onyx's B&B, we walked the three blocks. Five minutes later, when it began to sprinkle, I regretted that choice.

Onyx didn't complain, though. As a matter of fact, she was unusually quiet, and every few minutes, she glanced over her shoulder. When we arrived at the large Victorian home where she was staying, she rubbed her arms and scanned the area.

"What are you looking for?"

"I don't know. I just have this eerie feeling we're being watched."

I looked up and down the street. "I don't see anyone or anything. In fact, even for a Wednesday night, it's pretty quiet. Probably because of the rain. You sure you're not just delaying having to talk to Meacham about what happened earlier?"

"Not at all. He and I are good. We have our moments, but we understand each other, you know?" She knit her brows together, her head on a constant swivel. "Are you sure you're okay to walk back to your car in the dark?"

"Of course. This is Chattertowne, not L.A."

Probably best not to mention the crime rate had spiked over the past few years, what with the political corruption, vandalism, arson, and murder. Make that murd-*ers*.

"Okay, well, goodnight. By the way, you're coming to the hall of fame ceremony tomorrow, right?"

Was that nervousness and uncertainty I heard in her voice?

"Of course. You know I wouldn't miss it for the world."

"Thanks." She smiled, and her shoulders sagged in relief.

It just went to show that no matter how famous a person became, a part of them still needed to know they were liked, seen, understood, and valued.

"Hey, Onyx?"

"Yeah?"

"Welcome home."

Her smile broadened.

I gave a quick wave and headed down a side street in the direction of my car and City Hall. On the next block, two of the streetlamps were out. The sidewalk, lined with overgrown rhododendron bushes, was shrouded in darkness. What had been a slight breeze on the way to the B&B grew more intense with the increasing raindrops, swishing as it rustled through the leaves.

From somewhere behind me, there was a crack. I stopped to listen. When I heard nothing else, I resumed walking. A gust of wind blew my hair into my face from behind me. As I attempted to pull the strands away from my eyes, I heard a long creak.

Once again, I stopped.

Creeeeaaak.

I peeked over the hedge to my right and spotted an old swing swaying on the front porch of the old home.

I chuckled. My imagination was getting the best of me.

The sign on the fence marked it as the Ferguson homestead, built in 1898. The swing was empty. Unbidden, the image of the ghost of one of Chattertowne's early pioneers rocking back and forth appeared in my mind, but I immediately banished the thought.

I was spooking myself pretty good.

I still had two blocks to go until I turned onto Main Street, which was sure to have more lights and more people.

By then, the skies had opened up and the rain was dumping. Springtime in the Pacific Northwest. I knew better than to trust it to have the same weather for more than five minutes at a time. Not that I would have brought an umbrella. No true Washingtonian would be caught dead with one.

Caught dead.

That thought gave me an even stronger chill.

I picked up the pace, avoiding the newly formed puddles on the uneven cement. Tree roots had broken through in many places and had pushed up chunks of sidewalk in others.

Mental note: write article about the dangers of Chattertowne's uneven sidewalks, particularly for the elderly and disabled.

Another crack behind me, but I didn't slow down.

Onyx and her paranoia were contagious. No one had been watching us. No one had been following us. No one was following me.

Still, I shuffled faster.

I was so focused on getting to the lit area under the next streetlamp that I was airborne before it fully registered I'd tripped on a root. Just like with my car accident at Devil's Elbow, time seemed to slow between takeoff and landing. With a jarring thud, I hit the ground. My hands skidded along the wet pavement, undoubtedly shredding my palms, but the pain was delayed until my brain had time to catch up. Momentum rolled me ass over teakettle until I came to a stop wedged against a fence and under a shrub. Azalea, probably. Rainwater poured from the bush onto my face, and I was pretty sure I felt strands of spiderweb draped across my mouth and chin.

I blinked the water away from my eyes.

That's when the shadow fell over me, followed by the dark outline of a large figure looming above me, blocking what little light there was.

Chapter Twelve

As much as I wanted to scream, I didn't want to inhale spiderweb into my mouth. I also didn't want to ingest the spider that had made it, who was likely to be lurking nearby, unhappy I'd destroyed its house.

I brushed the rainwater and webs from my face with my hand. Pain seared through my lacerated palms.

"Owww!"

I didn't think I tasted spiderweb, but I definitely tasted blood.

Even in the dim lighting, I could see dark liquid dripping from my hands.

Before I could assess the rest of my injuries, I was hoisted to my feet.

"Help!"

"Audrey, it's me."

I'd have known that deep voice anywhere.

"Holden?"

He whirled me to face him. "Are you okay?"

"Why were you chasing me?"

"What? I wasn't chasing you. I was taking out my trash, and I saw you cross the street. I walked to the end of my block to catch your attention, and that's when I saw you bite it."

"Oh." I'd forgotten I was in his neighborhood.

He held my hands in front of him, palms up. "You really did a number on yourself."

"By number, I assume you mean a perfect ten for grace and style?"

He shook his head but couldn't hide the smile tugging at the corner of his mouth. "It's up there with some of your other spectacular falls, of which there are many. What the hell were you doing out here in the rain, anyway?"

"In my defense, it wasn't raining when we left."

"We?"

"I walked Onyx back to her bed and breakfast after having a drink at Louden's. Oh, by the way, she's in the wedding now. Anyway, I left my car down by City Hall, so I was just headed back to get it when I tripped."

He grunted. His mouth was firmly set.

"What?"

"Nothing. Here." He took off his plaid overshirt and draped it around my shoulders. "I have a first aid kit at my place. I'll get you fixed up, and then I'll drive you to your car." He linked his arm around mine.

"That's really not—" I curtailed my protest when I saw his determined expression.

When Holden had his mind set on something, there was no arguing with him.

His house was a craftsman-style, about a hundred years old. He'd bought it when he got his job as city manager, and for a brief period of time shared it with his ex-fiancée Emily. He'd decorated it in a style I liked to call Pacific Northwest man chic. Real wood furniture, dark green accents, uncluttered by anything that didn't serve a functional purpose. He was tidy, unlike me. Not that I was messy or dirty, but I didn't wash, dry, and put away every glass or dish the moment I'd swallowed my last bite, either.

He eased me onto the sofa and wagged his finger at me. "Don't move. I'll be right back."

My hands had been so badly abraded that I hadn't even noticed how messed up the rest of me was. When I'd pulled on my jeans that morning, they'd had a couple of small holes in them—the trendy kind, intentionally imbued by the manufacturer—but now the knees were threadbare and covered in blood.

He returned to the living room carrying a damp washcloth, gauze, a box of bandages, tape, antibacterial ointment, and the first aid spray with the green top that I knew was going to sting like a thousand bees.

"You're gonna hate me, but trust me. This is necessary."

"Can't we skip the spray?"

"No."

"Please?"

"No."

He cleaned my wounds one at a time, starting with my knees. He dabbed at the scrapes with the washcloth, gently pressing down, but not rubbing. His biceps bulged with each pat. He did that several times until he was satisfied that he'd gotten all the dirt.

He held up the spray. "This is gonna hurt, but just for a minute. I promise."

I grabbed the corner of his plaid flannel shirt and shoved it in my mouth. "Wewy."

"What?"

I spit out the shirt. "Ready." I shoved the shirt back into my mouth.

I hummed as he sprayed, tears streaming from my eyes.

"You okay?"

"Mmm hmm," I lied.

He wiped my cheek with the washcloth. "What are you humming?"

I let the shirt fall from my mouth. "Ow. *Safety Dance.*"

"I have no idea what that is." He blew on my knee where he'd just sprayed.

His breath was warm, but the sensation was cool. I felt a chill wash over me, and then a rush of warmth spread across my chest and neck. I suspected most of that had nothing to do with the spray and everything to do with his proximity as he tended to me.

"How can you not know *Safety Dance?*" I attempted to hum it more clearly.

"Nope." He sprayed my other knee. "Don't recognize it."

"It's an—ouch—80s classic."

"I'll take your word for it." He took my right palm and held it close to his face to inspect it.

I held my breath.

"Looks like you've got some gravel in there. I think we should run it under the faucet. See if we can't get some of that out with warm water before we take the washcloth to it. You okay to walk to the sink?"

"I'm fine."

I wasn't fine. I felt weak in the knees, and I was pretty sure it had nothing to do with my injuries.

Maybe it was because I'd never had a man caretake for me before.

Perhaps it was the post-adrenaline relief that I wasn't being followed by an axe murderer or a ghost.

It could have been gratitude combined with the little bit of alcohol I'd consumed at Louden's.

If I'd been willing to examine it, I'd have had to admit there'd always been an unspoken—well, mostly unspoken—chemistry between Holden and me, and at that moment I was feeling it from my head to my toes.

If I'd been willing.

But I wasn't.

He helped me to my feet, and I hobbled to the kitchen. Not a dirty dish in sight. Not a clean one either.

My drying rack was full of dishes that I'd probably use again before I got to putting them away.

Holden ran my hands under the warm water. It felt good. All of it.

"Audrey."

"Yes." My voice came out in a hoarse whisper.

What would he say? That he wanted to kiss me? That he wanted to see if there was really something between us? That even in this disheveled state, he thought I was the most beautiful woman in the world?

"Don't panic." His voice was steady but not calm.

Not what I was expecting. "Huh?"

"Don't look out the window, but I believe someone is in my back yard and they're watching us."

"Who is it?"

"I can't see many details. Looks like they're wearing a hoodie."

My brain switched from romance mode to fight-flight-freeze. As usual, I went into freeze mode.

"What should we do?" I asked through gritted teeth.

He tilted my chin to look up at him. Once again, I held my breath.

He leaned close and whispered in my ear. "On the count of three, I want you to get down. I'm going to try and surprise him by going out the back door."

Also, not what I was expecting, but I nodded.

"One. Two—"

I dropped to the ground in a squat. "Ow!" Pain seared through my knees.

"Three."

Timing had never been Holden's and my strong suit.

He looked momentarily confused and then raced through the back doorway.

I sat on his kitchen floor with my legs straight in front of me, trying to control my breathing. Bending my knees wasn't an option. I'd discovered that the hard way.

Onyx wasn't paranoid. I wasn't paranoid. Someone really had been following us. Following me.

I pulled out my phone and texted her.

Make sure the B&B doors are locked up tight. I think you were right. Someone was following us. Maybe it was paparazzi, but just to be on the safe side, double-check the locks.

A moment later, my phone buzzed with her reply.

For the first time in my life, I hope it's just paparazzi following me.

Holden burst through the back door, winded.

"Any luck?"

He bent over, with his hands resting on his knees. "Nope. I heard some running but couldn't see anything. The dude was fast."

"Why would someone be following me? I get why they'd be following Onyx. She gets followed everywhere she goes. She can't go to the grocery store or the gym without ending up in one of those 'stars, they're just like us' features."

Holden slumped onto the floor next to me and leaned against the cabinets. "Walk me through your day. When we left brunch after I told you about Wylie being brought in for questioning, did you go to the police station?"

"Not at first. I went to the *Current*. Onyx was waiting for me."

"Why?"

"She was worried Wylie was going to get arrested. Which turned out to be true. We went to the station to talk to Cole. She figured she could schmooze him with her charm and charisma."

"And? Did it work?"

"Hard to tell. Probably a little, but he was trying to play it cool."

"And how do you feel about that?" His brow arched.

"I feel nothing about that."

"Sure. That's why you flinched when you said it. Then what happened?"

"Then Jack and Miranda showed up. Jack said some things about Wylie having an inappropriate relationship with Laveda before she died, flat out accused him of tampering with the car and causing the accident. The next thing I knew, Miranda and Onyx were at each other's throats."

"Literally?"

"Literally. They had to be separated."

"Geez."

"Yeah. Then, Meacham Fields shows up in a Lincoln Town Car, and he's pissed that Onyx is throwing a fit about her high school sweetheart. The paparazzi are going nuts. We end up in Tacoma talking to Todd Wainwright."

Holden held up his hand. "Wait. Why Tacoma?"

"Oh. Because Onyx was freaking out over the idea Wylie might have to spend one minute in county jail, much less the whole night, and it was too late for a bail hearing today. She got Cole to agree to let him stay in a Chattertowne holding cell rather than be transferred, but he made no promises about tomorrow if we couldn't get someone to represent him asap. So, we met with Todd, and he agreed to come up here first thing and try to get him arraigned and out on bail."

"I don't blame Meacham for being unhappy about all of this."

"Yeah. They have a strange relationship. I can't quite figure out what the state of things is between them."

"So, then after you got back from Tacoma, you went drinking and now Onyx is a bridesmaid?"

"Miranda said she wouldn't be in the wedding if Wylie isn't kicked out.

You know Viv. She'll cut off her own arm before giving in to the pressure of someone else's agenda. Except our mother, of course."

"Of course. I guess where I'm struggling is I don't hear anything that makes me think someone would follow you. Other than photographers trying to get a shot of Onyx. But why follow *you*, and why here? You'd already left Onyx."

"Well, it's possible Meacham was following us to make sure Onyx was behaving, although I highly doubt that. Like you said, he'd have no reason to follow me. Could have been Miranda, since Onyx tried to choke her."

"What about Jack? Since he thinks Onyx is trying to protect the man he believes killed his girlfriend and attempted to kill him?"

"That's it!" I clapped my hands and then immediately regretted it. "Ow!"

"Good job, genius." He took my hands in his and gently placed his warm palms against mine.

It was surprisingly soothing and unsurprisingly unnerving.

"What if it wasn't Jack or Miranda? What if it were Hank?"

"Hank Dodd? Is he even in that kid's life?"

"Not really. At least, according to Cole. But maybe he thinks this is a way to get back into his son's good graces. Or Miranda's."

"Okay, but I guess I'm not understanding where you're getting this."

"Holden, I *saw* Hank Dodd tonight."

"You did? Where? How?"

"At Louden's. Did you know it was said that way? Loo-dens, not Loud-ens?"

"Yes."

"Oh. Well, I had no idea. Anyway, Hank was drinking there when we arrived. We made eye contact, and it wasn't friendly. And get this. *He* was wearing a dark hoodie. Could the person you saw in the back yard have been Hank Dodd?"

Holden sighed. He pulled his mouth into a tight line. "I used to play football with Hank Dodd. I know it's been fifteen years or so, and none of us are in the same shape we used to be—especially not Hank—but I also know back in the day he was the only guy on the team who could outrun me."

Perhaps he'd just outrun Holden one more time.

Chapter Thirteen

I picked up Onyx from her B&B just after eight in the morning, and we arrived at the Snohomish County Courthouse around eight-thirty. She was once again wearing Vivienne's Mariners baseball hat. On the way, I filled her in about the incident at Holden's house. She said when she'd gotten back to her room the night before, Meacham was already asleep, and he was still asleep when she'd left that morning.

That ruled out Meacham as the stalker from the previous night.

Todd Wainwright was waiting for us in the courtyard next to the veterans' memorial cauldron. There was a line of people waiting to get inside.

"What's all this about?" I asked.

"From what I've gathered, about half are jurors or prospective jurors and half are either press, ambulance chasers, or busybodies waiting to go through security." Todd glanced at his phone. "Chief Loveland texted that they're arriving in about ten minutes. I've already spoken to the District Attorney, and he says he'll be asking for bail. I assume you'll be covering that."

"Yes, of course. Whatever it takes." Onyx covered the brim of her hat and squinted. "Uh oh."

"What's wrong?" I asked.

She pointed across the courtyard. "Incoming."

Miranda and Jack walked toward the courthouse entrance. She caught sight of us, scowled, and veered in our direction.

"So, I hear that rather than kicking out a murderer and a pedophile from her wedding, your sister has opted to dump me in favor of his biggest defender."

"From what I hear, she didn't dump you. You tried to force her hand, and it didn't work."

"The man tried to kill my son!"

Todd raised his finger. "Allegedly."

"Allegedly, my ass." Miranda glanced at Jack. "Sorry for the language."

"It's fine," he mumbled. He had dark circles under his eyes, and his shoulders were sagging.

"You've been through a lot," Onyx said to Jack. "You look like you could use some rest."

"Don't talk to him," Miranda growled at her. "And don't tell me how to take care of *my* son."

Onyx flinched as Miranda spat out the words *my son*.

"She's right, Miranda. He doesn't need to be here. There are no witnesses called at preliminary hearings."

She pointed at me and then at Onyx. "Mind your own business. Both of you. I mean it. Come on, Jack."

He frowned and his shoulders slumped further, but followed her anyway.

"Poor kid," I said.

Onyx watched them for a long moment. "Yeah."

Todd slung his messenger bag over his shoulder, and I got a hefty whiff of his cologne. "I'm curious. I know the kid made the allegations, but is there any reason the mother might have an axe to grind with Mr. Barrett?"

"I don't think so," I said. "At least, not that I'm aware. But I've only been back in town a short while. Onyx, do you have any ideas?"

Onyx bit her lower lip. "Me? How would I know? I was gone longer than you were."

"True." Although her vehemence was a little over the top. "I can do some digging, but I have to be careful. She's been dating CPD chief Cole Loveland."

Todd's gaze flickered. "Has she now? Interesting." His phone buzzed. He looked at the screen. "Speak of the devil. Loveland says he's here with Wylie. Showtime."

* * *

It took us fifteen minutes to get through security. A few people waiting in line spotted Onyx when she had to remove the hat and put it in the bin with her purse and cell phone, but security ushered them away.

It was ridiculous that she'd gone unnoticed as long as she had. The hat didn't disguise her long hair or her curvy figure. It didn't hide the giant diamond ring on her finger or the fact that every item she wore—other than the hat—was designer. She might as well have been Clark Kent wearing glasses. And yet, it seemed to work.

We waited for two hours, but eventually, Wylie was arraigned. The charge was second-degree murder, and bail was set at five hundred thousand dollars. The prosecutor asked for a higher amount, but Todd successfully argued that Wylie was a well-known and respected member of the community. He was ordered to surrender his passport, and Onyx wired the cash to the court. By noon, Wylie was free on bail.

I'd seen Cole in the hallway at the courthouse, but he hadn't spoken to me. Something about the look he gave had left me feeling unsettled.

Todd was headed back to Tacoma, so I dropped Onyx and Wylie at Wylie's house. Whatever was going on between them, I wanted no part of it. Instead, I went back to City Hall.

Charlotte begrudgingly buzzed me back to Cole's office.

I rapped on the doorframe, and he looked up from his computer screen. "Hey there."

"Hey."

"I thought I'd pop in and see what's up."

He leaned back in his chair, which squeaked in protest. "Oh yeah?"

I indicated the chair next to me. "Can I?"

He gestured for me to sit.

Things hadn't felt this awkward between us since his very first appearance at a city council meeting, and I'd teased him about his hat and boots.

"How can I help you?" He clasped his hands in his lap. His mouth held a firm line.

"Did I do something wrong?"

"I don't know. Did you?" His gaze hardened.

"No? Why are you acting so strange?"

"I don't know what you mean."

I held up my hands in mock surrender. "Okay. Whatever."

"You and Onyx Carpenter seem to be pretty chummy all of a sudden."

"Is that what this is about? I didn't have a chance to warn you she was in town. I found out when you did. Same with Meacham. He just…showed up."

"That's not what this is about. I guess I'm just trying to figure out who you are."

"What?"

"When I met you, even when I was annoyed with you, there were a few things I discerned about you right away. One was that you were loyal. Another was that you cared deeply about doing your job well."

"Are you saying you're questioning those things now?"

"You're not being impartial, Audrey. You're too close to the story. You're so close that you're manipulating the outcome."

"How do you figure?"

"Where did you go last night?"

"You mean to the bar?" Or did he mean Holden's house?

"No. I mean, after you left my office."

"You know where I went. I took Onyx and Meacham to see Todd Wainwright."

"Right. So that you could help them bail out the prime suspect in a murder investigation. *My* murder investigation. That you're reporting on."

"Where is this coming from, Cole? All I did was accompany them as they hired an attorney. I didn't plead Wylie's case before a judge. I didn't post his half a million dollar bail."

"But you were there every step of the way. You're supposed to be observing, not interfering."

I stared at him for a moment. Something had shifted within him since I'd left his office the night before. What in the hell could have changed overnight?

"It's Miranda, isn't it?"

"What do you mean?"

I leaned forward. "I mean, she's unhappy that Onyx is working so hard to exonerate Wylie. And since she threw a hissy fit about Wylie being in the wedding, Viv has dropped her in favor of Onyx. If Miranda's unhappy, I'll bet she's chewing your ear off about it."

He flinched. Bullseye.

"Did you see Jack today? That kid's been through something. He looks like a zombie, and she's dragging him to the courthouse hell-bent on making Wylie's life miserable. There's no way he had anything to do with Laveda's death, but you've practically tried and convicted him already. You wanna talk about not impartial? Look in the mirror."

"You don't know what you're talking about."

I pressed my lips together. "Is that so?" I got to my feet. "I think it's interesting that Miranda was at the hearing today, but you know who I didn't see there? Laveda's parents. Seems to me, if they thought Wylie was capable of killing their daughter, they'd have been there. But you've got Miranda in your ear, and that's all you seem to care about."

"Audrey—"

I stomped out of his office without looking back. I brushed past a sneering Charlotte and out of the City Hall building.

I wanted to scream, but I waited until I got into my car.

As I slammed the door, I let out an "aaaaaaahhhhhh."

I felt a little better. And then I didn't.

I turned on my car and buckled my seatbelt.

Damn.

My own hypocrisy rang in my ears. I'd accused Cole of only caring about Jack, but where had my focus been?

I needed to go pay my condolences to Laveda's family.

* * *

A quick public records search for anyone named Volkova living in Chattertowne turned up nothing, but I found a Faddei and Ganna Volkov on

Pioneer Avenue. A few minutes later, I pulled up to the curb in front of five identical white cottages known locally as soapbox row.

Constructed in 1889, the small homes were built to house the women who provided laundry services for mill workers. Now they were subsidized as affordable housing for low-income families.

I double checked to make sure I had the correct house number. 333 Pioneer. It was the one in the exact middle. The yard was tidy, and the walkway was lined with tulips and hyacinths. In an upstairs window was a blue and yellow sign representing the Ukrainian flag.

I climbed the two front steps, opened the squeaky storm door, and knocked. After a moment, the door opened slightly. A little boy peeked out at me. He had the same greenish-blue eyes as Laveda.

"Hi, there. Are your parents at home?"

He blinked at me three times. He couldn't have been more than five or six years old.

"Symon, *khto bilya dverey* ?" A female voice called.

"*Ledi, babusya.*"

"Hello?" The voice called again, this time in heavily accented English.

"Hi, my name is Audrey O'Connell, and I write for the Chattertowne Coastal Current newspaper. I'm writing a story about Laveda, and I was hoping to talk to her parents."

"Symon, *zachynyty dveri.*"

The boy blinked at me once more and then shut the door.

I spoke into my phone. "Siri, what does *zakidney daveri* mean in Ukrainian?"

"Send the door as well," said the robotic voice.

Ouch. My pronunciation was terrible, but the translation gave me the gist of it. The woman told him to close the door because she didn't want to talk to me.

"Siri, what does *babusya* mean in Ukrainian?"

"It is a word that means grandmother."

Ah. So not the mother. Good to know.

I walked back to my car and glanced back at the house. The little boy was watching me from the upstairs window with the flag poster. I waved at him. He waved back.

I got into my car, but I didn't turn it on. I had a few hours before the Hall of Fame induction ceremony, I was in a tiff with my source at the CPD, and I was avoiding all things wedding-related, including my mother and my sister. I was a terrible maid of honor, no doubt about it.

While I contemplated my next move, a silver minivan pulled into the space in front of mine. A woman got out and shielded her eyes to stare at my car.

As she walked toward me, I pegged her to be in her late thirties. Her straight blonde hair was shoulder-length, and she was slim-figured. She rapped on my window with her knuckles, and then crouched to my level. She had the same eyes as Laveda and the little boy.

I lowered my window.

"Are you Ganna? Ganna Volkov?"

She held up her phone. She'd typed 9-1-1 onto the call screen, and her thumb hovered over the call button. "I am Ganna Volkova. My husband is Faddei Volkov. Now would you like to tell me who you are and why you are stalking our family before I call the police?"

Chapter Fourteen

"Like I told your, uh, mother?"

"Mother-in-law."

"Your mother-in-law. My name is Audrey O'Connell. I'm a reporter for the *Chattertowne Coastal Current*. First, I want to offer my condolences on your loss. There are no words when it comes to something like this."

"Thank you."

"I'm writing a story about your daughter, and I was hoping to speak to the family to get a more complete picture of who she was."

Ganna clenched her jaw. "You say there are no words, but still you want to write a story."

She had a point. "I saw the articles posted by the other regional papers, and they reduced her to a car accident victim. I'd like to paint a fuller picture. The young woman with hopes and dreams who left her war-torn homeland behind only to meet a tragic end."

She sighed. "Get out of the car. I will speak to you."

I raised the window and scrambled out of the car. "Thank you for giving me this opportunity."

She came so close to me that I smelled roses and garlic. "I am not doing this for you. I am doing this for Laveda and so that you do not write hurtful misinformation about Ukrainians."

"Oh, I wouldn't—"

She raised her hand to stop me. "Trust me, you would. I can tell by the words you use. Your intentions may be good, but your ignorance can be damaging."

I followed her to the front door, which she unlocked.

She poked her head inside the house. "Symon, *chas yty.*"

"Are we not going inside?"

"No. I am taking my son to the farmer's market. I promised him kettle corn. If you wish to talk, you will walk with us."

That hadn't been on my agenda, but it was likely my only chance to get insight into Laveda's relationship with Wylie from her family's perspective.

The farmer's market typically ran May through September, but this year, they were testing out April as well. Thankfully, the weather was cooperating.

Rhythmic thumping down the stairs was followed by the appearance of Symon.

"Hello, again," I said.

"Hello."

Ganna called into the house, "*Svekrukha ya ydu.*" She shut the door and locked it.

"Did you tell her to call the police on me?" I gave a nervous chuckle.

"Only if I do not return safely in an hour." A smile tugged at her mouth. "No, I told her I was going."

I glanced up at the house as we began to walk toward the market downtown. "I thought these only had two bedrooms."

"They do."

"You fit three adults and two kids in a two-bedroom?"

"We make do."

"I suppose it's better than the alternative."

"Which is?"

"Well, I just mean, you're not in a war zone. You're safe here." The moment the words left my mouth, I wanted to pull them back. I shook my head. "I'm sorry. That was insensitive."

"Hmm. Yes. It was. We fled Ukraine just before the invasion by Putin's army. It was not a war zone at that time. There was the looming threat of war, ever since the illegal annexation of Crimea, but no war. After the invasion, although it was horrific to watch what was happening in our homeland, we were grateful to be far away where we believed we were safe." A bitter laugh escaped her. "It seems violence has a way of seeking you out; you cannot hide."

"You believe Laveda's death was caused by violence, not by an accident?"

"I do not mean her death. I mean, the dozens of school shootings in this country since we relocated. Children are not safe here. There were even threats at Chattertowne High last year."

"What you're saying is very true. But specifically as it relates to how Lee died, do you believe it was an intentional act?"

"Who is this Lee? I do not know this Lee. I know my Laveda. Only Jack calls her Lee."

She hadn't answered the question, but I didn't want to push too hard.

"Lala."

I looked down at Symon, who walked between us. He was holding Ganna's hand.

"Lala? Is that what you call your sister?"

"Yes. My Lala." His big, round eyes stared back at me.

We got to the crosswalk and waited for the light to change.

"Symon, how old are you?"

He held up his free hand, fingers splayed.

"You're five? What a big boy you are."

He lifted his chin. "I am very big and strong." He flexed his tiny bicep and growled.

"Whoa. You are strong."

Ganna watched him with a sad smile.

"How long were Laveda and Jack seeing each other?" I asked.

"Oh, a few months, off and on."

"Oh, they weren't serious? I got the impression they were."

"Neither of them does anything halfway. Their relationship was very intense. She said she thought she might marry him."

"How did you feel about that?"

The light changed, and we began to walk again.

"I think they were too young, but is that not the way it is with young love?

They think they are grown when they are still children."

"And they met through golf?"

"Yes."

"She was pretty talented, from what I hear."

"Yes."

Well, this wasn't getting me closer to finding out about her relationship with Wylie. "Have you spoken with Jack since the accident? Has he talked to you about what he believes happened?"

"Wylie Barrett is in jail for causing the crash. They say it was not an accident. We wait for the judge to say."

Shoot. I didn't want to be the one to tell her Wylie had been released. "Can you think of any reason Wylie would want to hurt Laveda?"

Ganna glanced down at Symon. "I have heard the allegations."

"Do you believe them?"

"I do not know."

"Did you ever see anything…inappropriate…between them?"

"Of course not. If I had, I would have put a stop to it."

"Right, yes. I just mean that sometimes in retrospect, things that seemed innocent appear differently under the light of new revelations."

"I suppose I should try to examine things that way, but the truth is that would be very painful. My daughter has been—" She stopped and gulped air. "*Gone* less than forty-eight hours. My mind has yet to accept this fact. My heart has yet to accept this new reality. I am not even certain that understanding the why will matter. It will not change—" Once again, she stopped and gulped. Tears streamed from the corners of her eyes. She glanced again at Symon and then back at me. "I am done speaking on this for now. Please."

"Of course."

"Mama! Popcorn!" Symon pointed at the kettle corn booth.

"Yes, it is! Let us go and get you some popcorn. Just give me one second." She put her hand on my arm. "In Ukraine, my husband was a business owner. I was an accountant for a large corporation. We had a home, two cars, money in the bank. We had birthday parties and went to concerts. We celebrated holidays and spent time with friends and family. Laveda was in sports practices, and she was a top student. Our lives were good. We came here because we believed in the American dream and opportunities for our children to thrive. If you want to speak the truth, tell that story. Tell the truth. For us, there is no American dream. It is a nightmare, and I just want to wake up from it."

The whole way back to my car, I had a sick feeling. A heaviness. I'd seen Laveda one time before her death, and I felt sadness about it in a detached sort of way. Perhaps that was a byproduct of being a journalist. But also, Cole was right. I was too close to the story in some ways, and not close enough in others.

Laveda's story was more than the circumstances of her death. It was more than the death of one young girl, the salacious rumors about the man accused of killing her, and the celebrity adjacent to him.

Chapter Fifteen

It seemed as though the entire town had turned out for Onyx's induction into the Chattertowne High Hall of Fame…and then some.

As expected, media from all over the region, as well as paparazzi, were lined up along the north end of the school gymnasium.

She wasn't the only inductee, and I felt sorry for the others who had to share the marquee with her. There was the longtime owner of a local hardware store, a scientist who'd received acclaim for a global genetics project, and a female professional soccer player.

Onyx eclipsed them all. At least as far as the majority of the crowd was concerned.

"Audrey O'Connell, is that you?" A handsome silver-haired man waved at me.

"Mr. Hannah!"

He gave me a bear hug. "Please, call me Joe."

Joe Hannah had been principal of Chattertowne High for nearly twenty years when he finally retired.

"I'm not sure I'll ever be able to call you Joe. How's retired life?"

"Great. We bought a place on Whidbey Island. I fish all the time."

"That's awesome."

"I hear you write for the *Current* now?"

"I do. I was at the *Oregonian* for a bit but came back to town a few years ago."

"Fantastic. I'm sure your folks are glad you're back." His smile couldn't hide his pity. The sadness in his eyes said he recognized that was quite a step backward in my career. "Onyx has made quite a name for herself."

Ouch. That segue stung a little.

"She sure has."

"Speaking of." He jutted his chin toward the side door.

Onyx was no longer wearing Vivienne's baseball hat. She must have found someone to do her hair and makeup because she looked red carpet ready. Except her outfit. Instead of a sparkly gown, the woman had squeezed herself into her old cheerleader uniform. Her figure had filled out a bit since high school—both naturally and, I suspected, with the help of a plastic surgeon—so the shell top and short pleated skirt struggled to contain all her...assets.

Meacham wore a long black duster, a brown fedora, and mirrored sunglasses. He cowered a bit behind his wife, as if hoping to keep a low profile. The leopard print pantsuit underneath his coat didn't exactly scream discretion.

Onyx caught sight of me and waved me over.

"It was great seeing you, Mr., uh, Joe...Hannah."

He laughed. "Great seeing you, too, Audrey."

I scuttled across the gym, my sneakers squeaking the whole way. An area had been roped off to keep people from getting too close to Onyx and Meacham. My old friend Billiam was standing guard.

"Me again."

He grunted. "VIPs only."

"Onyx is asking me to join her."

He glanced over his shoulder. She was frantically beckoning me.

"See?"

He grunted again but unhooked the chain from the pole and stepped aside for me to pass.

"Thanks."

A third grunt was followed by silence. Apparently, *you're welcome* was too much to ask for in return.

Onyx squealed. "Can you believe how many people are here?"

Of course I could. This was the biggest thing to happen to Chattertowne since…well, I couldn't think of a time.

The MC for the evening called the event to order. Wisely, they chose to save Onyx's induction until after they'd honored the others. Whether people would have left early, I couldn't say, but the vast majority of spectators were only there for Onyx.

"And now, the final inductee of the evening. While she needs no introduction, I'm going to give you one anyway."

The crowd laughed.

"Over eighteen years ago, this young woman left Chattertowne for the bright lights of Los Angeles on a Greyhound bus with nothing more than hope and a dream. Oh, and that thousand-watt smile. Now, she's a global celebrity and successful entrepreneur, not to mention wife of a rock and roll legend. Please join me in applauding Chattertowne's favorite daughter, Onyx Carpenter!"

The place erupted. Onyx waved with both hands as she sauntered to center court. She smiled and waved for several minutes until the standing ovation finally petered out.

"Thank you Chattertowne, it is so great to be back here in my hometown, the place that will always hold my heart!"

More cheers.

"Thank you to the Superintendent, to the school board, to the Chattertowne High faculty, oh, I see Mr. Hannah over there! Hi, Mr. Hannah! Thank you for coming!"

Mr. Hannah's face was aflame as he waved at her and patted his hand over his heart.

"Hottest principal ever, am I right?"

Whoops and laughter.

"Raise your hand if you had a crush on Mr. Hannah." Onyx raised her hand. "Ah, see, I'm not alone. I wouldn't be who I am today without people like Mr. Hannah and the teachers of Chattertowne High. Even those who gave me detention. Mrs. Porter, I'm looking at you."

More laughter.

"You see, I'm just a regular girl—"

"Yeah, right!" someone shouted from the bleachers.

"I am! I was once a student sitting in those very stands. And while I loved it here, I loved this town. I wanted something more for my life. That's all it takes, you know? The seed of an idea that my life could be extraordinary. And then all the hard work of turning a dream into reality. But at the end of the day, when I take off the designer clothes and the makeup, I'm just a girl from Chattertowne, and I'm so honored to be from this place."

Once again, the entire gymnasium erupted into cheers and thunderous applause.

Onyx was presented with a plaque, and the photographer took photos of her with the MC.

"Babe?" She waved for Meacham to join her.

He walked toward her, waving into the stands.

The crowd went bonkers.

More photos were taken of the two of them, each holding one side of her plaque.

The MC spoke into the microphone. "Everyone, there are refreshments in the commons. You will get a chance to greet our honorees and get a cookie."

People began to file out.

Wylie emerged from the crowd and headed toward Onyx and Meacham.

Sensing potential trouble, I scuttled out onto the court.

"Congratulations, Onyx." Wylie wrapped her in a hug.

Meacham gave him a withering stare. "And you are?"

"Oh, sorry, I'm Wylie Barrett." He held out his hand. "So great to finally meet you, Meacham."

Meacham tilted his head with a grimace.

And then he swung a left hook into Wylie's jaw, sending him crashing to the ground.

The gym lit up like the Fourth of July as dozens of flashbulbs went off.

Meacham stood over Wylie and pointed down at him. "Stay away from my wife."

Chapter Sixteen

Cole and Billiam had rushed into the mayhem just after Meacham landed the sucker punch on Wylie. Billiam pulled Meacham a few feet away from Wylie, who was attempting to get up, swinging as he came.

Onyx stood in shocked horror, grasping her plaque to her chest.

She turned on Meacham. "How could you! This was my special night, and you've ruined it!"

"Babe—"

"No! I don't want to hear it!"

Cole helped Wylie to his feet. "Sir, would you like to press charges against Mr. Fields for assault?"

Wylie held up his left hand while rubbing his jaw with his right. "Can I think about it a minute?"

Onyx spun to face Wylie. "I'm so sorry he hit you, but please don't file charges. He'll get deported."

"I don't think that's how it works," I said.

My correction was met with a look of fury. "He's already had one strike. They said next time he's out of here and can't return for several years. This is his livelihood! If he can't tour in the States, his career is over."

"He probably should have thought of that before he knocked my block off." Wylie wiped his mouth and examined his fingers. Blood.

"Wylie, please. I'm begging you."

A look of confusion and hurt crossed Wylie's face. Perhaps a hint of betrayal.

I wasn't sure what he'd been expecting. No matter what he'd shared with Onyx in the past, or whatever feelings the past few days had rekindled, Meacham was her husband. It was clear that was where her loyalties lay.

I put my hand on her arm. "Onyx, maybe you and Meacham should skip the refreshments and head back to the B and B."

"I think that's a good idea," said Cole. "Wylie, you should head home as well."

Wylie stomped off toward the main exit.

"Good riddance," muttered Meacham.

Onyx gave an exasperated huff and marched off toward the side entrance. Meacham shrugged and wandered after her.

Cole shook his head. "No offense to your sister, but I can't wait for this wedding to be over so those two can leave town."

"You and me both."

"You golfing tomorrow?"

"Yes. I was hoping Wylie could give me some pointers, but then you arrested him."

He gave me a wry smile. "Sorry, I didn't consider your needs before doing my job."

"Very funny."

"What's funny?" Miranda was halfway across the basketball court with her heels click-clacking.

Honestly, who wore heels to a gymnasium?

"Audrey was just lamenting her terrible golf handicap."

Miranda flared her nostrils. "Now that your sister has chosen to side with a murderer, I'm no longer included in the scramble. I guess I'll go get a pedicure instead."

I looked down at her toes peeking out from her shoes. They were a glossy cherry red and appeared freshly painted.

I looked back up at her and arched a brow. "Sounds like a great way to spend the day."

She narrowed her gaze and looked down her nose at me. "You both are backing the wrong horse."

"Hey, I'm not backing any horse. I just support my sister's right to have the people in her wedding she chooses to have. You gave her an ultimatum, and it backfired."

"Even Onyx's husband knows what a creep Wylie is. I'll bet that punch felt really good."

I sensed Cole take a half step back. Coward.

Miranda must have noticed as well, because she whirled to face him, swaying on her heels. She reached for his arm to steady herself. "Aren't you going to give me a ride home?"

"Oh, I, uh, I think I need to stick around here a little longer." He beckoned to Billiam. "Officer Burton, can you give Ms. Dodd a ride home?"

"Sure thing, chief." He tossed a look of annoyance my way.

I refrained from sticking out my tongue at him like I'd done in school.

"You're leaving too, right, Audrey?" Miranda stared me down once again. "I think Cole has had enough of you today."

Cole frowned. "I can determine that for myself, Miranda, but thanks for your concern. Officer Burton will give you a ride home, and I'll give you a call later."

Her neck flushed with displeasure. She smoothed her blouse and gave a strained smile. "Don't forge-ehhhht," she sang as she walked away with Billiam hot on her heels. Literally. Her tone reminded me of Yzma from the movie *Emperor's New Groove*, with a slight growl punctuating the final syllable.

Cole sighed. "Most of the time when I'm investigating a case, I prefer not to know anything personal about the people involved. It helps me focus on the facts and not be bogged down by emotion. This time, I've got the worst of both worlds. I've got a woman I—"

"Hmm?"

"A woman I *know*, whose kid is a victim of a crime, and yet I know very little about the others involved. This time, not having grown up here puts me at a disadvantage." Cole shifted his weight between his feet.

I almost felt sorry for him. Almost.

Not enough to let him off the hook.

"If I may be so bold, I'd argue that you don't know Miranda as well as you believe."

"What do you mean?"

"Well, I see you as a man of integrity—"

"Thank you."

"I'm not done. I also see you as a man of intelligence."

"Also, not an insult. Why do I sense a *but* coming?"

"She's awful. You know that, right? I mean, how could you not know that?"

"That's not a very nice thing to say, especially since the woman nearly lost her son."

"If you'd asked my opinion prior to the accident, I'd have said even worse. This is my empathetic version. I really don't understand what you see in her."

"I really don't see how it's any of your business."

I held up my hands. "You're right. My bad."

"Besides, she's one of your sister's oldest friends."

"So, we're using Vivienne as the benchmark for good judgment? The woman is marrying someone who tried to kidnap her. All water under the bridge, now, apparently, but you get my point."

"Where is this nastiness coming from?"

That stopped me in my tracks. He was right, I was being nasty. I was all churned up and spewing out toxic barbs. What was with me? "I'm sorry. That was uncalled for."

He rubbed the back of his neck. "Look, weddings are stressful, and then you add in all the drama, and on top of it, a young girl is dead. I thought I had my guy, but what I was trying to say is, I just don't know Wylie well enough to know if he's capable of something like that."

"I have no doubt that most of us, when backed into a corner, are capable of a lot of horrible things. Including murder. The real question is, was Wylie really crossing a line with Laveda, and would he kill her to cover his tracks?"

Cole regarded me for a moment. "Off the record."

I nodded. "Okay."

He looked around to make sure no one was listening. After the fight had been broken up and Onyx and Meacham were gone, most people had left for the commons to get a cookie and some lemonade. A few people still lingered at the door, probably rehashing the evening's events.

He pulled me to the back of the gym, near the wrestling mat storage closet, where I used to make out with Marcus Washburn back in High School.

Judging by Cole's expression, making out with me was the furthest thing from his mind. "Laveda texted Wylie on the night of her death. Shortly before the accident, as a matter of fact."

"After they'd left 3F?"

"Yes."

"How do you know?"

"Laveda's parents provided a printout of the numbers she'd been texting and calling."

"And? Do you know what she said?"

"We never located her phone. We haven't yet gotten a warrant for Wylie's phone, and he's refused to unlock it upon advice of counsel, or to turn it over to us."

"I mean, can you blame him?"

"Innocent people shouldn't have to hide their texts, calls, and emails."

"That's one hundred percent false. Any defense attorney will say to not hand over anything you don't have to without a court order. Do you know what my Google search history looks like? If I were arrested for a crime and people saw that, it'd be straight to jail for me."

"I don't even want to know."

"It's because of the research I have to do for my job. Nothing scandalous, I assure you. So, you think you'll get the warrant?"

"I believe we will. The fact she was texting him right after she left an event where she'd been with him seems strange, right? I mean, I know he's her coach, but the idea of her texting him at night, it's kind of unseemly, don't you think?" He scanned my face. "What aren't you telling me?"

"Hmm?"

"Audrey, your face is telling on you like a Times Square billboard. You know something pertinent to the investigation, don't you?"

I pressed my lips tightly together and shook my head. "Mmm mnn."

"Out with it."

"We still off the record?"

"That only works in your line of work, not mine." He crossed his arms. "Spill it."

"I want to state for the record that I believe Wylie is innocent."

"So noted."

"When I went to use the restroom right before we left, I saw Laveda and Wylie in the hallway."

"What were they doing?"

"I just caught the tail end of it, so I don't really know. From what I saw, I thought maybe they'd been having an intense conversation, because she was…unsettled."

"Unsettled?"

"I don't know how else to describe it. She wasn't happy. She wasn't sad. She seemed…bothered."

"About what?"

"I have no idea. Like I said, I didn't hear any of their conversation. It just struck me as a little inappropriate. Not that I saw him touch her or anything. It was just the fact they were in a dark corner together. It really didn't sit right with me. I was—"

"Unsettled?" he repeated.

"Yeah. I assume the digital evidence you were referring to when you arrested him was the text from Laveda?"

"Yes."

"And?"

"And what?"

"What other evidence compelled you to arrest him?"

"I can't share all of that."

"Did you interview Jack?"

He flinched. Bingo.

"What did he tell you?"

"Let's just say that according to Jack, Laveda shared with him that Wylie made her uncomfortable."

"How so?"

"He said Wylie was acting obsessive. Possessive."

"All the essives, huh?"

"Something like that."

Suddenly, the lights in the gym went out, and we were standing in total darkness.

"I guess that's our sign to leave." Cole chuckled.

"Or we could stay here and make out." My laughter was met with dead silence. "Cole, I was joking."

"Shh." He grabbed my arm and pulled me to him. "Look," he whispered.

In the doorway stood a shadowy figure, highlighted only by the glow from the hallway. I couldn't see if they were looking at us, because I couldn't see their eyes. After a moment, the person turned and walked away.

"Was that—?"

Cole grunted. "Hank Dodd."

Chapter Seventeen

The next morning I awoke to the sound of someone banging on my door.

I grabbed the robe hanging in my bathroom and wandered downstairs.

The incessant knocking continued.

"I'm coming."

With a purported murderer on the loose, I probably should have checked to see who was pounding on my door at the ungodly hour of—I checked my phone—crap. Nine fifteen. Our tee time for golf was at ten. For some reason, my alarm hadn't gone off.

I opened the door to find my horrified sister.

"Audrey! We're supposed to be at the club in less than thirty minutes." She threw a shirt at me.

"I'm sorry. I don't know what happened. I swear I set my alarm." I examined the shirt. "I like big putts, and I cannot lie?"

She unzipped her hoodie. Her shirt read, *Who's Your Caddy?*

"Cute. Mom is going to hate these."

"She's not invited to this."

"Make yourself some coffee, and I'll go get cleaned up. I won't even wash my hair."

I ran back upstairs, threw the robe on my unmade bed, and flung open my closet door. Even though my mother belonged to the club, I didn't golf much and didn't exactly have the gear. The weather was typical for spring in the Seattle area, with a high of fifty-eight degrees and a thirty percent chance of rain. Not exactly skort weather, which was actually a blessing, since I didn't have time to shave my legs.

"Do you want creamer in your coffee?" Vivienne yelled from the kitchen.

"No, just black with a ton of whipped cream on top."

"You're so weird."

"What else is new?"

I settled on a pair of tan pants, the t-shirt, and a tan windbreaker. I pulled my golf shoes from a box on a high shelf.

I hustled into the bathroom and caught sight of my appearance. My hair's state mimicked how I preferred my martinis: shaken up and extra dirty.

I arched one eyebrow at my reflection and flipped my hair over my shoulder. "Blonde. Dirty blonde."

"Did you say something?" Vivienne was coming up the stairs.

"Nothing worth repeating."

"I put your coffee on your nightstand. I'll be waiting downstairs. You have fifteen minutes. Tops."

"I'm hurrying."

Once again, I stared at myself in the mirror, wavering on my promise to Vivienne about not washing it. I compromised with dry shampoo and threw it up in a bun.

A two-minute shower was enough to get the important bits clean. I brushed my teeth, concealed my dark undereye bags, and tried to cover a hormonal zit coming in on my chin. Just in time for the wedding photos. Of course. I swiped on some blush, lip gloss, and mascara.

After appraising my efforts, I gave myself a C plus. It would have been a B minus, but my mother graded on a curve, and her voice was constantly in my head.

I bounded down the stairs and grabbed my purse and keys.

"What are you wearing?" Vivienne eyed me with disdain.

"What?" I glanced down at my clothes. "What's wrong with it?"

"I can't tell if you look more like a park ranger or a serial killer."

"Serial killer? How do I look like a serial killer?"

"That beige windbreaker is the serial killer's jacket of choice."

"Well, then, maybe everyone will be intimidated by me, and we'll actually win today."

She laughed as we walked out the front door. "There's not a chance we're going to win. Rachel's a better golfer than you and I combined, but even she can't make up for our shortcomings. Lacey, Holden, and Yellin have an average handicap of less than ten, and when you add in Wylie the ringer, we've lost before we've started. Do you even have a handicap?"

"I don't even know how a handicap is calculated. Do you want a higher score or a lower score?"

Vivienne sighed. "It won't matter. The point is to have fun. Hopefully Rachel won't give up on us when she sees how bad we are."

"I know she's athletic, but I didn't realize she golfed that much."

"When have you ever known her to do anything halfway? She's even got a specialized wheelchair designed for golfing. It's called a paragolfer mobility chair. It raises her to an upright position for her swing."

"Technology is amazing," I said.

Vivienne grimaced. "Too bad it can't help you and me."

* * *

Vivienne and I arrived at the Chattertowne Golf and Country Club fifteen minutes before our tee time, which felt like a huge accomplishment, considering I'd been asleep in bed forty minutes earlier. She'd prearranged for me to rent clubs. Lacey had given her a set for her birthday, so she already had her own. She headed over to the golf cart area where Lacey, Rachel, and Yellin were waiting.

I walked into the pro shop, and once again, Ike was working the counter.

"Hey, dude."

I looked behind me to see if he was addressing someone else. There was no one there.

"Nice shirt." He smirked.

"Thanks."

"You were the one looking for Coach Barrett the other day, right? Did you find him?"

"Uh, yeah."

"Can't believe he murdered that girl."

My breath hitched in my chest. "I don't think he did."

Ike shrugged. "That's what everyone's saying."

"People shouldn't rush to judgment," I said.

Ike shrugged.

"My sister Vivienne O'Connell reserved a set of clubs for me."

"Oh, yeah, you're with the wedding group. Someone already checked you all in for your tee time." He scanned the length of me. "How tall are you?"

"I'm five-six."

"Right or left-handed?"

"Right."

He pulled out a set of clubs. "Try these. Stand up on that pad over there and take a few swings."

He indicated a raised platform.

The last thing I wanted was to be taking swings in front of Ike, but I needed to make sure the clubs were a decent fit if I was to have any chance of not embarrassing myself on the course.

As I climbed up the step, the bell on the front door jingled. A tall, gangly boy I recognized as one of the kids I saw playing basketball with Jack at the 3F event came into the shop. He was wearing a Chattertowne High basketball t-shirt and a pair of green Adidas track pants.

He nodded at Ike. "Hey, man. I need—"

"One sec, Austin, I need to finish helping this *lady* over here with her clubs."

Austin's eyes grew wide. "Oh, yeah, of course, sorry. I didn't see her there. I'll check out the, uh, shoes while I'm waiting."

An audience of one was bad enough. Two was humiliating.

"Okay, lemme see what you got," said Ike.

I pulled out the pitching wedge, positioned my feet, and dropped my head like my father had taught me to do.

"This feels weird. It's facing the wrong way."

Ike tilted his head. "You're holding it wrong."

"How am I holding it wrong? I'm just holding it like I always have."

He came closer. "Dude. Someone must have put a lefty club in your bag. Sorry about that." He took the wedge from me and handed me a different club. "Try this."

Once again, I positioned myself. This time, the club face was angled the right way. I dropped my head, wiggled my hips, and swung.

"Actually, not too bad. You've got some real power behind that swing. Must be your broad back and shoulders."

What every woman wanted to hear. "Thanks?"

If he noted my sarcasm, he didn't acknowledge it. "I did notice you rotate your left foot during your swing, which will cause you to slice the ball. You should sign up for lessons with Wylie. He'll have you swinging straight in no time. If he doesn't go to jail, I mean."

"I'll consider it." I'd considered it prior to today, but only so I could be competitive against Holden. After this, there was a good chance I'd never golf again. I replaced the club and swung the bag's strap over my shoulder. "Thanks for the pointers. I'll bring these back when I'm done."

"No rush. Good luck."

I glanced over at Austin, who was pretending to peruse the shoes. I knew he was pretending because he was intensely examining a peach-colored woman's shoe in his hand.

Outside the pro shop, it appeared everyone had arrived and was crowded around the carts.

Yellin's shirt read, *The Bogey man.* Lacey's said, *Let's Par-tee!* Onyx claimed she couldn't find hers, but I figured she just wanted to wear her form-fitting tank top instead. Rachel's shirt said, *Social Putterfly.* Wylie's was *May the Course be with You.* Holden's was the worst of all, *Tryna Catch Me Ridin' Birdie*, a punny play on a Chamillionaire song.

He eyed me up and down but said nothing, a smirk playing upon his lips. Probably judging my shirt and the rest of my golf attire, especially since he knew I rarely—like almost never—played golf.

Vivienne divvied up the group into pairs. Rachel was with Viv, although she wouldn't sit in the cart, she'd ride alongside in her paragolf chair. I was paired with Onyx, who was unusually sullen. I chalked it up to a late night, but it hadn't really been all that late.

Holden was paired with Yellin, which made me *so* very happy, because I knew she'd talk his ear off. Wylie rode with Lacey. I suspected that Lacey, being former assistant police chief, had some probing questions for her groomsman-bridesmaid-bridesman and the details surrounding his arrest so close to her wedding. I'd once been on the receiving end of Lacey's interrogation, and I wouldn't have wanted to change places with him for a million dollars.

Team Vivienne was headed to the back nine, while Team Lacey was starting at the first hole.

"Can you drive?" Onyx was scrolling on her phone and had already slid into the passenger seat.

"Sure. What's up with you?"

"Nothing." Her lips were pressed tightly together as her nails tippity-tapped on her phone screen.

"Have you golfed before?" Not that it mattered, since the deck was already stacked against us.

"No."

This was going to be fun. Playing a game I was terrible at, with a partner who'd rather be anywhere else, against a team of nearly scratch golfers.

Vivienne excitedly waved at me from the cart ahead of us, and I felt my irritation deflate. She was why I was doing this. It didn't matter how badly it went. The important thing was celebrating my sister and her special time.

"This day is important to Viv," I said to Onyx. "Let's try to make the best of it."

She set down her phone. "Sorry, you're right. I'm just so annoyed with Meacham right now, I can barely stand it. Can you believe he popped Wylie in the mouth last night? It's all over the tabloid sites this morning. Everyone's talking about my jealous husband and my high school sweetheart. The last thing I need is them digging into—" She stopped herself midsentence.

"Digging into what?"

"Nothing."

"Again with the nothing."

"Can we just drop it?"

"Sure."

Vivienne took a swing and shaded her eyes so she could follow the ball.

"Nice one." I clapped.

"It veered a bit further to the right than I wanted. It's right on the fringe of the fairway."

Rachel's chair raised her to the point of standing. She whacked the ball, and it sailed toward the green.

"You nearly hit the green on a par four!" Vivienne gave her a high five. "We may have a chance at this yet."

We were playing a nine-hole best ball scramble. With the rules Lacey and Vivienne had set for the day, everyone played their next shot from the location of the best of the previous shots. The caveat was that each player needed to have at least five of their shots used. That way, a team couldn't use only their best golfer's shots.

"Oh, my sweet summer child. We do not have a chance in hell. You haven't seen me swing yet." I laughed.

I stepped to the ladies' box and set my ball on a tee. I positioned my stance, trying to remember what Ike had said about over-rotation. I tucked my chin and stared at the ball.

"You gonna hit it or just look at it?" Vivienne said.

"No talking in my back swing. Or before my back swing, as the case may be." I adjusted my grip on the club, which I realized I'd been clutching so tightly my hands were starting to ache. I swung back and allowed the club to swing forward. Unfortunately, I completely topped the ball. I glanced around to make sure no one outside of our group had witnessed it.

"Try again, Audrey," said Rachel. "Just don't lift up your heels during your backswing. Keep them heavy until you're on your follow-through. Then you can lift your right heel as you pivot."

I followed her instructions and managed to get off a decent shot.

"Good job." Rachel applauded.

"Thanks. You're a good instructor. Okay, Onyx, you're up."

Onyx jumped out of the cart and pulled out a three wood. Despite the cold weather, she was wearing a white pleated skirt.

I walked back to the cart and slid my driver into the bag.

Onyx's phone began to ring. It was sitting on her seat.

"Onyx, it says Meacham is calling."

She swished her hips back and forth in preparation for her swing. "Can you bring it over here? Answer it on speaker."

I picked up her phone and swiped to answer the call. I selected speaker and held it up to her.

"Hey, babe, I can't really talk right now. I'm golfing and I'm about to tee off."

"Onyx, why the hell is TMZ reporting that you secretly had Wylie's baby and gave it away?"

Chapter Eighteen

Onyx dropped her club and snatched her phone out of my hand, quickly pressing the button to take the call off speakerphone. "What are you talking about?" She hissed into the receiver.

I couldn't discern what Meacham said in response, but he certainly wasn't whispering.

"We'll talk about this when I get back to the B and B." Her face registered distress. "I'll explain everything, please, don't—" She held the phone away from her face. "He hung up."

Vivienne placed a hand on her shoulder. "Onyx. Is it true? Did you really give Wylie's baby up for adoption?"

She shook her head. "How did they find out about him?" Onyx buried her face in her hands. "My life is ruined."

Vivienne's shoulders slumped. As much as I had empathy for Onyx, I felt terrible for my sister. All she'd wanted was to have a nice wedding, and all she'd gotten instead was a ton of drama.

Rachel observed us like we were a trashy reality TV show she couldn't look away from.

"Does Wylie know?" I asked.

"I was about to tell him the other night, but that's when the call came in about the accident at Devil's Elbow. He has a radio in his car, because he volunteers with Snohomish County Search and Rescue."

"Uh, I think he knows now." Vivienne jutted her chin toward the bottom of the cart path.

A golf cart with Wylie Barrett at the wheel was barreling its way toward us. A stunned-looking Lacey sat in the passenger seat.

"Hoo boy," I said under my breath.

Rachel's eyes lit up with even more amusement. This episode of *The Real Housewives of Chattertowne* was getting juicier by the minute.

The cart came to a screeching halt, and Wylie jumped out. "Are you freaking kidding me? My phone is blowing up. Tell me this isn't true. Tell me you didn't give away *my* child without even telling me it existed."

"I'm gonna give you guys some privacy." Vivienne hopped into the cart with Lacey, who made a quick U-turn. Impressive, considering golf carts aren't the most maneuverable of vehicles.

"I'm going with them." Rachel swiveled her chair and followed after Viv and Lacey.

Wylie and Onyx were in a standoff, neither one saying a word. His face was flushed with rage and grief, and hers with fear and shame.

"You two take my cart. I'll take this one." I pointed at the golf cart Vivienne had abandoned.

Neither of them acknowledged me. As I drove away, they were still in a silent standoff.

By the time I got back to the clubhouse, Vivienne had texted me that she and Lacey were taking Rachel to coffee, and I could join them if I wanted.

I'd also missed a call from Kayla at the bridal shop, letting me know my dress was ready to be picked up.

I swung open the door to enter the pro shop. Ike was talking to another boy I recognized from 3F. It was the skinny kid in glasses who'd been watching Laveda doing her dance workout. Both he and Ike jerked their heads in my direction.

Ike deftly slid something across the counter to the boy, who immediately shoved his hand in his pocket.

"Back so soon?" Ike glanced at the clock on the wall. "You weren't supposed to be done for a couple hours."

"Something came up." I hoisted the clubs off my shoulder and leaned them against the counter. I turned to the boy. "You were at the 3F meeting the other night, weren't you?"

"Yes, ma'am."

I didn't want to discourage good manners, but the ma'am part bruised my ego. "Ouch. I didn't realize I was *ma'am* years old."

The boy's eyelids flew open. "I'm so sorry, I didn't mean to offend you!"

I waved him off. "It's fine. So, you must be pretty devastated about Laveda."

The boy's Adam's apple bobbed up and down. "Why do you say that? I mean, it's sad, but I didn't know her very well."

"Really? I had the impression maybe something was going on between the two of you."

Ike grunted a chuckle. "He wishes."

Pink crept up the boy's neck. "She was nice. She sat next to me in English, that's all. We were friends."

I glanced behind him. "Are you golfing today? You don't have any clubs."

He made a furtive glance in Ike's direction. "Oh, uh, I was thinking about starting."

Ike cleared his throat. "Yeah. He was asking about lessons."

My internal lie detector was going off like crazy, but I couldn't pinpoint why. "Sport of kings."

The boy gave me an incredulous look. "Uh, I think that's horse racing."

"Hmm. You could be right. Well, thanks for the clubs. I only got one shot off, but they handled pretty well."

Ike gave a curt head nod. "How about this. I'll make a note that you're owed a free rental since you didn't really get a chance to use them."

"That's so nice of you. Thank you."

"What can I say, I'm a prince of a guy." He lifted his left brow, and his lascivious smile had me wanting a hot shower to rinse off the film it left behind. "Hope to see you soon."

"Oh, uh, not if I see you first, ha ha." I wasn't joking. When I returned later in the day for the rehearsal dinner, I'd be sure to keep an eye out to avoid him. Something about Ike really gave me the creeps.

A golf cart squealed into the lot, practically leaning on only two wheels. Yellin was driving, and a traumatized Holden clutched the handle on the side of the passenger seat. She parked the cart in front of the pro shop.

"I see your group decided to call it quits after Wylie left," I said.

"We finished the hole, but Lacey was gone, too, so it didn't make sense to keep playing," said Holden.

Yellin grumbled. "I woulda kept going, but Holden felt it was in bad taste after the brides noped out."

"He has a point."

"Where are you headed?" he asked.

"My bridesmaid dress is ready, so I'll probably go pick it up from Kayla's."

"I'm glad I don't have to wear a dress. Lacey said I could wear a pantsuit. The only problem is it kind of makes me look like the Jolly Green Giant."

"Oh, I'm sure it's not that bad." I wasn't sure at all, but it seemed like the right thing to say under the circumstances.

"I think we're all at a bit of a disadvantage with this color scheme," Holden said.

"Are you wearing a green suit?" I asked him.

"Hell no. I'm wearing a black suit, dark green shirt, and a black tie."

He looked great in dark green. It contrasted nicely with his medium-brown complexion and deep brown eyes. Just picturing it made me feel flustered.

Yellin narrowed her gaze. "You feeling all right, Audrey? You look a little feverish."

"Oh, I uh, I think I had too much caffeine this morning."

The corner of Holden's mouth twitched. He'd known me long enough that he could read me like a book.

I glanced around. "Uh oh."

"What's wrong?" he asked.

"I just realized I rode with Vivienne."

"I'd give you a ride," Yellin said, "but I have an appointment in Bellevue." She lowered her chin and her volume. "A *waxing* appointment."

"Oh. Well, you don't want to be late for that."

"I can take you," said Holden.

"Thanks. You can just take me home, and I'll grab my car."

"She said my tux should be in this afternoon, so I might as well come with you. Besides, I took today off, so I don't have anywhere I need to be until the rehearsal."

"Well, I'm off to Bellevue. I'll see you both later." Yellin gave an abrupt arm raise and marched off toward her car.

"I'm parked over there." Holden pointed across the lot.

The boy in glasses came out of the pro shop. He did a double-take when he spotted me, and then looked at Holden. He scurried across the parking lot, clutching his jacket closed.

"What was that about?" asked Holden.

"My intuition tells me nothing good."

* * *

Kayla had my dress hanging in a dressing room when we arrived at the bridal shop. Holden's tux had arrived as well, so she'd put his in the room next to mine.

I had to admit, she'd done a fantastic job with the alterations. Everything fit my body where it was supposed to be snug, without making me feel like a Renaissance wench in a corset or an overfilled muffin oozing over the rim of the tin.

I exited my dressing room just as Holden stepped out of his. My breath caught at the sight of him. He was a sharp dresser as a city executive, but these days he'd been wearing mostly construction gear.

The off-the-rack suit had been tailored as if made for him, a testament to Kayla's skills. He was broad-shouldered with large biceps, but at five foot ten, he didn't have the height to justify the size of suit needed to accommodate them.

"Close your mouth, Audrey." He gave me a teasing smile.

"I've never seen you in a full suit."

His eyes perused my gown. "You clean up nice, kid."

"Thanks." I couldn't hide the note of disappointment in my voice as I picked an invisible piece of fluff off the dress.

"Audrey."

"Hmm?"

"Look at me."

I raised my gaze to his.

His brown eyes warmed. "You look beautiful."

I quickly looked away, embarrassed about my transparent insecurities. "Thank you."

Kayla rushed into the room. "You guys both look amazing."

"All thanks to you," I said. "I really can't thank you enough for saving me from looking like moldy guacamole."

Kayla laughed. "It wasn't that bad. I thought you were pulling it off, actually." Her face told another story.

"We both know that's a lie."

"Okay, you're right. It was awful. I'm glad we were able to find a replacement." She moved to the back of Holden and, with her fingertips, adjusted his jacket. "How does that feel? Not too tight, I hope."

"Nope, it's perfect."

"Audrey, Onyx's dress is ready also. Do you think she'll be able to come in and try it on before I close at five?"

Holden and I exchanged glances.

"What's wrong? What did I miss? Don't tell me she's dropped out of the wedding now, too."

I sighed. "No, I don't think so. At least, not that I'm aware. She's dealing with some…personal issues. Let me call her really quick."

I pulled out my phone and dialed her number.

After a couple rings, Onyx answered the call with a pitiful voice. "Hello?"

"It's Audrey. You okay?"

She sniffled. "Not really."

"I hate to bug you, but I'm at Kayla's picking up my dress, and she says yours is ready to be picked up."

"Can you grab it for me?"

"She really prefers you try it on, to make any last-minute adjustments."

"I'm sure it will be fine. Just please bring it to me."

"At the B and B?"

"I'm at Wylie's. Meacham won't answer his phone." Onyx wailed like a kid in the park who's lost their mom. "His last text to me said he wants a divorce!"

Chapter Nineteen

I suspected Holden's offer to drive me to Wylie's to give Onyx her bridesmaid dress was less about consideration and more about fascination with the unfolding drama and not wanting to miss the show. I didn't blame him. The whole thing was bound to get tabloids across the world panting for more.

Wylie's home was a cedar wood late-70s split-level that sat atop a steep driveway on a ¾ acre parcel about a mile from Lake Pilchuck and about two miles from the town of the same name.

Lake Pilchuck had initially been founded in the late 1800s as a logging community. After World War II, Seattle socialites discovered the lake's untapped beauty, and summer homes began popping up along its shores. By the late 1960s, the town was mostly blue-collar, with many working for Boeing until the layoffs of 1970 and 1971. The economy of the town didn't recover until the mid 70s, just in time for the next recession.

Now a bedroom community of the Seattle/Bellevue tech hub, Lake Pilchuck had finally started to come into its own.

I was familiar with the area because my friend Shelly had grown up in the house next door to his. Both homes looked down upon—literally and figuratively—the neighborhood below, which my friend's parents called "Scuzzville." I'd never been a fan of class warfare, but I could see how the neighborhood had gotten its not-so-affectionate nickname.

It was understandable how HOAs got their bad rap, but at least the bylaws encouraged some yard maintenance. It wasn't that the residents of "Scuzzville" didn't own lawnmowers—they did, usually more than one, often on display in the front yard—they just rarely used them. I'd have hay fever attacks waiting for the school bus after a sleepover at Shelly's house because the grass and weeds were knee-high.

It was the kind of place where even fences didn't make good neighbors. Chain link and barbed wire barely restrained angry, barking dogs and nearly feral children like the McQuaids. There were four McQuaid kids, three brothers and a baby sister named Carrie. Carrie was in my grade, and she was so mean that a rumor circulated that she'd been the inspiration for the Stephen King movie. Never mind that the original film (and the book it was based on) were released in the 1970s, long before she was born.

There was Michael "Mickey" McQuaid, the one who'd died in a motorcycle accident going over a hundred miles an hour around Devil's Elbow, Anthony McQuaid, who went to the Walla Walla State Penitentiary for the 2007 armed robbery of Chattertowne's state liquor store (prior to Washington voters privatizing the sale of liquor in 2011), and the third brother, Christopher, who worked as a quality control inspector at Boeing.

Carrie, the youngest, terrorized her classmates—including me, although I learned early on to give her a wide berth—through all twelve years in the Chattertowne public school system. She then went on to (I presumed) terrorize her classmates at Stanford, where she'd gotten a full-ride scholarship, moved on to Harvard Law, and now sat on the bench as a Ninth Circuit Court of Appeals judge with a reputation for fairness and equitable application of the law.

My mother, an avid gardener, liked to say Carrie was like a Creeping Juniper plant: She somehow not only survived growing up in rocky soil surrounded by weeds, but she also managed to thrive. I didn't inherit my mother's green thumb, so I took her at her word that the analogy fit. I also made a mental note to buy a Creeping Juniper plant in hopes I might keep it alive.

"These driveways must be terrible in the winter," said Holden as he drove the steep incline.

"The worst. Once I slept over at Shelly's during a snowstorm. Not only did her father have to park his car at the bottom of the driveway and hike up to the house, but we also had a bird's eye view of all the cars sliding into the ditch. It turned into a demolition derby."

"The things that amuse you."

Before we even got up the stairs to the front doors, Onyx was standing there to welcome us.

"Making yourself at home, I see."

She squinted her bloodshot eyes. "Where else am I supposed to go? My husband wants to divorce me. Besides, I owed Wylie an explanation. I've owed him one for a really long time, actually."

She ushered us into the entryway. One set of stairs led down to the basement. The other led up to the kitchen and living room.

We followed her up the stairs to where Wylie was sitting in a leather armchair in the corner. It was a recliner, but he wasn't reclining. In fact, he was leaning forward, arms resting on his thighs, hands tented. His left foot bounced frenetically. His expression was one of vacant shock, like when the information taken into a brain overloaded it so much it all seeped out until there was nothing left but the residue of a reality that no longer existed and the knowledge that time would forever be sorted into before and after that moment.

"How you doing there, bud?" My casual greeting did nothing to ease the awkward tension in the room.

He shrugged, foot still bouncing.

I handed Onyx her dress, zipped into a garment bag. "Technically, Kayla is closed this weekend, but she says if you try this on and there are any issues, she'll come into the shop tomorrow to make minor alterations."

She waved a dismissive hand. "I'm sure it will be fine."

Holden shifted his weight but stayed silent.

"I know it's none of my business—"

"You're right, Audrey, it's not." Onyx pursed her lips.

I looked between the two of them. "If there's anything else I can—"

"See you at six."

Her dismissal was firm.

"Onyx, I'm here if you need to talk."

Her expression softened. "Thanks. And thank you for bringing the dress. We'll see you at the rehearsal."

I wouldn't say we slunk out of the house like chastised puppy dogs, but it was pretty close. Okay, I slunk. Holden sauntered, as usual.

"Where am I dropping you?" he asked as we descended the driveway.

"Home. I rushed out of the house this morning, and I think I may have forgotten deodorant." I sniffed my armpit. "I definitely forgot deodorant."

"I'm so glad you feel comfortable being yourself around me," he said, drily.

"What, you worried the romance is gone?"

He snorted. "A couple ill-timed kisses do not constitute romance."

Ouch. "Speaking of romance, am I the only one who thinks this Miranda-Cole relationship makes zero sense?"

Holden gave me a side eye. "Jealous?"

Now it was my turn to snort. "As if."

He squeezed the steering wheel. "Seems to me there's a *there*, there."

"With Cole and me? There's definitely no *there*, there. I'm the burr in his boot, that's all."

Holden cocked an eyebrow. "Interesting turn of phrase."

"It's the whole cowboy persona he's got going on."

"Yeah, I get that. I guess I'm just wondering *why* you're the…burr in his boot."

"I dunno. It's been that way since he got here."

"And you don't think it has anything to do with sexual tension? And don't make that face at me, Audrey. I know you too well."

"What face?"

"The one where you try to pretend that what I'm saying is absurd when you know damn well it's the truth."

I shifted in my seat. I shifted back again.

"You're uncomfortable with the idea, but that doesn't mean I'm wrong," he said.

"I'm not uncomfortable with the idea, these seats are just weirdly molded."

He shook his head.

"What do you care anyway?"

He pulled off the road, put the car in park, and turned to look at me. "Did you seriously just ask me that?"

I didn't know what to say. I blinked at him, willing some clever retort to make its way into my mind. No such luck.

He stared at me for a moment, closed his eyes, and heaved a sigh. His lips pressed together several times, but the words never came. When he turned to look at me once more, his brown eyes were hooded and heavy.

"Every time I think we understand each other, you prove me wrong." He shifted the car into gear and turned on his signal.

"What does that even mean?"

"You're proving my point." With that, he pulled back onto the highway.

* * *

I couldn't get the conversation with Holden out of my head, no matter how hard I scrubbed it with shampoo in the shower.

Was he trying to tell me something? Was I that obtuse? He'd once answered that question with a flirty *you're not obtuse, you're acute.* At this moment, however, I felt pretty clueless.

There wasn't a universe where Holden and I actually ended up together, was there? A timeline where we lived happily ever after and had curly-headed babies with his slow smile and perfect teeth and my innate klutziness?

I couldn't see it. Not that I could see an alternate universe in which Cole and I played Roy Rogers and Dale Evans, singing *Oh give me a home where the buffalo roam* as little cowgirls and cowboys ran around free on the range.

"What is happening to me right now?" The naked woman in my bathroom mirror stared back at me with a wide-eyed gaze and a foamy bouffant atop her head. She obviously didn't have any more clarity than I did.

"Are you talking to yourself again?" Vivienne shouted through my bathroom door, which was slightly ajar.

"Ack!" I covered my bits. "You can't just barge in here! I'm in the shower."

"I didn't barge in there. I announced my presence. *Now* I'm barging in. I won't look."

"Gah, it's like when I was in high school, and you were in middle school. I never had any privacy."

"You should learn to lock your front door, then, if it bothers you so much." She hopped up on the counter. "I need a favor."

"Of course you do," I muttered.

"What was that?"

"I said, what can I do?"

"You can tell me why Lacey and I shouldn't drive down to City Hall tomorrow and forget this whole idea of a country club wedding with a bridal party comprised of a murder suspect out on bail, his ex-lover slash baby mama in the middle of an internationally televised scandal, Lacey's cousin who has the volume control of a toddler, and then there's you and Holden, whose chemistry is so intense I'm worried you're both going to spontaneously combust as soon as he grabs your arm to escort you down the aisle."

"What are you talking about? There's nothing going on with Holden and me."

"Oh, right. So the fact that he looked like he wanted to eat you for breakfast this morning was my imagination?"

"I'm not going to dignify that with a response." Mostly because I didn't have a good one.

"And of course, we can't forget the fact every time my boss sees you and Holden together, he looks like he wants to punch a wall."

I dropped my washcloth. "Cole? What do you mean? What did he say?"

"He didn't have to say a word. It's written all over his face."

"I doubt that's true. He's always annoyed with me, that's all."

"I have eyes, Audrey. Anyway, back to my initial query."

"Well, the first reason you shouldn't call off your wedding for a quick ceremony at City Hall is because City Hall is closed on Saturdays."

"You know what I mean. This whole wedding at the country club thing is turning out to be a disaster. Maybe we should elope."

As her maid of honor, my job was to lie to her if I had to in order to get her down the aisle. "Viv, even if every single thing went wrong, I'd still never tell you to call it off. This is about you and Lacey. So if the caterer gave everyone food poisoning, the country club burned down, and your minister broke his leg five minutes before the ceremony, it would still be worth it."

She laughed. "I sure hope none of those things happen. That would be pretty awful. But thanks, Audrey. I needed to hear that. The show must go on!"

Unfortunately, the one thing I didn't account for was yet another murder.

Chapter Twenty

I arrived at the club fifteen minutes before the rehearsal was set to begin. Yellin was the first to greet me with a hearty, "Audrey's here!"

Lacey was smiling at Vivienne and tucking a strand of her platinum blonde hair behind the ear of her bride-to-be. Viv wrapped her arms around her fiancée with a blissful grin, and I felt a heaviness leave my body that I hadn't even realized I'd been carrying.

I'd spent my entire life looking out for my baby sister. All I'd wanted was for her to be healthy, safe, and happy. Her expression told me my job was done. She was no longer my sole responsibility. Now it was Lacey's turn to watch over her, protect her (from herself and others), and keep that smile on her face.

I caught Holden staring at me from across the ballroom. His thoughts were inscrutable from his expression. I struggled to maintain eye contact with him. He made me feel seen in a way that wasn't comforting. It was unsettling. I felt exposed.

Worse yet, I had no idea what he thought about *what* he was observing.

Onyx sashayed into the room with Wylie, bringing up the rear. He still wore the catatonic expression I'd seen earlier that afternoon at his house. Hopefully, he'd pull himself together in time for the wedding on Sunday. The last thing Vivienne needed was a morose man greeting her as she walked down the aisle.

It's not that I didn't have empathy for him. He'd been heartbroken when Onyx had left all those years ago, but he'd eventually moved on. Not in a relationship, nothing significant or long-lasting, at least, but he'd put one foot in front of the other and made a life for himself. He had a home, a career, and a purpose with 3F.

With her return, Onyx had not only dredged all those buried hurts and brought them to the surface, but she'd also revealed to him that the loss was even greater than he'd known. Discovering he had a child—one that he might never know because he wasn't given the opportunity to weigh in on the decision—had to have been messing with his head.

Onyx marched up the aisle toward Vivienne and Lacey. "Hello, ladies. Sorry we're late."

I knew this version of Onyx. It was *the fake it 'til you make it* version, and she'd improved her façade over the years, being in the public eye. Deep down, she was a wreck. I was certain of that.

She was in the middle of a public scandal, her husband was threatening to divorce her, and clearly, Wylie wasn't handling the baby news well.

Thankfully, my mother was adept at handling crises. She clapped her hands and began directing the rehearsal. Judging by the deer in the headlights expression on the minister's face, he was relieved someone was taking charge. Poor guy probably never officiated a wedding with quite so much drama.

Lacey's mom had passed away when she was young, and her father, former Chattertowne chief of police Andy Kimball, was still in prison for his part in the recent political scandal that had rocked city hall and the criminal enterprise behind it. Not to mention he'd incited and compelled his own daughter into committing the crimes for which she'd spent several months in lady jail.

Since she didn't have a close family member to walk her down the aisle, Tony Bianchi had offered. Tony's version of escorting her didn't include touching of any kind, but instead, they just walked next to each other like strangers who happened to be moving in the same direction. The two of them ambled down the aisle like they were headed to the counter to order a burger. As they reached the minister, Bianchi slapped her on the back and took his seat on the right in the front row.

Rachel was paired with Yellin, so Yellin had to keep pace with Rachel's electric wheelchair. It was less of a graceful floating down the aisle, instead more of a race to the finish line.

I stifled a giggle.

Next up was Onyx, escorted by Wylie, who was still in such a stupor that she practically had to drag him to the makeshift altar that the country club had wheeled to the front of the room.

As Best Man and Maid of Honor, Holden and I were the last to go before Vivienne walked down the aisle. We hadn't spoken since he'd dropped me off that afternoon.

Holden held out his arm, and I hesitated. Movement in the back of the room caught my attention. Cole was hovering near the door, and his gaze was laser-focused on me.

What was he doing there? Investigating? Had there been a development in the case? Was he there to arrest Wylie...again?

That was the last thing this wedding needed.

"Audrey Jeanne!" My mother clapped her hands. "Snap out of it. It's your turn."

"Yeah," Vivienne said from behind me. "The sooner we get through this, the sooner we can start drinking."

"Amen to that," murmured our father.

I turned away from Cole to look at Holden. He looked back at me, and what I saw in his gaze surprised me. His brown eyes were filled with hurt and confusion.

He'd been an enigma for so long, and now he was giving me a glimpse into his soul. It rattled me so much I had to look away.

"Any day now, Audrey," my mother sang through gritted teeth.

I took a deep breath and looped my arm through Holden's without looking at him. *I'm walking down the aisle toward the altar arm in arm with Holden Villalobos.* Even telling this to myself didn't make it feel any less surreal. I also sensed Cole's gaze boring through the back of me. The whole thing was like an out-of-body experience.

And I had no idea what I felt or thought about any of it.

The rest of the rehearsal went by in a blur. There were a lot of yadda yaddas, you go here, now we do this, you may kiss your bride, and finally, what everyone wanted to hear: let's eat. And drink.

We made our way next door to the club restaurant, where a section of tables had been cordoned off for our group. The rest of the dining room was open to the public. Because the weather was cooperating, meaning it wasn't raining, the patio was open as well. The heat lamps were on, though, since it was still only a brisk sixty degrees, and the temperature was dropping.

The club overlooked the eighteenth hole, which was a floating green in the middle of a manmade water feature. The sun had already set, though, and the course wasn't well lit, other than the fountain in the middle of the pond.

My father had opened a bar tab for the bridal party under the password *Viva la Vida*. It had been Vivienne's idea, as a sort of portmanteau of their names—Viv and Lacey—but also a nod to the meaning of the phrase, long live life, which they said embodied their new mantra now that Lacey had been released and they were free to be married. They'd also asked on the evites that any social media posts or photos from the wedding include #VivaLaVida.

I didn't have the heart to bring up the Coldplay song of the same name, which was loosely inspired by the French Revolution and Louis XVI, who lost his head in the guillotine. Not the most romantic tie-in for a wedding.

Holden was once again keeping his distance from me. I couldn't tell if he was mad at me, hurt, or both. I hadn't even had time to process the shift in his attitude.

Meanwhile, Cole was lurking at the entrance to the restaurant. It was clear he hadn't been invited to the rehearsal dinner, because he hadn't ventured into the area marked off for the wedding party.

"What can I get you?" asked the bartender as I slid onto a stool.

"Not sure. Any suggestions? Oh, and—" I looked around and lowered my voice. "The password is viva la vida."

He nodded and gave a half smile. "I already noticed you. I know you're with the wedding party." He winked.

Aww, dang. A winking bartender. All I wanted was something to take the edge off, and now I had to deal with this.

"The brides have requested a specialty cocktail to be served this weekend," he said. "We're calling it the CGCC green jacket."

"What's in it?"

"Bourbon, chartreuse, fresh thyme, and a squeeze of lime with a sugar rim."

"Have you tasted it?"

"I have."

"And?"

He rubbed his chin. "Imagine soaking a lime popsicle in booze, dropping it in grass, and then rolling it in sour candy."

"You're not selling it."

"I'm giving my honest feedback. It's up to you what you choose to do with that information."

"I'll take a vodka martini, extra dirty, blue cheese olives, please."

His smile broadened. "Ooh, extra dirty. Just how I like my women. I get off at nine. Maybe by ten you could—"

Cole hopped onto the stool next to me. "Hi, honey. Sorry I'm late."

The bartender held up his hands. In one, he held a martini glass; in the other, he held a dishrag. "Hey, man, sorry. I didn't see a ring." He circled to the other side of the bar to work on making my drink.

"Funny how he apologized to you, but not to me," I said.

Cole grimaced. "Not surprising with guys like that."

"Not that I don't appreciate the rescue, but what's with the skulking?"

"What do you mean? I'm not skulking."

"You've been hovering near the entrance since the rehearsal ended."

"I wasn't hovering near the entrance. I was hovering near the exit. I don't want to make a scene, but I need to talk to Wylie Barrett before he leaves tonight."

"I knew you were working. Why do you need to talk to him?"

He looked down his nose at me. I inferred from his expression that he had no intention of answering that question.

"Come on. I won't say anything. I just want to know what to expect. Are you going to arrest him again? If so, that will really throw the wedding into turmoil. Can't it wait until after they say *I do?*"

"I'm not here to arrest him. Unless there's something on his phone that *warrants* it." He gave me a pointed look. "Get it? Warrants it?"

I gasped. "You got a war—"

"Shh." He gently placed his hand over my mouth and looked around, presumably to see if anyone had been listening.

I pulled away his hand. "First, you did not just shush me! Second, we are not so long past a global pandemic that I want anyone putting their hands on my mouth."

"Sorry. I don't have a lot going for me in this investigation other than the element of surprise. I don't want Wylie sneaking out of here before I can serve the warrant."

There was a sudden commotion out on the patio. Through the glass doors, I spotted an enraged Meacham Fields screaming at Wylie. His face was magenta, and veins popped out of his neck. Wylie, still dazed from the morning's revelations, took two steps backward. Onyx stood between them, attempting to push Meacham away from Wylie.

Most of what was being said was unintelligible, but the tone was undeniable.

Vivienne slid open the door, and suddenly Meacham's words became crystal clear.

"You're a dead man!"

The flash of a paparazzi's camera illuminated all three of their shocked faces.

Chapter Twenty-One

By the time Cole and I made it to the patio, Wylie was gone. Onyx stood frozen in place, with horror plastered across her face, clearly humiliated over such a public airing of her dirty laundry. I approached her and put my hand on her arm.

Meacham was panting, his hands still balled in fists of rage. At least this time, he hadn't decked Wylie like he had at her hall of fame ceremony.

"Where's Wylie?" Cole asked.

Neither of them responded.

Vivienne pointed into the darkness, toward the golf course. "He took off that way. It was so strange. He's been a zombie all night, and then suddenly, with that camera flash, it was like he was a spooked horse. He just took off running."

Cole scanned the edge of the patio. "Where's the photographer?"

Once again, Meacham and Onyx ignored him, still in their own post-traumatic trances.

Vivienne shrugged. "I didn't see. The flash kind of blinded all of us, and then Wylie bolted, and the crowd started forming."

Lacey joined her on the patio and placed a protective arm around her. "You okay?"

Vivienne's laugh was bitter. "You sure you don't want to elope?"

"If that's what you want, but I don't think it is."

Vivienne's shoulders slumped. "I just want to be married."

"I know you do. Me too. And we will be, in less than forty-eight hours." Lacey kissed the top of Vivienne's head.

I walked over to Onyx and touched her arm. "Hey, you're welcome to stay at my place tonight. Might be best to create some space for cooler heads to prevail."

She threw a glare at Meacham. "Thanks. I think that will be best."

Meacham shook his head. "I can't believe you're doing this to us."

"Me doing this to us! You're the one who said he wants a divorce!"

"You know I didn't mean it, I never do, but if you're gonna keep sneaking around with your ex, I just might follow through." He turned and walked into the restaurant.

Tears filled Onyx's eyes. "Stupid idiot." She turned to me. "Not you, Audrey, obviously."

"I didn't think you meant me."

Lacey slid the patio door shut and stood with her back to the bar, blocking the view of four of us from prying eyes.

"What happened?" I asked.

Onyx shook her head, tears spilling down her cheeks. "I've made a mess of things, that's what happened."

"What did Meacham say?" Vivienne asked. "I didn't even see him arrive."

"That's because he popped out of nowhere. I don't know if he was hiding in the bushes or what. Wylie and I were discussing our...situation, and suddenly Meacham was in his face, screaming that he wanted to kill him."

"What is the situation?" I asked gently.

"She sniffed. "I'm not ready to talk about it quite yet, if that's okay."

"Of course," said Vivienne.

"I stuffed a lot of big feelings about it a long time ago, and now it's all blown up in my face and I need a little time to sort it all out."

"Totally understandable," I said. "Like I told you this afternoon, I'm here if and when you want to talk."

"Thanks." She sniffed. "Do you think I'm a monster?"

"What? No, why would you say that?"

"Because I gave up my baby to pursue my career."

"Onyx, listen to me. You were, what, eighteen or nineteen years old yourself. You were a kid having a kid. Do I agree with the shenanigans surrounding Miranda lying to Hank and Jack all these years? Absolutely not."

"I don't think I'm the mother type, you know? I'm not sure I ever will be."

"And that's okay," I said. "Really. Things are a mess now, but they'll calm down."

"I hope so. Audrey, thanks for offering to let me crash at your place. I don't think I can deal with Meacham tonight. I need to stop by the B and B to get a few things. Hopefully, Meach isn't there. I don't know what I'd say to him."

"I'm just going to finish here and then I'll head home," I said.

Onyx gave Vivienne a quick hug. "I really am sorry I've made a mess of things. I'd understand if you want me out of the wedding."

"Not even a little. But I do agree that you and Meacham and Wylie need time and space to calm down and process what's happened. I hope you're able to decompress at Audrey's tonight. I know when I'm overwhelmed, everything feels more manageable after a good night's sleep."

"I hope you're right." Onyx gave a sad smile before walking into the restaurant.

I turned to Vivienne. "We can still try to salvage the night."

Her expression was grim. "I don't think so. I just want to go home and pray that tomorrow things are better."

As Lacey escorted Vivienne inside, Cole joined me on the patio. I spotted Holden watching us from inside the restaurant, stony-faced.

"Welp, guess you didn't get to serve your man the warrant," I said.

Cole put his hands on his hips. "Appears that way. Although, you know me. I don't give up that easily when I want something."

"What's your plan?"

"How about you and I go back to the bar, you swig down your martini, and we go looking for Wylie?"

"You had me at martini."

* * *

By the time Cole and I headed out to the parking lot, most of the bridal party had left. It was, after all, difficult to have a bridal party without either of the brides.

Holden had hung around sipping his whisky for a few minutes after the hubbub. He'd been brooding, which for most men was a quality I didn't particularly admire, but somehow he'd managed to make it look sexy and mysterious. My observations had come in furtive glances, however, as I tried to pretend I didn't notice him at all.

"What kind of car does Wylie drive?" asked Cole, scanning the parking lot.

"Uh, some sort of luxury SUV. Lexus, maybe. Dark gray."

"Could it be a Lincoln?"

"Sure."

"Like that one?" He pointed at a vehicle parked on the right side of the lot.

"Exactly like that one."

Cole began walking toward the car, and I followed.

"So Wylie never left?" I asked.

"Well, his car didn't. If this is indeed his car." Cole reached the driver's side door and attempted to open it. Locked. He peered into the driver's window.

I peeked into the rear window. "It's his car. His clubs are back here. I recognize his *Caddyshack* gopher driver cover from this morning."

Cole walked around the car.

"What now?" I asked. "Can't you just wait until after the wedding to serve him with the warrant?"

"No, he might get wind of it from his attorney and delete the messages. If he can avoid being served, he won't have to abide by the warrant."

"Todd Wainwright would never advise him to break the law."

"I'm not saying he would. But he could let him know it's coming, and Wylie could act to protect himself."

"True."

"Do you have Wylie's number?"

"I do." I pulled out my phone and selected Wylie from my contacts. The phone rang several times before going to voicemail. "Not answering."

"Maybe give Onyx a call. See if she's heard from him."

I pulled out my phone. "I can try, but if she thinks I'm helping you go after him, she'll be resistant." I selected Onyx's number from my call log.

"Well then, don't tell her."

After two rings, the line clicked. "Hey, I'm just gathering my things at the B and B. I'll be there soon."

"No rush. I'm still at the club. You haven't heard from Wylie, have you?"

"Not since he stormed off. Why?"

"Oh, I thought maybe you'd run into him and given him a ride. His car's still here in the parking lot."

"That's weird," she said. "Did he come back into the restaurant?"

"No, I've been here the whole time. And he's not answering his phone."

Her end of the line was silent.

"Onyx? You there?"

"Yeah. I just had to catch my breath."

"What are you thinking?"

She exhaled. "I'm thinking my husband was pretty angry tonight."

"Wait. Meacham isn't there with you either?"

Cole's left brow arched.

"No. And I don't think he's been back here since he was at the club."

I held the phone against my chest and addressed Cole. "She says Meacham hasn't been back to the B and B."

"So now we have two men unaccounted for."

"What was that?" Onyx's muffled words rumbled against my chest.

"Sorry. I was just telling Cole what you told me. He's a little concerned. Do you think Meacham would have gone after Wylie?"

"I don't know. Maybe? But what I don't understand is why Wylie didn't just get in his car and drive away."

"If he didn't drive anywhere, and you didn't pick him up, he probably went somewhere on foot."

"I'm coming back there."

"Why?"

"We need to look for him. I've got a sick feeling in my gut that he's not okay. We need to find him." She disconnected the call.

"Onyx is coming back here to help us look for Wylie."

"Normally, I'd say that's a bad idea, but this is a pretty large course and it's dark. I'd call Bianchi to come back here, but I know he had quite a few drinks before his wife came to pick him up."

I typed something into my phone.

"Who are you texting?"

"No one. I was googling how large the course is."

"And?"

"It's nearly two hundred acres. That's double the size of the Hundred Acre Wood, and that place was huge."

"Where's the Hundred Acre Wood?"

"You know, Winnie the Pooh lived there. And Tigger and Piglet. Oh, and Kanga and Roo."

"I cannot believe we are actually having this conversation."

"Oh yeah, how could I forget Eeyore? You two would get along well, Cole. Similar temperament."

"I see you've got jokes tonight."

"I've always got jokes. You just don't usually find them humorous."

"That is true." His expression became pinched.

"What?"

"Maybe you should call Holden and see if he's available to search for Wylie. I don't want to take any of my guys off patrol if this turns out to be a nothingburger."

I bit the inside of my cheek to prevent myself from making fun of his use of the term nothingburger. "I suppose I could call him. He's kind of annoyed with me right now."

"Why?"

"Uh, you know, I'm not really sure, and apparently the fact I don't know is part of the reason he's mad at me."

Cole gave a knowing nod. "Ah. One of those. The old, *if you don't know, you haven't been paying attention,* Catch-22. Of course, the answer is obvious to anyone with eyes."

"What do you mean?"

"He's in love with you, and he doesn't quite know what to do with his feelings."

"No. That's not it."

"Who are you trying to convince? Me or yourself?"

"I'm not trying to convince anyone. Holden and I are friends."

He scoffed. "I saw the way he was looking at you before he walked you down the aisle tonight. That didn't look like friends."

"What do you care, anyway?"

It was the second time that day I'd uttered those words, and they didn't land much better with Cole than they had with Holden.

"What do I care?" He shook his head and then nodded with his lips pressed together. "Right. What *do* I care?" He tsked. "Maybe the better question is *Why* do I care?"

My mouth went dry. He was angry. I'd seen him annoyed lots of times, but he was actually angry. At me. My heart thumped wildly in my chest.

"Cole—" I reached toward him, but he stepped back. "I...I don't understand."

"Clearly."

Fuuuuuudddddgggge. What was happening? Both Cole and Holden were acting out of sorts, and I had neither the insight nor the bandwidth to deal with it.

"Just call him. Please." His tone was terse.

My fingers trembled as I selected Holden's number from my recent calls. I considered putting it on speakerphone, but bearing in mind the current tension between Cole and me, I didn't want to risk Holden saying something that would make the situation worse.

After two rings, he answered. "Hey there."

"Hey. Are you sober?"

"Is this a booty call?"

A wave of relief about not having him on speakerphone washed over me. The last thing I needed was for Cole to give me an *I told you so.* "Sorry, no. I just meant are you sober enough to drive? I'm still at the club, and Wylie's car is here in the parking lot, but no one knows where he is. Do you think maybe you could come back to help look for him?"

"He probably took a rideshare home."

That hadn't occurred to me. I held the phone away from my ear. "He just brought up a good point. Maybe Wylie called a car to get him."

Cole nodded. "He's right. We should check his house."

"My friend Shelly's parents still live next door to him. Let me give her a call. Hey, Holden? I'll call you back in a minute."

"No need. I'll head that way. I'll see you in about fifteen."

He hung up before I could respond.

I dialed Shelly.

"Audrey? Everything okay?" She sounded groggy.

"Yes, I'm sorry to wake you up, I didn't realize how late it is."

"It's okay, what's up?"

"Do you think your parents are asleep?"

"Not my mom. She stays up late reading every night."

"Could you call her and ask if it looks like Wylie's home?"

"Yeah, sure, I guess. But why?"

"I'm looking for him. He's in Vivienne's wedding, and he kind of stormed off from the rehearsal dinner. No one can get ahold of him. I just want to make sure he's okay."

"Oh, geez. Okay. Let me call her, and I'll call you right back."

"Thanks." After the call disconnected, I looked up at Cole. "She says she'll call me after she talks to her mom."

He tipped his chin. "Got it. And Holden?"

"He's on his way."

"Good." Only it didn't sound like he thought it was good. It sounded like he'd rather get a root canal.

A few minutes later, Sheila called back. "Mom says it's dark over there. Has been all night. She also said she usually sees his headlights when he comes up the driveway. It shines into her living room window. Nothing tonight."

"Okay, thanks. I'll talk to you later." I disconnected the call.

"I take it he's not home," said Cole.

"Her mom says it's dark at his house, has been the whole evening."

His expression was grim.

A Toyota Prius with a glowing rideshare sign in the windshield turned into the parking lot and pulled up to the curb. Onyx hopped out, and the car drove away.

"Any news?" she asked, bundling her coat against her body. "Geez, it's getting cold out here."

"Holden's coming to help look for him. I called my friend Shelly, whose parents live next door. He hasn't gone home from what her mom can see."

Onyx blanched. "I don't feel good about this at all."

Cole tilted his head. "I'm curious. You don't know where your husband is, either. Why aren't you concerned about his whereabouts?"

"I'm concerned. Of course I'm concerned. Not for his well-being, though. Meacham has survived being held in a Russian jail, three crazy stalkers, two overdoses—"

"And a partridge in a pear tree?" It slipped out before I even realized I was saying it. "Sorry, bad joke."

"Jokes are usually funny. Anyway, he's like a cockroach. You can't kill him. I'm more worried about what he might do to Wylie. I've never seen him so mad. Which is dumb, because my relationship with Wylie happened long before I met Meacham."

"I'm guessing it has less to do with rationality and more that he's upset and fears losing you."

She flared her nostrils. "You know that Bonzerkind song *Tube Temptress?*"

"Of course. Everyone does. It won a Grammy, didn't it?"

She shook her head. "Nope. It did get nominated for a VMA, though."

Cole clapped his hands. "I know that song. It goes like, *green eyes the shade of hazardous waste told me she was toxic. The next thing I knew I was watching the clock tick midnight in the garden never good, only evil. Drowning in my shame from which there's no reprieval.*"

"I'm pretty sure reprieval isn't a real word," I said. "But I will give him points for not dangling his preposition. And kudos to you, Cole. That was quite a performance."

"He wrote that song about a one-night stand he had three days after we got back from our honeymoon. He couldn't even be faithful for one week. Now he has the audacity to be angry about a child I gave away eighteen years ago? It's the height of hypocrisy."

So much for the fantasy of being married to a rock star. Even though I'd heard all the stories and the rumors, I'd assumed it was a persona he had to keep up. In fact, Onyx had often made jokes about it to the press. She'd say something like, *oh yes, Meacham has a dozen mistresses. I invite them over for tea every Tuesday.* It never occurred to me that she would stay with an unfaithful husband. She'd always struck me as too proud and self-assured for that.

Not to mention, what kind of idiot cheated on Onyx freaking Carpenter?

Meacham, apparently, was that idiot.

Holden's car pulled into the lot. He'd changed into joggers and an oversized hoodie. His mouth was set firm as he sauntered over to where we stood on the sidewalk.

"Thanks for coming," said Cole.

"No problem. What's the plan?" He wasn't making eye contact with me.

Cole looked up at the sky. The clouds were covering the moon. No stars were visible either.

"It's pretty dark. I say we split into two groups. Onyx, you come with me. We'll take the front nine. Audrey, you go with Holden, take the back nine."

Why was he putting me with Holden when he knew we'd been having issues? Was this a punishment of some sort?

"Can't we ride in the golf carts?" asked Onyx.

"The pro shop is closed. They have all the keys," Holden said. "We could try to hotwire them."

Cole gave him a stern look.

Holden held up his hands. "Kidding. Obviously."

I wasn't convinced that he'd been kidding.

Cole held up his phone and waved it around. "Call me if you come across anything." He touched Onyx's elbow to guide her in the direction of the first hole.

Holden turned to me. "Ready?"

"Mmhmm."

He began walking back toward the clubhouse.

"Where are you going?"

"To search the back nine."

"The tenth hole is over there." I pointed to my right.

He chuckled. "You know we don't have to start at the tenth hole, right? Might as well start at eighteen and work our way backward."

It hadn't occurred to me, but I had no intention of giving him the satisfaction of knowing that.

"It's just like you," he said.

"What is just like me?" I walked quickly to keep up with his stride.

"You're so linear."

"Is that an insult? Somehow it sounds like an insult."

"It's not an insult. It's an observation. Of course, you'd start at the beginning, even if that means doubling your efforts."

"Dude. Either way, we have to walk the same distance."

He stopped and I nearly bumped into the back of him.

"Did you just call me dude?"

"It felt appropriate in the moment."

He began walking again, but at least he'd slowed his pace. "Eighteen is over here, just past the putting green and the fountain."

I gasped. "The water. We should look in the pond. He'd been drinking. Maybe he fell in."

Holden walked off the path and toward the water hazard and the floating green for hole eighteen. I held my breath as we made our way to the edge. The fountain had been turned off for the night, including the lights.

"What's that? Out there? I think I see something floating in the water."

"Where?"

I pointed. "Just past the fountain to the left. It's actually moving this way."

"Audrey, it's moving this way because it's swimming. It's a duck."

I strained my eyes. "So it is. It was hard to tell from here."

We walked back to the path. The red tee box—typically considered the ladies' tee box—was empty, so we made our way toward the white tee box. A little way past that was the blue tee box for the most advanced players with the longest drive range. Nothing was out of place as far as I could see.

We continued walking toward the seventeenth green.

"I learned the craziest thing recently that I was convinced was a joke, but it turns out its true."

He glanced over his shoulder. "What's that?"

"They move the holes. Practically every day."

"Of course they do."

"What do you mean, of course they do? I'd never heard that in my life."

"Can you imagine what the greens would look like if day after day people tromped around the same hole? What did you think was happening?"

"I thought the hole was where it was. That means every time you golf a course you won't know where the flag is supposed to be. That's literally moving the goal posts," I said.

"It's not literally moving the goal posts, because they are flagpoles, and this isn't football."

"You know what I mean."

We continued along the path to the sixteenth green. I had heard it was an especially challenging hole because of the bunkers and the woods that abutted the fairway.

Holden kept walking toward the tee boxes, but I stopped when I felt my phone buzz in my pocket. It was a text from Cole.

Anything?

I responded with **Not yet. You?**

Nope.

"Hey," I called to Holden

"Yeah?" He turned around.

"I think we should walk down the middle of the fairway. That way we can see both the path and the rough on the other side."

"Okay."

He lumbered up the hill, and I followed him. I scanned the wood line but saw nothing out of the ordinary. Of course, it was pretty dark.

He abruptly stopped walking, and I nearly ran into his back.

"I need to ask you a question."

"That sounds ominous. Shoot."

"If you can't be honest with me about what's going on between you and Cole, could you at least be honest with yourself?"

"That's not a question. It's a declaration of war.'

"The fact that you see it that way tells me everything I need to know." He turned around.

I grabbed his arm and pulled him to face me. "What is happening right now? You've been acting strange all day."

It took everything in me to maintain eye contact under his penetrating and unwavering gaze. When he broke eye contact, the relief I expected didn't come. My chest still ached.

"Never mind."

"Holden."

"Let's just get back to the task at hand."

"Fine." I turned on the flashlight and once again focused on the trees. Something caught my eye, glinting in the woods. I walked toward it, shining the light straight ahead.

Suddenly, the ground disappeared beneath me. Sand flew everywhere, as I tumbled and rolled, finally coming to a stop face-first in the bottom of the sand trap. I spat sand from my mouth and tried to wipe it from my eyes.

"Oh, no." Holden looked down at me from the edge of the sand trap, rubbing the back of his neck.

"I'm okay. I just have sand in every single crevice, but I don't think I'm actually hurt."

"I'm glad, but that's not what I was talking about." He jutted his chin. "Look behind you."

I rolled to my right and stared into the face of a very sandy and very dead Wylie Barrett.

Chapter Twenty-Two

By the time Cole and Onyx reached us, Holden had hoisted me out of the trap and attempted to brush much of the sand off me.

Onyx's knees buckled at the sight of Wylie's dead body. She collapsed to the ground and began sobbing. I knelt next to her and put an arm around her heaving shoulders.

Cole made his way carefully down into the hole and checked for a pulse.

"I already tried," I said. "I couldn't find one."

Not to mention, Wylie's eyes were open and unblinking.

Cole pulled out his cell phone and called dispatch, requesting an aid car and backup. He then shone his light across Wylie's body. The light glinted off a metallic object a few feet away.

"Is that a golf club?" I asked.

"It is. An iron. And it appears to have blood on it."

I moved closer to the edge of the bunker and shone my own phone's light on the club.

Onyx's wails grew louder, combining with the incoming sirens.

Paramedics were the first to arrive from the nearby fire station. I rejoined Onyx and Holden.

Two EMTs jumped into the bunker. They also attempted to locate a pulse but found none.

I once again had my arm around Onyx, who was rocking back and forth.

Over and over, she repeated the same phrase, "I never should have come home."

"This isn't your fault," I said.

"You and I both know that's not true. If I hadn't come home, Wylie would still be alive. Oh gawd, do you think Meacham did this?"

"I can't answer that. You know him better than anyone."

She sniffed. "Where would he even get a golf club? I don't think he's ever swung one in his life. And he's not very strong. I mean, I think I could beat him at arm wrestling. But then again, he was *really* upset."

"And he did threaten to kill Wylie."

She stopped and considered that. "That's true. He did. Although, it sounded more like the kind of thing you say in the heat of the moment, right? People never really mean it."

People killed in the heat of the moment all the time, but it wasn't the right time to mention that.

I looked over at Holden. "Are you okay?"

His mouth twisted to the left. "I don't know what I am. I think I'm in shock."

Onyx's phone rang in her hand. She looked up at me, wide-eyed. "It's Meacham."

Holden sat up. "Answer it!" He whistled at Cole and beckoned for him to join us.

"Meach, baby, what have you done?"

As Cole emerged from the sand trap, he gave Holden a curious stare.

"Meacham," Holden whispered, pointing at the phone.

Cole's eyebrows both jumped, but he didn't say anything. He moved closer to try and hear the conversation.

"You know exactly what I mean. Where are you?" She listened for his response. "No, I was *at* the B and B. You weren't there."

Cole leaned closer to Onyx. I felt a flutter of jealousy, but immediately tamped it down. He put up his hand to indicate he wanted Meacham to stay where he was.

"Don't go anywhere," Onyx said. "I'm coming there. I need to talk to you."

Cole gave her a thumbs-up.

She hung up the phone. "He's definitely drunk. Maybe high. He said his chauffeur drove him around for a while so he could clear his thoughts before going back to the B and B."

"It's possible," Cole said. "I need to talk to him, though. Do you mind if I come with you?"

"Sure, but I'm not sure he'll be able to string two sentences together in this condition. Afterward, can you drop me off at Audrey's? I'm staying at her place tonight."

I'd kind of forgotten that I'd made that offer. So much had happened since then, and I was exhausted. Still, I couldn't rescind the offer, especially now.

"Sure," said Cole. "That would make me feel better anyway. I'm not sure it's safe for you to be alone with your husband."

The look on her face told me she hadn't considered the possibility he might hurt her, and deep down she didn't believe it. Maybe she just didn't want to believe it.

Tony Bianchi arrived with Billiam in tow and cordoned off the area. Billiam stood guard, trying to look official and intimidating to anyone who might dare to move past him.

Bianchi appeared sober, so either he held his liquor really well or he'd had enough time, water, and food for the effects to wear off. He dismissed the paramedics, since there was no need for lifesaving measures, and an ambulance was coming to remove the body.

He then pulled the four of us aside to ask about the events of the night.

He started with Cole and Onyx because Cole said he was in a rush to get to the B and B. He was worried Meacham might get spooked and take off before he could question him about where he'd gone after his fight with Wylie.

Neither Cole nor Onyx had much to say anyway, considering they weren't the ones who'd found Wylie's body. Onyx explained that she'd returned to the club to help search for Wylie, and that her husband hadn't been at the bed and breakfast when she left, but he was there now.

After Cole and Onyx left, Bianchi turned to Holden and me. "You said you were together the whole time you were searching, correct?"

"That's right," said Holden.

I nodded.

CHAPTER TWENTY-TWO

Bianchi shone his flashlight in my face.

"Hey!"

"Sorry. I just noticed something was off about you. You're covered in sand. I take it you were the one who found him?"

"Up close and personal."

"Should I ask how it was you came to be in the sand trap?"

"I'll give you one guess."

"Well, Audrey, knowing you as I do, I'd hafta say you probably fell in there."

"Bingo." Holden touched the side of his nose.

"I was looking at the tree line and didn't see the hole."

"It's ten feet across and six feet deep."

"I'm aware. I rolled down the entire thing."

"She rolled into Wylie," Holden added.

"Tony, we can assume that the bloody golf club lying next to his bleeding head is the murder weapon, right?" I asked.

"In a murder investigation, we should never assume anything. In this case, though, it's a pretty safe conclusion. We'll know more after the autopsy and forensic testing."

"I bring it up because that is a left-handed club." I pointed at the sand trap.

He looked over his shoulder. "Officer Burton."

"Yes, sir?"

"Can you take a peek at that club?"

Billiam moved around the bunker. He shone his flashlight. "What am I looking for?"

"Notice anything unusual about it?"

He stared at it for a moment. He tipped his head to the right. "Looks to me like it might be a left-handed nine-iron."

I gave Bianchi a *told ya so* grimace.

"Well, that is an interesting fact." He crossed his arms over his chest. "Who was golfing in your scramble today with lefties?"

I looked at Holden, who shrugged.

"No one in our group," he said.

I shook my head. "Not ours either. But I do have a theory."

"I'm all ears," said Bianchi.

"Last night at the Chattertowne High Hall of Fame ceremony, Meacham took a swing at Wylie."

"Yeah, I was there. And he threatened him tonight. So?"

"It was a left hook. I'm pretty sure Meacham is left-handed."

* * *

Onyx wasn't at my house when I arrived. I texted her for an update, and she said she'd decided to stay at the bed and breakfast with Meacham. It was a surprising turn of events, considering he was now the prime suspect in her baby daddy's murder, but then who really could understand the inner workings of a marriage?

I'd washed my face and changed into a tank top and lounge pants when my doorbell rang. I peeked out my bedroom window and spotted Cole's car parked in front of my house.

When I opened the door, he was leaning against the frame, looking haggard. Unusual for him.

"I was just about to go to bed. So, Onyx decided to stay with Meacham tonight. What's up with that?"

He pointed at my living room. "Can I come in?"

"Sure." I opened the door wider for him to walk through.

He slumped into a chair and pulled off his hat, setting it in his lap.

I sat on the couch. "You okay? You look exhausted."

"I'm dog tired, and I suspect I won't be getting much sleep tonight."

"What's going on? What happened when you got to the B and B?"

"Well, Meacham was passed out drunk in the bed. Hopefully, he's just drunk. Anyway, he was still wearing the clothes he'd had on at the club when he'd confronted Wylie. Not a bit of blood spatter that I could see. That makes no sense if he whacked Wylie over the head. With a blow hard enough to kill him, I might add. Head wounds bleed. A lot."

"I'm aware." A picture of my high school sweetheart's fatal head injury came unbidden to my mind. I hadn't really ever dealt with that trauma, too caught up in trying to find his killer. Which I had. And I didn't want to think about that at the moment. Especially not this particular weekend.

I shivered.

"You cold?"

"This house is pretty drafty. I guess that's what happens when it's over a hundred and thirty years old." It wasn't a lie, just a deflection. "So, you don't think Meacham killed Wylie?"

He rubbed the scruff along his jaw. "I don't know what to think. Everything points that direction."

"That's convenient."

He looked at me. "What do you mean?"

"What are the odds of two murders in Chattertowne within days of each other that are perpetrated by different people?"

"The answer should be the odds are low, but the murders of last fall say it's not out of the realm of possibility."

"I suppose that's true."

He was referring to a series of crimes that had occurred several months earlier, ranging from graffiti to arson to murder to murder-suicide.

"But logically we know that Meacham wasn't in town when Jack and Laveda were in their accident, so he couldn't have tampered with Jack's car," I said.

Cole shrugged. "He'd have no motive anyway."

"Right. But also, who had motive to try and kill Jack and/or Laveda? Besides Wylie, if he were actually trying to cover up an affair or inappropriate behavior with Laveda."

"Remember, the most obvious answer is usually the truth. The obvious answer is that Wylie killed Laveda and injured Jack, so someone probably killed Wylie in revenge," he said.

"Even though Meacham is the most obvious suspect because he literally threatened to kill Wylie tonight? Couldn't he have just cleaned off the blood from his clothes?"

"Maybe." Cole grimaced. "Dammit, I should have taken his clothes. I wasn't thinking clearly. Can you text Onyx and let her know I need those clothes for testing first thing in the morning? She can't let them be laundered before I have a chance to see if there's blood on them."

I pulled out my phone.

Hey, Cole needs to test Meacham's clothes to verify they have no blood on them. Don't let them get washed before he can do that.

My fingers hovered over the screen. "What time should I say you're going to pick them up?"

"I'll stop by on my way to work. About eight-thirty."

He says he will come by around 8:30 in the morning.

I waited for a response, but it never came.

"How am I going to tell Viv that Wylie's been murdered? She was worried enough that the threat of him being in jail on her wedding day was going to ruin everything. This is just…"

"If it were me, I'd call her now. She should hear it from you before she hears it on the Chattertowne grapevine. I'd say morning is too late."

"Ugh. I can't give this kind of news over the phone."

"Understood."

Cole's phone rang. He checked the caller ID. "It's Miranda."

"You should probably take that." Or just ignore her. That would be preferable.

He accepted the call. "Hey there." He nodded in response to whatever she'd said. "It's true. How did you hear?"

Miranda's voice wasn't loud enough for me to decipher her words.

"I see. No, I wouldn't say it ends my investigation into whether Wylie was involved in the accident. I need to get those answers, not just for Jack's sake, but also for Laveda's family." He paused to listen. "I *have* been making progress. I'm sorry it hasn't been fast enough for your liking."

Trouble in paradise?

A strange look crossed Cole's face. "I can't speak to the details of an ongoing investigation."

Ooh, Miranda was sure to hate that response. I must have telegraphed my satisfaction because he scowled at me.

"I understand. I'll be in touch." He disconnected the call and blew out a long sigh.

I waited for him to fill me in, hoping I didn't look too eager for the scoop.

"You look like the cat that ate the canary," he said. "Not my favorite look on you."

"Sorry. You already know I'm not a fan of hers. I shouldn't gloat, though."

"No. You shouldn't gloat about the demise of my almost-relationship."

It wasn't my fault giddiness at the thought bubbled up. I couldn't control it. At least that's what I told myself. "She's obviously concerned that you won't continue to pursue the investigation into Jack's accident."

"Which, as you heard me tell her, isn't the case."

"There's something else."

"Is there?" His mouth twitched at the corner, a tell I'd recently identified.

Cole's poker face was infinitely better than mine. Even better than Holden, who I'd always struggled to read. Discovering this indicator of hidden thoughts felt like a coup, especially since interpreting people's body language had never been my strong suit.

"Yes. She said something, and it was almost like the proverbial lightbulb went on above your head."

"Is that so?"

"So, now you're being cagey?"

"Audrey, I'm investigating two crimes. Two murders. They may or may not have been perpetrated by the same person. They may or may not be related." He held up his hand when I opened my mouth to argue. "They probably *are* related. But my job is to explore all possible scenarios."

"But you don't want to share your theories with me."

"I've shared as much as I'm comfortable sharing. Now, you should probably go speak to your sister."

"You don't want to come with me? They're staying on the sailboat tonight, and you know how much I hate going down to the marina."

"Go with you to tell Vivienne that her wedding has run into yet another complication? No, thank you. Let me know if she decides to postpone."

* * *

"Do you think we should postpone?" Viv asked Lacey through tears.

Lacey wasn't crying, but she was still visibly upset. This was atypical, as she usually was pretty stoic. The events of the previous several days were taking their toll on both the brides.

I'd broken the news to them about Wylie's murder as gently as I could, but it was impossible to say those words without devastating impact. Their friend was dead.

"We'll do whatever you want to do." Lacey squeezed Vivienne's hand.

Viv looked at me. "Audrey? What do you think?"

"I think this decision is completely up to the two of you."

"I know that. I want to know what *you* think. What would you do if it were you?"

I exhaled. "If it were me, I'd wait until the morning of the wedding to make the decision. You sent out evites just a few weeks ago. You can send a cancellation that way at the last minute if you need to."

"What will change between now and Sunday afternoon? Wylie won't be any less dead," Vivienne said. "I assume Onyx is a mess. She'll probably drop out of the wedding."

"She was upset. Of course she was. She was also very concerned with whether Meacham was responsible."

"I mean, of course it was Meacham. Who else could it be?" said Lacey.

"You were assistant police chief. You know how this works," I said. "Would you jump to that conclusion?"

"As an officer, no, I wouldn't. As a person with common sense who isn't bound by investigative integrity that has to hold up in a court of law, absolutely. Every day, I had to set aside the obvious answer to ensure my biases and assumptions didn't taint the case."

"You know it's funny. Tonight, Cole said, *the most obvious answer is usually the truth*. Do you think that's leading him down the wrong path?"

Lacey pondered the question. "Hard to say. He's not totally wrong. Most female victims are killed by a spouse or boyfriend. For men, that's not typically the case. It used to be that the majority of murders were committed by a family member or acquaintance. In the past several years, those stats have become a little cloudy. For the bulk of murders these days, the relationship is unclear. That doesn't mean they're a stranger, but it could be someone who's not a friend either."

"So if you put your police chief—" I corrected myself before Lacey could. "Sorry. *Assistant* police chief. Put that hat on for a moment and tell me what avenues of investigation you'd be pursuing."

Vivienne shook her head. "She doesn't need to be picking at any scabs. That job left its scars."

"It's okay, Viv. There were a lot of things about that job that were important to me. I made an impact." Lacey blew out a breath. "I'd say you kind of have to hold both cases in your hands at the same time. Separate hands, but still. My gut says they're connected. The law of probability says they're connected. Whether murder A and murder B are motivated by the same thing or murder A resulted in murder B would be my primary focus."

"But how do you figure that out?"

"I'd make a chart. List out every suspect for each murder—and I mean every possible suspect, from the kids at the 3F meeting to the paparazzi who've been following Onyx around—along with their motives. If you don't know their motives, leave that blank. Then cross-reference them to see if any single suspect emerges for both cases."

"Maybe we should do that now," said Vivienne. "Three heads are better than one."

"It's nearly midnight. You've got to be exhausted," I said. "It's your wedding weekend."

"It won't be if we don't figure this out," said Vivienne. "This may be our only chance to save this wedding. Besides, I doubt I'll sleep much tonight. Lacey?"

"I'm down. It will be nice to feel useful again."

"Oh, babe." Vivienne kissed Lacey's cheek. "You're useful every day."

Lacey chuckled. "Thanks. Just what everyone wants to hear from their wife. Useful."

Vivienne whispered something in Lacey's ear, which caused pink to creep up her neck.

Lacey smiled broadly. "I suppose useful isn't a bad thing."

Vivienne clapped her hands together. "Okay. Let's solve a murder!"

Chapter Twenty-Three

Lacey drove to the all-night pharmacy and returned to the boat with poster board—which we laid on the dining table—and multicolored permanent markers. Jack and Laveda's accident suspects were in blue, while Wiley's murder suspects were in green.

Who cut the steering lines in Jack's car and why?

1. **Wylie: Having an inappropriate relationship with Laveda?**
2. **Someone who had a crush on Laveda (boy in glasses?): jealousy**
3. **Other attendees at 3F: motive unknown**
4. **Friends of Jack: prank gone wrong**
5. **Unknown person or persons with unknown motive**

Who murdered Wylie and why?

1. **Meacham Fields: Wylie's relationship with Onyx, also their newly discovered love child**
2. **Husband of one of Wylie's female (adult) golf students: anger or jealousy over possible affair?**
3. **Laveda's family member (mom or dad?): revenge for her death**
4. **Attendees of 3F: unknown motive**
5. **Unknown persons with unknown motive**

"Wait. I just thought of something."

Vivienne and Lacey looked up from the posters to stare at me.

"If Laveda's parents are on the list, Jack's parents should be on the list as well."

Vivienne nodded. "I can't imagine Miranda killing anyone, but if we're gonna put her on the list, we should put Jack, too. while we're at it. He lost his girlfriend and nearly lost his life. Revenge isn't out of the question."

Lacey added all three names to the list.

1. **Hank Dodd: Anger over his son's accident, has been seeing skulking around**
2. **Jack Dodd: Anger over his accident and girlfriend's death**
3. **Miranda Gadling Dodd: Anger over her son's accident**

"Lacey, there's more to it than that with Miranda," I said.

"Like what?" asked Vivienne.

"Like the fact she was booted from your wedding because she didn't like that Onyx was defending him."

"She wasn't booted from the wedding. She gave me an ultimatum about dropping him from the wedding or she'd quit."

"Same result. Miranda is a social climber, and she saw the wedding—along with the press coverage Onyx's appearance would bring—as her opportunity to get noticed. Maybe she even saw it as her ticket out of this town," I said. "Now that opportunity is gone, and she may have seen Wylie as an obstacle to her agenda."

"Why get herself kicked out if that's what her goal was?" asked Vivienne. "Having Wylie in the wedding after his arrest didn't change the press coverage. In fact, it probably increased the interest."

Lacey pursed her lips. "My guess is that it never occurred to her we'd choose Wylie over her. She's angry because she thinks he was responsible for the accident and can't understand why we don't see it that way. Onyx taking her place in the wedding probably added insult to injury."

I nodded. "I agree."

"What's the deal with Miranda's social climbing anyway?" asked Lacey.

"She's got a lot going for her. Why try so hard?"

Vivienne leaned back. "I've known her since we were in elementary school, and that's been her M.O. for most of that time. I know her parents didn't have a lot of money. She never wanted to do sleepovers at her house because she lived in Scuzzville."

"Scuzzville? What the heck is Scuzzville?"

Vivienne's cheeks flushed. "It's a terrible name we used to call her neighborhood because the houses weren't well-maintained, and the kids were a little rough around the edges. We really shouldn't call it that; it's a bad habit that needs to be broken."

"Yeah, it came up earlier today when Holden and I took Onyx's dress to her at Wylie's. It's so unkind. I'm ashamed we haven't put a stop to it before now," I said.

Lacey crossed her arms. "I can see how being mocked for living in a less desirable neighborhood would drive a person to put a lot of distance between themselves and their old life."

I'd spent so much time disliking Miranda's attitude that I'd never really given much thought to why she behaved that way. I was part of the pain and shame that had fueled it in the first place. I owed her an apology.

"Back to the suspect list. Are we saying we *don't* believe Wylie cut the steering lines in Jack's car?" Vivienne looked at Lacey. "You knew him better than either of us. Was he capable?"

"Everyone's capable of doing all manner of evil under the right circumstances." She gave a sheepish look. "You know firsthand that people aren't always as they present themselves." She picked up Vivienne's hand and kissed it. "Thankfully, you were forgiving and didn't murder me over it."

"Even taking that into account," I said, "logistically, I think it was nearly impossible for Wylie to do it. Turns out he was with Onyx after 3F. So, unless she was an accessory to his crime, he couldn't have cut the lines. Although, I suppose it's possible the lines were cut before the event even started. Wylie was the last to arrive, claiming he had to pick up donuts. Cole told me that the forensic investigator thinks perhaps the line was cut, but wedged into position for the fluid to drain slowly, not all at once. That way, as they drove, the line got jostled and began leaking at a more rapid pace. If Wylie cut the line before bringing in the donuts, some of the fluid could have leaked while everyone was in the gym, but most would have been lost during the drive."

"That would mean there could be steering fluid in the parking lot where Jack's car was parked," said Vivienne.

"Only one way to find out," said Lacey. "Let's take a drive."

* * *

We arrived at the church around one in the morning. The surrounding neighborhood was quiet, with only streetlamps and porch lights to illuminate the area. The church was situated on a hill, with the main entrance at the top of the hill and the multipurpose/gymnasium entrance down below.

Lacey drove us in her car because 1) she's a control freak and 2) she said I'm not a good driver. I decided not to argue the point. This time.

She pulled into the parking lot in front of the lower entrance. "Any idea where the kid was parked?"

"Honestly, I didn't notice his car when we arrived. Cole drove. I was so focused on how nervous he was, because it seemed so unlike him."

Viv and Lacey exchanged a look I couldn't decipher.

"What?"

"Nothing." Vivienne suppressed a grin.

I climbed out of the car and began scanning the parking lot. Most of the lines were faded, and there was a lot of gravel. It hadn't rained a lot since the accident, which worked in our favor, but I had no idea what I was looking for.

"Anyone know what color power steering fluid is?"

"It should be pink or reddish," said Lacey.

"In the dark, everything's the same color," quipped Vivienne.

It was true. I thought I found a small puddle, but when I shone my phone's flashlight on it, it turned out to be oil.

For forty-five minutes, we wandered the lot.

The sound of an approaching vehicle caused me to freeze. I looked at Viv, who was also frozen in place.

Lacey was across the parking lot, out of whispering range.

Suddenly, the car's headlights cut out. The car crept toward us, only the low hum of the engine and the occasional pop of gravel signaling its advance.

"What should we do?" whispered Viv.

"I don't know," I hissed back at her.

"Technically, we aren't trespassing, right?"

"I don't know, you're the one who works at the police station."

She scoffed. "Yeah, but you're the one obsessed with rules."

The car came to a stop, engine still purring, headlights still dark. A window rolled down and a glaring Maglite shone through the window, straight into my face.

I covered my eyes. "Ack!"

I thought I heard a mumbled cursing.

The light turned off, as did the car's engine. The car door slammed, but I was still too blinded to see who was walking toward us.

"What in the world are you ladies doing out here at nearly two A.M.?"

"Cole?" I squinted. "Is that you? I can only see spots."

"Sorry about the flashlight."

Lacey wandered over to where we were huddled. "This isn't what it looks like."

Cole guffawed. "I highly doubt that."

"What are you doing out so late?" I asked. "I thought you went home."

Once again, Vivienne and Lacey exchanged a look. Viv smirked, and Lacey cocked her right eyebrow.

"Oh, for the love of—what is with you two?" I demanded.

Cole shook his head. "I don't want to know. And I asked you first."

"Well..." I said. "We might sorta be looking for power steering fluid."

He briefly closed his eyes. "And why would you be looking for power steering fluid in an empty church parking lot in the middle of the night? Like I even need to ask."

Vivienne put her hand on Cole's shoulder. "Here's the thing. See that woman over there?" She jerked her head in Lacey's direction.

Lacey waved and gave Cole a sheepish grin.

"That woman, the one who is so patiently going along with my shenanigans? I'm trying to marry her in about thirty-six hours, but members of our bridal party keep getting arrested, dropping out, or dropping dead. Or all of the above. Oh, and just so you know, if this thing does end up happening, I'll be expecting you to fill in for Wylie."

Cole's gaze widened, with a hint of horror passing across his face. "Okayyy. So am I to assume you're investigating where Jack's car began leaking power steering fluid?"

"Yes."

"Why would you assume I hadn't already done that?"

"It's not that we assumed that," I said. "It's more that we assumed if you had, you weren't going to share the info with us anyway."

"Now *that* is a fair assumption."

"Look," said Vivienne. "We can do this the easy way or the hard way. You don't want us interfering in your investigation—"

"Correct."

"However, you also know me well enough by now, and you certainly know my sister well enough—"

I grimaced.

"To know that we aren't easily deterred when it comes to something as important as this. Do us all a favor and say we can work together to solve this."

"Okay."

Vivienne shook her head. "I don't want to hear all the reasons why we should stay out of it, and let you do your job—"

"I said OKAY."

She stopped. She looked at me with her head angled. "Did he just say okay?"

"He did," I said.

She looked at Lacey, who nodded. "He did."

"I did."

Viv lunged to hug him. "Thank you. Thank you. You won't regret it!"

CHAPTER TWENTY-THREE

"I already am," he mumbled from under the full weight of her enthusiasm.

* * *

A plan was made to meet at my place at nine-thirty the next morning. First, Cole was going to pick up Meacham's clothes from the B&B and drop them off at the Washington State Patrol's crime and forensic lab up in Marysville. It was the closest place outside of Seattle set up to do that kind of testing.

I'd gone home and fallen right into bed without even changing my clothes. I dreamt of rolling in endless sand pits filled with dead bodies.

Vivienne, knowing me as well as she did, showed up with a triple-shot vanilla latte and an apricot raspberry muffin from Abigail's. Oh, and she brought Lacey, too. Lacey drank her coffee black and unsweetened. Judging by her tired expression, she needed all the caffeine she could get.

"Mom's mad," announced Vivienne.

"I know. She texted me. I haven't responded."

Our mother had heard the news about Wylie's death via a post in the Chattertowne crime and community group on Facebook. She wasn't thrilled she had to read it online, rather than hear it straight from her daughters.

I hadn't even submitted an article to the *Coastal Current* for publication yet, which was why I'd also gotten an early morning text from my editor, Nicholas Anderson. He was understandably annoyed, but he cut me a little slack when I told him I'd send a story by noon. I did, after all, have a first-hand account of most of the previous nights' events, so that had placated him a bit as well.

When Cole arrived, he was agitated. "Did Onyx ever reply to your text?"

I pulled out my phone. "No. But it looks like she did read it."

"Interesting."

"Why?"

"When I got there, she said she never saw your message. She says while she and Meacham were eating breakfast, the B&B owner took his clothes and washed them. She says she didn't tell her to do it."

"Hmm. It looks like she didn't read the message until seven-thirty. Maybe she's telling the truth."

"I took the clothes anyway. They were in the spin cycle when I arrived, but maybe we'll get lucky and there will be something."

"Yeah, *if* Meacham bludgeoned Wylie. If testing reveals nothing, it won't answer the question."

"I had to try." Cole looked at my half-eaten muffin on the table. "Any more of those pastries?"

"There's a ham and cheese croissant on the kitchen counter," said Vivienne.

After he left the room, Lacey lowered her voice. "Is Onyx trying to cover for Meacham?"

Viv shrugged. "Who knows. She may be worried that he killed Wylie, and even though she's upset about Wylie's death, Meacham is her husband."

"If he's guilty, that would make her an accessory after the fact. That would be dumb," said Lacey. Once a cop, always a cop.

"People do a lot of dumb things for love," I said.

"True statement." Cole returned with the croissant in hand. "Someone said something about a chart?"

Vivienne pulled out the posters we'd made the previous night and laid them on my coffee table.

Cole looked over them for a moment. "I was kind of hoping you'd have found something I hadn't. The only entry on both lists is an unknown person with unknown motives."

"Yeah, we noticed that," I said. "I guess that means the two crimes were committed by two different people."

"Maybe." His forehead was crinkled as he stared at the lists.

"What aren't you saying?"

"I think there's something missing from both lists."

"What's that?"

"What if it were a golf student of Wylie's in competition with Jack or Laveda? Someone who would benefit from them being out of the picture. Or a parent who wanted their kid to get the attention Jack and Laveda have been receiving from Wylie."

"That makes sense for the accident, but not for Wylie's death," said Lacey.

He nodded. "Unless Wylie suspected them. Or, the accident didn't actually change the amount of attention they were getting. Then they might realize it wasn't that Jack or Laveda were the obstacles, but that Wylie didn't think their golfer was worth the extra attention."

It was a viable theory. "So the golfer—or their parent—killed Wylie out of anger?"

"Right."

Vivienne asked the question that was on my mind. "Do we know of any of his students that might fit that bill?"

"I don't, but I know who might," said Cole.

"Jack."

He nodded at me. "Jack."

* * *

Somehow, Cole talked me into accompanying him to Miranda's house to talk to Jack. Whether he wanted me there as a buffer between him and Jack or him and Miranda, I had no idea, but I suspected I wasn't Miranda's favorite person at the moment either.

Vivienne and Lacey were scheduled for facials and a couples massage at noon, and I insisted they not cancel. We assured them as soon as we had any information, we would pass it along.

As we approached Devil's Elbow, Cole slowed the car.

"Hey, can you pull over for a minute?" I asked.

"I can. The question is why?"

"Humor me."

He pulled onto the side of the road just past one of the steep driveways along that stretch. I got out of the car and walked along the edge of the street in the direction of the curve. Behind me, Cole's door opened and closed.

"You planning on letting me in on what you're looking for?"

I glanced over my shoulder. "It was dark the last time I was out here, and there were firetrucks, ambulances, police cars...I wanted to see the scene in the daylight."

He'd caught up with me. "If you're looking for power steering fluid, you're out of luck. You know it was drizzling that night. Also, the bulk of the fluid was in the gully where the car landed. Forensics found a decent amount down there."

"Really? I guess I'd assumed it dripped out the whole way here and there wasn't much left by the time they hit the curve."

"Probably most of it did, but what was left drained out after the crash."

"No matter." I waved my hand dismissively. "I'm not looking for fluid anyway. I'm looking for skid marks."

He went silent.

I stopped and turned to face him. His expression was bemused.

"What?"

He knit his brows together. "What made you decide that was important?"

"I don't know. I've been thinking about my own accident out here, and how much rubber was on the road afterward. I just wanted to see for myself where Jack started to brake, if at all."

"I see."

I gasped. "That's what you were doing last night! You came out here. Were you looking for skid marks, too?"

"I was. I was looking over the accident report, and I didn't see a mention of it. I wasn't sure if it was overlooked or what."

"So is your thought that if there are no skid marks then…what? You can't possibly believe he meant to go off the road. Do you actually think he might have tried to take himself out and bring Laveda with him?"

He shrugged. "Just following all possible theories."

"Has he ever indicated that he's not handling the pressure well, and might possibly…nope out? As the kids say."

"There's no doubt that the pressure is intense. I've witnessed the toll it takes on him. If I had seen anything to indicate he was a danger to himself, I would have intervened. Was I concerned about him? Sure, but he's trying to become a pro golfer. That's not an easy path. He's seemed to handle it as well as can be expected."

"Definitely not easy. He claimed not only did the steering go out, but possibly the brakes as well. If they did, there wouldn't be any marks."

"Right. But the brake lines were intact according to the forensic examination, so there should be evidence of braking."

"What did you see when you were here last night?"

"It was too dark. I looked, but I gave up and decided to come back later. That's when I found you and the other two Keystone Cops milling around the church parking lot."

I began walking toward the curve. With a name like Devil's Elbow, I'd have thought the area would feel spooky, like something out of the *Blair Witch Project*. Instead, the sun was peeking through the trees, and although the area was wooded and mossy, it was kind of pretty. Fuzzy buds were beginning to sprout on a magnolia tree at the bottom of someone's driveway. I caught a floral whiff that smelled nothing like what I'd imagine a devil's elbow might smell like. Sulfur and sweat, plus maybe Axe body spray.

A car rounded the corner coming from the opposite direction. The driver locked eyes with me and then looked behind me at Cole, who was pantomiming for him to slow down.

"Oh, to have that kind of power," I mused.

"It's not power. It's responsibility."

"Okay, Spider-Man." I pointed at the street. "Nothing here."

We walked closer to the drop-off.

"Would you look at that." Cole folded his arms.

About ten feet from the edge were very distinct tire tracks. At the beginning of the tracks, the marks were dark but lightened as they headed straight toward the embankment.

Chapter Twenty-Four

We pulled into Miranda's driveway about five minutes after visiting the crime scene. Well, the accident scene, at least. It had answered one question for me, which was, had Jack been able to brake going around the corner. The answer was that he'd attempted to stop, but the inability to steer had propelled the car careening over the embankment. There wasn't even a curve to the tracks, indicating he'd lost one hundred percent of his ability to steer.

As I'd stood at the edge, I had a flashback to the night I was in the car that sailed over that very embankment. "Those poor kids," was all I could muster as tears streamed down my face. Laveda's last moments were undoubtedly terrifying in a way no one should ever have to experience, much less a sixteen-year-old girl with the brightest of futures waiting for her.

It was imperative that we figure out what had happened, for Laveda's sake. For her family's sake. For that little brother who would never again get a hug from his "Lala."

Miranda and Jack lived in the single-story home she and Hank had purchased during their marriage. I trailed Cole up the walkway to the front porch.

Jack answered the door wearing a Def Leppard t-shirt. I suspected he'd never actually listened to the band. His hair was mussed, and his eyelids heavy with fatigue. His pallor was anemic, and he still had dark circles under his bloodshot eyes.

"Oh, hey. My mom just went out. I don't know when she'll be back."

"Actually, I was hoping to talk to you, Jack. Mind if we come in?" said

Cole.

He looked warily at me. "I guess."

We followed Jack into the living room, which appeared to be recently remodeled. The floors were a faux wood gray plank, with gray walls and white molding. The furniture was gray velvet. I'd seen similar décor in a lot of flip homes in the area. Because the Puget Sound housing market was so hot, investors were buying up every rundown property they could get their hands on, yanked out the carpet, Formica countertops, and any hint of character to gray-ify every surface. The goal seemed to be neutrality or modernization, but the effect was stark and soulless.

Cole and I sat on the sofa, while Jack plopped into a recliner in the corner. "Is this about the accident?"

Cole leaned forward. "I have some news."

Jack rubbed the back of his neck. "Is it about Coach Wylie dying? My phone's been blowing up about it all morning."

A flicker of surprise crossed Cole's face. "You don't seem very upset about that."

Jack flinched. "Honestly, I'm not sure how to feel about it. The dude killed my girlfriend, and he almost killed me."

"That hasn't been established."

Jack's expression hardened. "Are you saying you don't believe me?"

"Not at all. I believe you that you have reason to believe he was responsible. My job is to verify that, even in light of Wylie's death. Maybe even more so because of his death."

"You think someone else could have done this?" he asked.

"I think we have to consider that possibility. Is there anyone else you haven't mentioned who might have a motive to hurt you or Laveda? Maybe a competitor? I hear you're up for a scholarship. Who might benefit if you're unable to accept it?"

Jack considered the question. "Maybe Conner McCloud."

Cole pulled out a notepad. "Who's Conner McCloud?"

"He's on the golf team. I guess technically he's number two, but he's so far behind me, I doubt he'd get the scholarship. He may be delusional enough to believe that, just like he was delusional enough to believe he had a chance with Lee."

Cole sat up in his chair. "He was interested in Laveda?"

"Yeah, but it wasn't mutual. Just because she was nice to him didn't mean she would dump me to be with him."

A thought niggled in my brain. "What does Conner McCloud look like?"

"I dunno. Nothing special. Skinny. Glasses."

My pulse quickened. "Was he at 3F the other night?"

Jack's brows pinched together. "Probably. Yeah, I think so."

Cole turned to me. "What are you thinking?"

"If it's the boy I'm thinking of, he was in the pro shop yesterday when I turned in my clubs after the best ball scramble debacle."

"So? He golfs."

"That's the thing. He was in there without clubs, talking to Ike. I asked him if he was golfing, and Ike said he was asking about lessons. They both made it sound like he'd never golfed before. I sensed there was something off about the interaction, but I couldn't put my finger on it."

Jack balled his right hand and punched his left palm. "If he hurt Lee, I'll kill him."

Cole held up his hands. "Whoa. I'm an officer of the law. I'm going to pretend I didn't hear that. If Conner is responsible, he will be held accountable. Just let me handle this the right way. The *legal* way. If I have to arrest you for murder, your mother will never forgive me."

The side door leading into the kitchen from outside slammed shut. Miranda stood in the entrance to the living room.

"You're damn right I'll never forgive you if you arrest my son. He had nothing to do with Wylie's death."

* * *

It took a few minutes for Cole to talk Miranda off the ledge long enough to explain what was happening. Once she understood that he was trying to protect Jack, she calmed down...well, calm for Miranda. She always ran a bit high-strung.

After we left Miranda's, we stopped at Julia and Jack's drive-in for a late lunch of burgers and fries.

As we waited for our food, I fought the urge to grill him about their relationship again. He'd been cagey about it and noncommittal, but it was obvious they'd been spending a considerable amount of time together recently. It just didn't make sense to me.

Was he finally seeing the side of her I'd known since we were kids? Did it matter? And probably more to the point, why did it bother me so much?

"Penny for your thoughts," he said between bites of a Jack's deluxe cheeseburger.

"Haven't you heard? Inflation is off the charts. You're gonna have to come back with a better offer."

He gave me a crooked smile. "You can be funny when you let yourself."

My mouth dropped open, and I made an offended gasp. "A lot of people think I'm funny."

"I just said you can be funny."

"Yeah, but the way you're saying it, you act like me being funny is rare."

"I think you're always saying and doing things that are funny, just not always intentionally. Usually, when you're taking yourself too seriously, which you do a lot."

My mouth gaped further. "That is rich coming from you."

He held up his hands. "Let's reset. I meant to compliment you, but it came out wrong, and I'm sorry. Can we start over?" He held out his hand for me to shake.

I could have dug in my heels and made him pay, but what good would that have done?

"Fine."

I shook his hand. His smile reached his eyes, which held a mischievous grin.

"Let's try a new topic. What do you think about Conner McCloud being the culprit?" he asked.

"It makes sense. More than the idea of two different bad actors, which has always seemed far-fetched to me. What do you think?"

"I'm reserving judgment. That reminds me. I need to figure out where we're going."

Cole called the station to get Conner McCloud's address. He lived about three blocks from Chattertowne High School, and five from the church where the 3F event had been held.

We pulled up to the Edwardian two-story home around three.

Cole knocked on the door, and a little girl in braids opened it. I figured her for about eight or nine years old.

"Hey there, is Conner home?"

"Conner!" For a little thing, she had quite pipes on her.

Conner came down the hallway. When he spotted Cole and me, his eyes widened, and he froze in place.

"Conner, I'm Chief Loveland—"

"I know who you are. I saw you talk at 3F."

"I'd like to ask you a few questions about Laveda Volkova and Wylie Barrett."

He hesitated. "Sh-should I have a lawyer?"

Cole tilted his head to the right. "Do you feel like you need an attorney present? We just wanted to ask you some questions."

He glanced over his shoulder. "I don't know what to do. My parents aren't home right now."

"If you're uncomfortable speaking to me, we can just set up a time for you to come down to the station with your parents and your attorney present."

"At the police station?" This seemed to rattle him even more. "Oh, uh, maybe we can talk for just a few minutes."

"I don't want you to feel pressured."

He shook his head. "It's okay. Just for a few minutes." He repeated the phrase, as if reassuring himself.

The McCloud house's interior was consistent with its exterior: antique furniture, vases filled with dried flowers, and, judging by the tickle in my nose, a hundred years of dust.

"Achoo!" I put my finger against the tip of my nose. "Sorry."

CHAPTER TWENTY-FOUR

Cole gave me a disturbed look. "Bless you. Do you need a tissue?"

"Do you have one?" I sniffed.

"No, actually, I don't." He turned to Conner. "Tissue?"

"One second." Conner scurried out of the room.

"This place smells like the old antique store my great-grandmother used to drag Viv and me to when we were little."

"In a comforting way?" Cole asked.

"In an old musty way. Achoo!"

Conner came scurrying back into the room with a box of tissues. "Here you go. You must have pretty bad allergies or something."

I took a tissue from the box and dabbed my nose. "Or something."

I eased my way onto a brocade scalloped-edge sofa that was probably filled with horsehair based on its firmness and the latent odor of barn. Cole made the mistake of dropping down onto the sofa, and he actually rebounded.

"Whoopsie!" I giggled. "Careful there, cowboy. This thing bucks like a rodeo bronco."

He narrowed his gaze at me and adjusted his hat. Did he mean to do that, or was it a psychosomatic response to me calling him a cowboy?

To Conner, he said, "I understand you're on the golf team at Chattertowne High, and that Wylie was your coach."

"Yes." Conner sat on his hands, and still they fidgeted beneath him. "I can't believe he's dead."

"What did you think of Wylie?" asked Cole.

"What do you mean?"

"Was he a good coach?"

Conner nodded. "Sure. I mean, he definitely had his favorites."

"Like Jack?"

"Yeah, and a few others."

"Laveda?"

Conner nodded vigorously. "Oh, yeah, he definitely liked her."

"What do you mean by that? Do you think any lines were crossed?"

He shrugged. "Dunno. But he paid her a lot of attention."

"Did you ever see anything that made you think something inappropriate was going on?" I asked.

"They just seemed…close. Maybe it was innocent."

"Does the girls' golf season coincide with the boys' season?" asked Cole.

"Yes. Both teams play in the spring."

"So you were around Laveda quite a bit? In training and such."

"I wouldn't say quite a bit. We all golfed the same courses."

"And you and Laveda were good friends?"

"I wouldn't say *good* friends. I knew her. I've known her since she got to the States."

Cole was taking his time with this kid, letting him sweat a bit.

"What did you think of her?"

"She was cool."

Cole's brow arched. "Another *Cool*."

"Yeah, uh, I mean, she was nice to me."

"Are you sure it wasn't more than that?" Cole asked.

"What do you mean?"

I leaned forward. "The other night at 3F, I noticed you watching her do her little dance routine workout thingy."

He shifted. "So?"

"I think you liked her as more than a friend," I said.

Pink crept up his neck. "Like I said, she was cool. But she had a boyfriend."

"A boyfriend who nearly died the night Laveda did," Cole interjected. "Maybe you didn't realize she'd be in the car with him. Maybe you thought you could get rid of Jack and have her all to yourself."

"That's not true! Of course, Laveda and Jack rode together. They were always together." He shook his head. "You don't really think I killed Laveda and Coach Wylie, do you?"

"I don't know what to think, Conner. If Jack had died in the accident, who on the golf team was most likely to benefit from that?"

Now Conner had begun to look green. There was a good chance he might vomit.

"I'm number two, but that doesn't mean…I would never…" His voice trailed off.

"You lied about being a golfer when I saw you at the pro club. Why?" I demanded.

"I don't know. I panicked."

"About what?" Cole pressed.

The pressure of our tag team was getting to him. Beads of sweat were forming at his temples. "I would never hurt anyone, especially not for a scholarship."

Cole's face registered a *gotcha* smile. "Who said anything about a scholarship?"

The remaining color drained from Conner's face. "I think I want that lawyer now."

Chapter Twenty-Five

Cole left his business card with a quaking Conner. He decided not to bring him to the station for questioning since Conner was supposed to be babysitting his little sister, and if he left, she'd have been all alone.

Cole gave strict instructions that Conner was to be at the police station first thing Monday morning with his parents and his attorney.

"A lot of good that will do for Viv and Lacey's wedding on Sunday," I muttered as we drove back to my house.

"What was I supposed to do? Leave a little girl alone in the house? Conner's a minor, too. It's better this way. If it turns out that he's the killer, we want to do everything by the book."

I sighed. "I know."

He pulled his car into my driveway. I checked my phone. I had a text from Vivienne asking for an update that I didn't want to have to give her.

"It's four o'clock," I said.

"Yes."

"That means exactly twenty-four hours from now, the wedding is supposed to start. Whether it does or not is another matter. I guess it was unrealistic of me to think we could solve this case in a day."

"You're right, that is unrealistic, especially since technically it's two cases."

"Two related cases."

"Maybe. Probably. Do you think they'll really postpone the wedding?"

"That or elope. Either way, my mother is going to have a conniption."

Cole chuckled. "I haven't heard the word conniption since I was a kid."

"So, what's your plan?"

"I'm going to go home. Make myself some dinner, turn on the television to watch the Mariners lose—again—and then I'll check in with the crime lab to see if they were able to get anything from Meacham's clothes."

"On a Saturday night?"

"There's a guy named Jerry who's going through a divorce, so he's been working extra hours."

"Well, I guess Jerry's burden is our benefit. If he finds blood spatter on the clothing, perhaps this case will be solved yet."

"I'm not sure that arresting Meacham Fields for murder will calm things down around here."

"True, and Onyx will be sideways, so she'd probably drop out. Viv is so concerned about things being even."

"I hate to break it to you, but things are already uneven. Wylie's death makes five total attendants. And your sister is threatening to make me take his place."

"Shoot, you're right. Maybe it's better if Onyx drops out." I put my hand on the door handle. "Can I ask you a question?"

"I suppose, although such an open-ended question makes me nervous."

"What do you like about Miranda?"

"Oof. Right between the eyeballs, I see. Well, I don't know her that well. We met at the Senior Center's Santa pancake breakfast in December. She makes a mean blueberry pancake."

"That's it? Blueberry pancakes? You don't strike me as the *way to a man's heart is through the stomach* type."

"I can't speak for most men, but I'm a pretty simple guy."

I scoffed.

"What?"

"Nothing about you is simple. I've been trying to figure you out since that very first city council meeting."

He stared at me for a moment. "You've been trying to figure me out? Why?"

"I don't know. Because you're not from here. Because you intrigue me, because—"

"I intrigue you?"

"Okay, intrigue might be too strong a word. Mostly, you infuriate and aggravate me." I laughed.

He reared back a bit. "Whoa. That escalated from a compliment to an insult pretty quickly."

"I didn't mean it like tha—"

"How did you mean it?"

"Cole, I—"

"I gotta go." He stared pointedly ahead.

"Okay. I guess I'll see you tomorrow?"

He continued staring out the windshield.

"Okay then. Have a good night."

I shut the car door, and he backed out onto the street without making eye contact. The encounter left me with an icky, sinking feeling. I stood in my driveway like a lost child. The events of the week had taken their toll, and my throat felt like it was being squeezed. Shoot. I was about to cry.

Across the street, a car door slammed. Holden looked at me with an expression I couldn't quite decipher. Hurt? Confused? Angry?

How long had he been there? Had he been waiting for me? Had he watched Cole and me as we talked in the car? Had he seen me staring forlornly after Cole as he'd driven away?

"Well, that was enlightening," he said in a clipped tone as he walked toward me.

"Holden? What are you doing here?"

"I came to see how you were after last night. I didn't realize I was interrupting a date."

"It wasn't a date. We were interviewing witnesses and a possible suspect."

His demeanor shifted. "You have a suspect? Who?"

"I can't say."

Immediately, his face clouded over. "Oh, I see. It's just a secret you have with Cole."

"It's not like that. I think there are…complex legal ramifications that make me talking about it a bad idea."

"Whatever, Audrey." He turned his back.

"Wait. Why are you leaving?"

When he turned around again, his eyes were sad. "The writing's on the wall. I've seen it."

"What does that even mean?"

But he just walked back to his car, got in, and drove away.

I stood in my driveway for a moment. It was too late to go after him, since he was already gone, but my brain was finally catching up, and I felt the need to explain or to defend myself.

A gust of wind blew my hair into my face. I looked up where dark clouds were quickly moving in above me. The sky was taking on a moody purple hue, a telltale sign of a storm.

Ominous. Foreboding. Appropriate for how I was feeling.

I dragged myself into the house and locked the door behind me. I didn't bother turning on the lights since there was still a bit of diminishing daylight left, and I just wanted to go to sleep.

Somehow in the span of mere minutes, I'd managed to alienate both Cole and Holden.

The worst part was I had two more people to upset. Three if you counted my mother. Might as well get it over with.

I walked upstairs to my bedroom and changed into sweats. I pulled on my Pilates socks with the grippy bottom—I'd started wearing them in the house after a slip down the stairs a few months earlier—and flopped on my bed to FaceTime Vivienne.

"Hey," she said when she answered.

Lacey hovered in the background. "What's the good word?"

I was about to open my mouth when Vivienne said, "There is no good word, is there? I can tell by your face."

I exhaled. "Here's what I can tell you. Cole has a man at the crime lab who's working late today to test Meacham's clothing. As soon as he knows something, he'll call me. I think."

"What do you mean, you think?" asked Vivienne.

"Well, when he left, he was unhappy with me. As was Holden."

For the third time in a day, Vivienne and Lacey exchanged a look.

"I really wish you'd either stop doing that or tell me what's going on."

Vivienne gave me a bemused smile. "Do you really not know?"

"Know what?"

"You're in a love triangle."

I guffawed. "In order to be in love triangle, the two other people have to actually like you."

Lacey smiled as she shook her head. "For someone so smart, you sure can be clueless."

"You wouldn't be the first person to make that observation, but could you be more specific?"

Vivienne sighed. "Honestly, Audrey. I can't tell if you're being purposely obtuse or coy, or if you really don't see it."

Obtuse. There was that word again. Maybe it really did apply to me. "Could someone please spell out for me what I'm apparently too dumb to understand?"

"Don't look at me," Lacey said. "I'm staying as far away from this situation as possible."

"Coward." Vivienne's statement might have been harsh, but she punctuated it with a kiss on Lacey's cheek. She turned back to the screen. "I'm pretty sure Holden's been in love with you since high school. At least on some level. And Cole, well, I've been working with him for a while. Do you know how often he asks about you?"

"Cole asks about me?"

"Yes."

"Not in a, *hey, where's your sister going to be today, so I can avoid her* sort of way?"

Vivienne rolled her eyes. "No. In an *I'm thinking about your sister and want to talk about her* sort of way. And it's pretty much every single day."

Somewhere in the back of my mind, I'd wondered if either of these scenarios were possible. The idea that both of them were not only possible but probable was more than I could wrap my brain around.

"I can't deal with this right now. Let me get back to the update."

"Fine," said Viv, "but inevitably you're going to have to deal with it."

I waved my hand. "That's later Audrey's problem. Today's Audrey wants to solve these murders so your wedding can happen. Cole and I went to look at the accident scene. We found skid marks."

Lacey poked her head into the frame. "What did they look like?"

"Straight. No curve. Terrifying when you imagine those poor kids trying to stop and not being able to turn the wheel."

"Really awful," said Vivienne.

"Anyway, after that, we went to talk to Jack. He gave us the name of a kid who might have a motive for both crimes."

Vivienne's gaze widened. "Really? Who?"

"Don't say anything," Lacey interjected. "If he's a minor, you have to be really careful."

"That's why Holden's currently mad at me. I refused to tell him."

"I'm sure that's not the only reason," said Vivienne.

Disregarding her quip, I said, "Lacey, am I allowed to give a vague description?"

"I suppose that would be okay."

"It's someone connected to Jack, Laveda, and Wylie through school, golf, *and* 3F."

"That makes a lot of sense," said Lacey.

"Unfortunately, Cole has to wait for him to come into the police station with his parents and attorney...on Monday."

"Monday!" Vivienne cried. "We really are going to have to call off our wedding, aren't we?"

A concerned-looking Lacey put her arm around Vivienne. "We still have time."

"Not much! We have to give people a heads up if we're going to cancel."

A thumping sound came from downstairs. Or was it a crash? I jerked my head to look in the direction of my closed bedroom door.

"Audrey? Everything okay?" Lacey asked.

"I don't know. I thought I heard something downstairs. It's probably just the wind." Branches from the pine tree outside my bedroom window whipped against the pane.

"Are you expecting anyone?" asked Vivienne.

"No."

"I don't like this," she said.

"Me neither." Lacey shook her head. "Want me to come check it out?"

"It's probably nothing. But stay on the phone with me as I go look."

I carefully twisted the knob on my bedroom door. It squeaked like something in a haunted house movie.

"You should definitely get that door greased," said Lacey.

"It never sounded so ominous until now."

I pulled open the door and began to tiptoe down the stairs. Viv and Lacey watched quietly, both of their expressions intense and wide-eyed. It wasn't helping me to stay calm with their nervous faces staring at me, waiting to see whether the boogeyman was gonna get me.

As I reached the landing, I flipped on the entryway light switch. I looked to my left and to my right and then back again. I waited to see if any shadows would move in either the kitchen or the living room, but nothing happened. The only sound was my heavy breathing and wind whistling through the drafty house.

"What do you see?" whispered Vivienne.

"Nothing yet."

I padded around the corner and peeked into the kitchen. Nothing appeared out of place.

As I stepped across the entryway toward the dim living room, a floorboard creaked underneath me, and I gasped. A spike of adrenaline coursed through my body, causing my heart to race and tingles to spread from my chest to my fingertips.

"What was that?" said Vivienne.

I slowly inhaled and exhaled, trying to calm my breathing. "It was just this old creaky house. I need to talk to Renee about having someone come out and put weatherstripping around these windows and doors. It's so drafty I can hear the wind whistling like they're open."

As I moved into the living room, I heard a crunch beneath my foot, immediately followed by a sharp pain.

I howled.

"What's wrong?" "What happened?" Viv and Lacey both shouted at me through the phone.

I dropped to the floor and grabbed at my foot. Even in the dimness of the room and the tears stinging my eyes, I could see that blood was beginning to soak my sock.

"I think there's glass on the floor. I stepped on it."

"Glass? Are you okay?" Vivienne asked.

"I'm definitely cut. I don't know how badly yet."

"Where did it come from?" asked Lacey.

I scanned my surroundings. Pebbles of clear glass spread across the wood floors. It looked like spilled diamonds. A few feet from me, under the sofa, was a round object the size of a large grapefruit. I extended my arm to reach for it.

"There's something…under…here," I grunted and continued stretching my hand.

"Show us," said Vivienne.

I turned the phone so they could see what I was trying to grab. "Can you see it?"

"Sort of. Is that a rock?" asked Lacey.

"I think so." I crawled closer and grabbed it. "Yeah. It's a rock. It's got some writing on it."

"What does it say?" asked Vivienne.

"It's hard to see. I need to move close to the light."

I scooted a bit across the room, the pain in my foot searing. "Ouch."

"Be careful!" Vivienne's voice cracked with emotion.

I held the rock into the light. In black Sharpie three words were written:

Leave him alone

The wind blew harder, and then the lights went out.

Chapter Twenty-Six

"Leave who alone?" Vivienne repeated for the third time since she'd arrived at my house. "Who could they mean?"

"It could be any number of people." My bandaged foot was propped on the coffee table in front of me. "I feel like it has to mean Conner, right? He's the new primary suspect."

"Does he know that?" asked Vivienne.

I shrugged. "I think so. He asked for an attorney to be present before being interviewed again."

Lacey stared at the candle—honeysuckle scented—flickering on the table next to my foot. It was the only light in the room. The power had been out for thirty minutes with no sign of the wind letting up.

"What do you think, sweets?" Vivienne asked her.

Lacey was still deep in thought. "Something's off."

"Of course something's off." I waved my hand toward the broken window where the rock had been cast. "Somebody's decided *I'm* the problem in this scenario, even though none of it has anything to do with me. I'm just an innocent bystander."

"Ha. I don't know about innocent, but you're right, it doesn't make sense that someone would threaten you to back off when you're just along for the ride." Vivienne tucked her platinum blonde hair behind her ears. She always did this when she was unsettled. "What if this isn't about the investigation at all?"

"What do you mean?"

"What if it's about Cole? What if it's about romantic jealousy?"

"You mean…you think Miranda did this because I was with Cole today?"

"Maybe." She turned to Lacey and furrowed her brow. "Really? Nothing? You have no response to anything I'm saying?"

"I'm thinking."

Vivienne turned back to me. "Did you call Cole?"

"Not yet."

"Audrey, this is vandalism. No. It's terrorism."

"That's a bit extreme."

"Call him."

I sighed, but pulled my phone out and did what she asked.

He answered on the first ring.

"That was fast."

"How can I help you, Audrey?" His clipped tone and cold demeanor were worse than his relentless banter and clapbacks.

I swallowed hard. "Uh, a rock came through my living room window."

"It's windy. A lot of stuff is getting blown around."

"Well, this one had a message written on it."

"Are you serious?"

"Yup."

"What did it say?"

"It said *leave him alone.*"

I heard the sound of jangling keys in the background. "I'm on my way."

He disconnected the call before I could say anything else.

"I guess he's coming here," I said.

Lacey considered me for a moment. "Tell me again about your day from the time I last saw you this morning."

I recounted how Cole and I had driven to the crime scene, we'd observed the skid marks, then gone to Miranda's to talk to Jack. After speaking with Jack, we'd gone to lunch, and then to Conner's. After that, he'd brought me home. Holden was here, as I'd said, and that hadn't gone well.

"I guess I hadn't realized Holden had been here right before you went inside," said Lacey.

"Yeah, me neither," said Vivienne.

"What difference would that make?"

Vivienne and Lacey exchanged looks.

"What now?"

"Could Holden…" Vivienne didn't finish her question.

"Could Holden what?" What was she getting at? "You don't think Holden threw a rock through my window." I laughed at the absurdity.

Vivienne gave me a pointed look. "You said that he was upset about you being with Cole. Maybe Cole is the one you're supposed to leave alone, and Holden's the one telling you to do it."

"No." I shook my head. "Nope. No way."

She shrugged. "You sure?"

"A thousand percent."

"Okay."

But Vivienne didn't look convinced.

I turned to Lacey. "Is that what you were thinking?"

"No. I was thinking maybe Onyx did it in defense of Meacham."

"One problem with that," came a disembodied voice through my broken window.

Vivienne and I both screamed. I flailed my arms and my foot jerked, knocking over the candle. Hot wax spilled onto the coffee table, extinguishing the flame in the process. The living room plunged into darkness.

"Oops." Cole chuckled. "Didn't mean to startle you."

"Cole!" I yelled. "Not cool."

"Sorry, I was just checking out the window, and I heard you talking."

Lacey stood from the sofa and turned on her phone's flashlight. "Where's the lighter?"

"In the kitchen."

"It is okay if I come in?" asked Cole.

"The more the merrier," I muttered.

Cole entered the house right as Lacey relit the candle. He removed his hat, and water drained off the brim.

"Sorry, it's really pouring out there. Hailing, too." He removed his coat and hung it on the rack. Then he removed his shoes. "Wet and muddy."

"Watch out for broken glass," I said. "Viv tried to sweep it up, but there was a lot."

Cole's expression was tight. "Where's the rock?"

I pointed at the side table.

He pulled on blue latex gloves. "Did you touch it?"

"Of course I did."

He sighed. "What about you two?"

Lacey sat on the sofa. "Absolutely not."

"Good, so we should only be dealing with two sets of fingerprints, not four."

"Can you even get fingerprints off a rock?" I asked.

"This one has a fairly smooth surface, so possibly." He lifted the rock and examined the writing. "So, the question is, who is the *he* that you're supposed to be leaving alone?"

"Right."

Vivienne clicked her tongue. "Maybe *you're* the he."

Cole jerked his head. "What? Why would I be the he?"

"Because Audrey spent the day with you. Perhaps your girlfriend is jealous. I've known Miranda a very long time. If she feels like something or someone is threatening what she sees as hers, she can get vicious."

"She's not my girlfriend."

"Does she know that?" asked Vivienne. "Because when she was still in my wedding, she referred to you as her significant other and wanted to make sure you'd be seated next to her at the reception."

"Significant other? Where would she get that idea?"

I clamped my lips shut. Our argument that afternoon had been about Miranda, and I didn't want to add any fuel to the fire. Better to let Vivienne tell him how it was.

"Well, Cole, from what she told me, you two were exclusive. Saw each other almost every day. What would you call it?"

If I weren't in pain from my foot getting sliced by glass, freaked out by someone vandalizing my home with an ominous warning, and stressed about the wedding that was in danger of being cancelled, I'd have been more inclined to let her pursue her line of questioning. After all, I wanted the answers too. I also wanted to know how long he'd been standing outside my broken window listening to our conversation.

Had he heard Vivienne's theory that Holden might have been trying to warn me away from spending time with Cole? Would Cole have also thought that was an absurd notion? And what would he have thought about the idea of being in a love triangle with Holden and me?

But I had a more pressing question. "What did you mean when you said it couldn't have been Onyx warning me away from pursuing Meacham as a possible suspect?"

He sat in the chair next to mine. "I got a call from the crime lab. Not a single trace of blood or other biologics from more than one male person."

"But you said yourself that since it was washed, a lack of evidence wouldn't exonerate him."

"True. However, trace evidence *was* found on his clothes. Toothpaste mixed with what is likely Meacham's own DNA. Rum. Rhododendron pollen. Lipstick with female DNA, probably Onyx. If the clothes were washed well enough to get blood out, they wouldn't also still have all these other elements."

Lacey's expression was grim. "So you are eliminating Meacham as a suspect?"

"Not officially, but I believe investigative efforts should be focused elsewhere."

"Okay, so where?" I asked.

"Things are coalescing pretty well around one suspect. Conner McCloud."

Lacey nodded. "That must be the kid you were talking about. Sounds right to me as well."

"So, what does that mean for us?" asked Vivienne. "For the wedding. If Conner won't even be available to sit for a police interview until Monday, do we cancel?"

Lacey grabbed her hand. "I say we sleep on it. How about you stay here with Audrey. I'll head back to the boat. You're not supposed to see the bride before the wedding anyway, right?"

CHAPTER TWENTY-SIX

Vivienne laughed. "Since when are you a traditionalist?"

"I'm not, but I can see how spending the night apart before your wedding day can make it more special. Besides, that way, Audrey won't be alone."

"If you're sure—" Vivienne was cut off by her phone ringing. "Hello?"

Someone on the other end of the line was speaking, but I couldn't hear their words.

"Oh no!" Vivienne covered her face with her left hand.

"What is it?" Concern etched Lacey's face.

Vivienne said into the phone, "Okay, please keep us posted." She hung up, and her shoulders slumped.

"What happened?" asked Lacey.

"That was the golf club events manager. The power is out. I guess a transformer blew. They don't know how long it will be until the power gets restored." Tears began to stream down her face. "Well, I guess that's the final nail in the coffin. The wedding is off!"

Chapter Twenty-Seven

Lacey tried to reassure Vivienne that the wedding could still happen even if the entire building blew away. She made her promise not to send out a cancellation notice until the situation could be reevaluated in the morning.

Vivienne agreed, but I knew my sister well enough to know she'd already made up her mind. In order for Lacey to talk Viv out of canceling in the morning, she'd have to pull off some sort of miracle.

Cole took an old cardboard box and covered the broken window, holding it in place with duct tape. It would have to do until I was able to get someone out to replace the glass. It was going to be expensive, that was certain. Probably not covered under my renter's insurance policy either.

A text from Lacey's slip neighbor, Nicholas Anderson—also my editor—about the wind down at the marina sent her scurrying out the door after giving my sister a goodnight kiss.

After Lacey left, Vivienne yawned, said goodbye to Cole, and said goodnight to me before heading upstairs.

"So much for me getting any sleep tonight," I said.

"Why is that?"

"Because she's going to insist on sleeping in my bed, even though I have a perfectly nice guest bedroom set up. And she's a cover hog."

"At least she doesn't snore."

"No. She whimpers."

Cole chuckled. "Not sure that's much better."

"Thank you for coming over so quickly."

"Of course."

"Don't say *of course* like you weren't irritated with me when you dropped me off earlier today."

He squinted at me. "I find you baffling."

"That makes two of us."

"Two of us who find you baffling?" His mouth twitched, but he didn't smile.

"Oh, I'd say there are more than two people who find me baffling. Which is confusing as hell to me, because I have no poker face, and I feel like I'm pretty straightforward."

His gaze dropped to his feet. "Is Holden one of those people? Who finds you baffling, I mean. Or does he understand you better than I do? I know you've known each other for a long time."

My mouth went dry. "I would say Holden probably finds me more annoying than perplexing, but I could be wrong."

"I believe you are." He looked up at me from underneath heavy lids.

"Perplexing? Annoying?"

"Wrong." Now he was looking straight at me.

"Speaking of perplexing," I murmured.

His left brow shot up. "You find me perplexing?"

"Mmm hmm." I pressed my lips together.

He took a step closer. "What do you want to understand about me?"

Over a year's worth of questions vanished from my mind in an instant.

He tilted his head to the right and blinked at me. "No questions?"

"The last question I asked didn't go over very well."

"You mean about Miranda?" He took another step closer.

"Yes," I rasped. So much for playing it cool.

A smile played upon his lips. He tipped the brim of his hat backward, showing a twinkle in his eyes. "Am I making you nervous?" He took another step forward until he was looking down at me.

I swallowed. "N-no."

His smile broadened. "I don't believe you."

"W-What are you doing?"

"Calling your bluff." He began to lean closer.

"Audrey, are you coming?" Vivienne called from the top of the stairs. "I need you to snuggle me and tell me everything's going to be okay."

Cole took a half step back, and I let out a half-gasp, half laugh. "Just a minute." My voice cracked.

"You okay? Your voice sounds funny."

"Yep. Give me one sec."

Cole stepped back further. "I'd better go."

I stepped toward him and put my hand on his forearm. He looked down at it and then up at me.

He seemed to be trying to convey something through his eyes, but I couldn't tell if it was regret or relief that nothing had happened between us.

"Lock the door behind me." His voice was gruff. "I'll check on you in the morning, see if this wedding is actually going to happen."

I removed my fingers from his arm. "Okay. Thank you for coming."

"You already thanked me." He gave a quick wave and slipped out the door.

I turned the deadbolt behind him.

"Audrey?" Vivienne called again.

"On my way." I blew out the candles and walked up the darkened stairway.

By the time I got to the top of the stairs, I was winded, but it wasn't from the ascent.

Something had shifted in the vibe between Cole and me, and I had no idea what to do about it.

Or if I should do anything at all.

* * *

By Sunday morning, the storm had passed. The power had come back at my house at 3:27 am. I knew the exact time because all my bedroom lights came on. I checked my phone as I turned them all off.

It had taken me a while to get back to sleep, unlike Vivienne, who'd taken a sleepy time gummy and was purring like a kitten.

I was still a card-carrying member of Nancy Reagan's *Just Say No* campaign, blithely ignoring that the over-the-counter nighttime sleep aid I took on occasion was likely far more addictive, so I resorted to counting sheep. Actually, they weren't sheep. They were all the questions I wished I had the nerve to ask Cole while I had the chance. Now that the moment had passed, what were the chances I'd ever get another opportunity to ask them?

When Vivienne's alarm went off at seven, I'd only gotten a total of four hours of sleep.

"Do you think Salon du Monde has power?" she asked through a yawn and a stretch.

I groaned. "Only one way to find out. Why don't you text Travis?"

She grabbed her phone from the nightstand. "I had the strangest dream."

"Hmm," I said into my pillow.

"You're gonna want to hear this."

I rolled over and opened one eye. "What?"

She was typing into her phone. "Good news. Travis says the salon has a generator, so he'll be able to do my hair at ten no matter what. Mom is at eleven, and he'll spruce you up at noon."

"That is good news."

Vivienne's expression told me she caught my sarcasm. "It is. Now, my dream. You and Cole."

"Me and Cole what?" She had my attention.

She gave me a suggestive nod. "You know."

I sat up, propped against a pillow. "No, I don't."

"You and Cole were together in my dream. *Together.*" She raised and lowered her eyebrows.

"Why?"

She scrunched her nose. "Why? What kind of question is why? Because you guys like each other. That's why."

I folded my arms across my chest. "What were we doing in your dream?" I suspected she didn't really have a dream; she just wanted me to spill the tea about what had happened after she'd gone to bed.

"Audrey, if I have to spell it out for you, it really has been too long."

I'd had enough of that topic. "On a more important note, happy maybe wedding day."

She screwed up her face. "Do you think it's in bad taste to go ahead with the wedding, all things considered?"

"Vivienne O'Connell, when have you ever made decisions based on what other people may think?"

She laughed. "True. I thought you were gonna say 'when have I ever made decisions that were not in bad taste.'"

"That maid of Honor dress you picked out for me was pretty bad."

She threw a pillow at my head. "You're just boring."

"When Onyx and Meacham leave town, the murders get solved, and you are happily married, I'll be thrilled to go back to living a boring life."

She blew her bangs from her face. "You and me both." Vivienne's phone rang. "It's mom."

"You should probably answer it. She's a giant stress ball about this wedding roller coaster."

"Hey, Mom." Vivienne paused to listen. "Okay. Okay." She closed her eyes and inhaled. She opened her eyes as she exhaled. "Okay. I'm with Audrey. I'll have her go check it out. I will. I *will*. Yes, I'll see you at the salon at ten. Okay. I love you too. I know. I know. Love you, bye." She disconnected the call and set her phone on the nightstand.

"What am I going to check out?"

"The club. Mom called the coordinator, and she said the power was still out, and they only have a limited generator, so they're trying to improvise. She doesn't trust that they have things under control, and she's hoping you'll go over there to make sure their backup plan is sufficient."

"So, you're going ahead with the wedding?"

"I am. We are. If people don't want to come because they think it's tacky to move forward with it, I will totally understand. But I want to marry Lacey. Today. Even if no one shows up." Her gaze widened, and she hopped off the bed. "I'd better start getting ready!"

"I think you're forgetting something."

"What's that?"

"You should probably tell your bride the wedding is on." I laughed.

She pointed at me. "You're right!" She grabbed her phone off the nightstand and began furiously typing. She looked up at me. "Don't forget to be at the salon by noon at the latest."

"I won't forget."

"I mean it, Audrey, don't be late!"

* * *

The spring sunshine reflected off wet roads covered in errant branches and debris that I dodged and weaved all the way to the country club.

When I arrived, the scene was pure chaos. It was a good thing my mother sent me down to check things out instead of Vivienne, or worse yet, going down herself.

Golfers were everywhere, some on the putting green, some waiting for their tee time outside the pro shop, and some driving their carts around the nearly full parking lot like Lewis Hamilton at Monaco.

On the restaurant and reception side, staff were unloading tables and chairs from a rental truck and hauling them inside. The coordinator spotted me and ducked behind a potted plant.

"You know I can see you, right?"

The woman gave a nervous chuckle and stepped from behind the Ficus, smoothing her skirt. "Audrey, hello. I didn't expect anyone from the wedding party to be here yet." She examined my jeans, sweatshirt, and no makeup. "Shouldn't you be getting ready?"

I jerked my thumb over my shoulder. "My dress is in the car. My mother sent me down to see how things are going and to find out if you need any help. She tried calling, but the phone lines seemed to be down."

"Yes. No phones, no electricity. We've got the kitchen running on the generator, so the food should be prepared as planned, but as you can see, most of the lights are out." She held up her hands to indicate the dark reception area.

"What about candles?"

"That's our plan. I have someone running to find any stores that are open for business. They tried the grocery store, but they're out of power. They're headed to the hardware store next. Fire code enforcement prefers battery-operated flameless candles, but if worse comes to worst, we can scrounge up enough candles to light this place up."

"Okay, I'll let my mom know. I'm sure she has candles that she can contribute."

"Perfect. I know this isn't ideal for Vivienne and Lacey, but I promise I'm doing everything I can to make the most of this bad luck."

"We appreciate everything you're doing."

She gave me her cell phone number so that we could reach her to get updates.

I was headed back to my car when I spotted Ike behind the dumpster. He wasn't alone. He was arguing with someone.

I crept closer and hid behind a juniper bush.

Austin, the tall boy who'd been in the pro shop when I'd gone in looking for Wylie earlier in the week, was towering over Ike. "Dude, I need this."

"Like I told you, my supplier is having a hard time getting it. It's a hot commodity."

"I've got the NBA elite camp in less than a month. This is my shot at getting drafted."

"I get that, but this stuff is selling like hotcakes. It's the best thing since the Clear."

Clear. Where had I heard that before?

"Ike, man, text me as soon as you get it. Please. I'm begging you."

"I will. You're first on my list. By the way, how did that other stuff work out?"

Austin's neck turned pink. "I chickened out."

"Aww, dude, why? You were so excited. It's so easy, too. Plop plop. Let the good times begin."

"I know, but I decided I want my first time to be with a girl who can keep her eyes open. Know what I mean?"

I knew what he meant, and it made me feel like I was going to vomit. He was talking about some sort of date rape drug, like Rohypnol.

I scurried back to my car and climbed inside. With trembling fingers, I searched *Clear* in my phone's browser. The first result that came up was for an identity verification system, mostly used for getting through TSA lines faster at the airport.

I adjusted my search to *Clear for athletes*.

Bingo.

I read aloud from the Wikipedia article. "Tetrahydrogestrinone (THG), known by the nickname The Clear, is a synthetic and orally active anabolic-androgenic steroid (AAS) which was never marketed for medical use." The article went on to say that it was developed in secret as a designer drug with the specific aim of avoiding detection in blood and urine tests and had been used by a number of high-profile athletes prior to its discovery.

What if Wylie had discovered that Ike was dealing drugs out of the pro shop and confronted him?

I gasped.

And what if Jack had learned Ike was supplying steroids to Austin, and that's why Ike cut the power steering lines in his car?

I needed to talk to Jack again.

I turned on my car just as Ike emerged from behind the dumpster. He jerked his head in my direction.

We made eye contact.

His gaze narrowed, and he tilted his head slightly. His expression held a darkness that caused a chill to run across my arms.

Chapter Twenty-Eight

I put my car into reverse and backed into the aisle. My tires squealed slightly as I raced out of the country club parking lot.

I pressed a button on my steering wheel. "Call Cole Loveland."

"Calling Cole Loveland," responded the electronic voice.

The phone rang four times before his voicemail message said, "You have reached Cole Loveland, Chattertowne Chief of Police. If this is an emergency, please hang up and dial nine-one-one. Otherwise, leave a message and I will return your call as quickly as possible."

Beep.

"Cole, it's Audrey, although you probably already knew that from caller ID. I think I know who killed Laveda and Wylie. Cole, it's Ike. I saw him today with a high school kid behind the dumpster at the country club. I overheard them talking about some sort of steroid, I think. Also, I'm pretty sure Ike sold the kid a date rape drug. He said he didn't use it, though. Anyway, think about it. Jack finds out that Ike is selling steroids and other drugs, which goes against everything he stands for with that anti-drug use campaign he started. Ike tries to silence him. But maybe Wylie also finds out somehow and confronts Ike, so he kills him. Wait, then why would Jack accuse Wylie of cutting the steering lines? And why wouldn't he mention Ike as a possible suspect?" I gasped. "I know! Because Laveda was the real target! That's why she was talking to Wylie that night after 3F. She was telling him what she'd learned about Ike. That's how he knew, and that's why he confronted him. Why Wylie didn't mention it, I don't know. Maybe he didn't put the pieces together until the night of the rehearsal. Anyway, I'm headed to Miranda's house to talk to Jack. Maybe when you wake up, you can meet me out there. Bye."

I was pretty dang proud of myself for piecing the whole thing together. My gut had been telling me all along we were looking for a single killer, but in my defense, it had been nearly impossible to find someone with a motive to kill both Jack and Wylie without this final bit of information.

Other than Conner, of course.

As I considered the case against Conner, however, it looked weak in comparison to the case against Ike. Sure, Conner had a motive to get Jack out of the way, both for the golf scholarship and the girl. But would he really try to kill Wylie? I suppose if Wylie had somehow found out that Conner had cut the lines, he might have confronted him, and then maybe Conner panicked. Still, after this morning's revelations about Ike, the Conner theory was seeming less and less likely.

I pulled into Miranda's driveway and turned off my car. I took a deep breath.

My conversation with Cole last night led me to believe things weren't serious between him and Miranda, but that didn't mean she wouldn't be furious with me if he fully ended things with her because of me. If she even suspected there was possibly something happening between Cole and me, she'd probably want to kill me.

I really needed to stop casually throwing around that phrase. Too many people had actually been killed.

I tromped up to her front door and rang the doorbell. After a few moments, Miranda opened the door. She was fully dressed, with her hair and makeup done. As a matter of fact, she was wearing a green dress. She was ready for Vivienne's wedding.

"Let me guess. Onyx dropped out because of Wylie, and now Viv needs me to step back in." Her mouth curved slightly in a victoriously smug half-smile.

Didn't see that coming. How awkward. "Uh, you know, I haven't spoken with Onyx yet this morning, so I'm not sure where things stand with that."

"So, why are you here?" She put a hand on her hip and leaned against the doorframe.

"I think I may know who's responsible for Jack and Laveda's accident and Wylie's death."

"What? Who?" She wobbled, her knees slightly giving way.

"Are you okay?" It wasn't the first time lately that I'd noticed her having balance trouble.

She straightened. "I'm fine."

"Aren't you going to invite me in?"

She scowled but opened the door wider and ushered me to come inside.

I sat in the same spot I'd been the previous morning. "Do you know Ike from the pro shop at the country club?"

"Of course."

"He's dealing drugs."

She placed a hand across her chest. Her hand was trembling. "What? drugs? Are you sure?"

"I saw it with my own eyes. Well, not exactly with my own eyes. More like I heard him talking about it with some kid who's trying out for the NBA."

Her gaze widened. "Austin? What was he buying? Cocaine? Heroine?" She lowered her voice. "Fentanyl?"

"Oh, no, not those kinds of drugs, at least, not that I am aware. He was buying steroids. Or, more accurately, trying to buy them. I guess Ike's having a hard time getting them. I don't know if it's pills or what, but I guess it's like one of those undetectable kinds of performance-enhancing designer drugs. Like Clear."

Color drained from Miranda's face. Her eyes shifted back and forth. "You think whoever killed Wylie…they did it because he discovered he was selling drugs out of the club?"

"That's the theory. Wylie confronts Ike, and whack. Poor Wylie."

"And Jack's…accident?"

"Well, I know Jack is heavily involved with Safety First, so obviously if he discovered Ike was supplying athletes with drugs, he'd do something about it, right?"

"Of…of course."

"I was in the pro shop a couple days ago, and Conner was there without clubs. I asked him if he was golfing, and he said he was thinking of taking it up. Ike said he was thinking of signing up for lessons. When Cole and I were here yesterday, Jack said Conner is number two on the team. Maybe Ike got nervous that Jack was onto him and would blow the whistle, and that's why Ike cut the power steering lines."

Miranda's chest rose and fell at a rapid pace. "I'll kill that punk Ike myself."

"There's another possibility."

"Which is?"

"What if Jack didn't know? What if Laveda is the one who found out, and she was the real target? I saw her talking in private with Wylie the night of the accident. Maybe she told him what she suspected."

Miranda pressed her lips together and flared her nostrils. "But then why wouldn't Wylie say something? He'd have to have known that Ike was a possible suspect."

"Probably because Jack accused him of causing the accident, and it threw him for a loop? Besides, I think it's more likely that Wylie wanted to investigate Ike himself before reporting it to anyone. I'm sure he likes Ike." I chuckled to myself.

"I don't think any of this is funny."

"It's not. At all. I was giggling because I said he likes Ike."

"So?"

"You know, the slogan for Eisenhower's campaign?"

"Who?"

God bless the Chattertowne public school system.

"Never mind. It's not important." I glanced into the kitchen. Two cases of blue Gatorade were stacked on the counter. "That's a lot of Gatorade."

Miranda waved her hand. Once again, it was shaking. Was it nerves? Or something else?

"It's pretty much all Jack drinks," she said. "Those two cases will barely last a couple weeks."

A thought niggled in the back of my mind, but then it quickly evaporated.

Miranda glanced at her Apple watch. "Aren't you supposed to be getting ready for this wedding? It's eleven-thirty."

"Eleven thirty! It can't be." I looked at my phone. 11:36. Shoot. It was after 11:30, and I was supposed to be at the salon to get my hair done at noon. I jumped up. "I gotta go. Are you coming to the wedding?"

Miranda pushed out her lower lip into a pout. "I'm not sure I'm welcome."

"You're welcome. I know Viv wants you there." I held up my index finger. "As long as you don't start any drama."

Miranda's laugh was sharp. "Tell that to Onyx. She's the one always starting drama. Thank goodness Jack—" Miranda's mouth shut faster than a rat trap.

"Thank goodness Jack, what?"

"Nothing."

"I'm curious. Humor me."

"Oh, uh, I was just going to say thank goodness Jack didn't have a mother like that."

Weird. "You're not exactly drama-free, but whatever you need to tell yourself. I hope we see you at the wedding." It was mostly a true statement.

"Maybe."

I got in my car and backed out of her driveway just as Jack was pulling up in Miranda's car.

He rolled down his window. He still looked exhausted, and his eyes were barely open. "Hey. Everything okay?"

"It will be. I was just here to tell your mom I think I've solved the case of your accident and Wylie's murder."

His lids flew open. "How did you figure it out?"

"Long story. Your mom can fill you in. I'm supposed to be getting my hair done for my sister's wedding."

He was still staring at me as I rolled up my window. Just before I drove off, I noticed him take a swig from a blue Gatorade bottle, and once again, a thought flashed through my mind.

As I drove toward Devil's Elbow, the thought returned and began to coalesce. An image of Jack handing Laveda a blue Gatorade bottle as they left the 3F meeting caused me to slam on my brakes. Thankfully, no cars were behind me.

Had the Gatorade bottle been recovered from the scene of the accident? Had it been tested?

I drove further and pulled off the side of the road about ten feet from the deadly curve. I put the car in park and called Cole again. Once again, it went to voicemail.

No point in leaving another message.

I dialed Tony Bianchi's number.

"Bianchi."

"Hey, Tony, it's Audrey."

"I know. It says on the readout. What can I do you for?"

"Do you have access to the police report from the accident at Devil's Elbow involving Jack Dodd and Laveda Volkova?"

"I'm at my kid's baseball game, so I don't have access to it at the moment, and then I have to be at the club for the wedding. I can pull it up tomorrow."

"Shoot."

"What exactly are you wanting to know?"

"I was curious if a Gatorade bottle was found at the scene and—if so—was it tested."

"I don't need to look at a report to give you that answer."

"Oh, good. So what can you tell me?"

"There was no Gatorade bottle found in the vehicle. I inventoried everything myself. Jack kept that car meticulously clean. Not like most teens, where they've got old fast food bags and discarded wrappers all over the place." A cheer went up in the background. "Nice hit, Marco! That was my kid. He got a base hit. Tied game in the bottom of the eighth inning."

"Congratulations." There was probably a more appropriate response, but I was focused on getting answers. "What about outside the car?"

"What?" Tony yelled over the crowd.

"Did you find anything related to the crash outside the car? Could there have been a Gatorade bottle that wasn't collected?"

"I suppose if it were in the car and fell out into the ditch during the crash, it might have been missed, but nothing was noted on the road other than the skid marks."

I opened my car door and walked toward the curve, keeping an eye out for oncoming traffic. "Talk to me about the skid marks."

"Audrey, where are you? It sounds like you're outside."

"I'm at Devil's Elbow."

"Why, may I ask? Especially since your sister is getting married in less than four hours. Does Chief know you're there?"

"I left a voicemail for Cole. I'm starting to think we have this whole thing wrong."

"What does that even mean?"

I stood at the spot where the skid marks were beginning to fade. "The skid marks. I assume you got photos."

"We did. Both that night and the next morning, since it was hard to see them in the dark."

"Were they analyzed by anyone?"

"What are you getting at? Audrey, we know what happened in the accident, we're just not sure who caused it."

"I'm not sure that's accurate. Is it possible to tell the difference between skid marks and acceleration marks?"

Bianchi went silent. "Are you saying what I think you're saying?"

"I don't know."

He muttered an expletive. "Skid marks start out light and get darker as the person slams on the brakes harder. Acceleration marks start out dark and get lighter as the vehicle gains momentum."

"Tony."

"Yeah?"

"You and Cole need to get out to Devil's Elbow as soon as possible."

Bianchi disconnected the call after promising to hunt down Cole as soon as the game was over and meet me at the scene.

I threw my phone into the front seat of my car.

I walked to the edge of the road and looked down into the deep ditch. Even though the sun was trying to peek through the trees, the growth was thick, and it was still pretty dark.

I was going to have to climb down to look for the Gatorade bottle.

Thankfully, I wasn't in my wedding clothes. I had no doubt that Viv was going to be furious at me for missing my hair appointment, but if I was right, the case would be solved before the ceremony.

What better wedding gift could I give her?

I slowly climbed down the hill, muddy from the storm. I grabbed at a root that turned out to not be strong enough to hold my weight. It pulled loose from the hillside, and I fell backward. Because of course I did.

When I landed, I felt a hard object beneath me. I rolled to the side and pulled the item out from under my rear.

A blue Gatorade bottle.

A car approached the curve slowly. Had to be Cole or Bianchi.

A door slammed and as I looked up a face peered over the edge.

Not Cole or Bianchi.

"I thought I might find you here."

Chapter Twenty-Nine

Jack Dodd observed me from above. Gone was the good boy façade; in its place was a cold-blooded murderer who appeared convinced he'd gotten away with his crimes.

"I've been looking for that bottle. Thanks for finding it for me. How about you toss it up?"

"You drugged her."

"Is that a question?"

"I know you drugged her, and I know you got it from Ike."

"You think you know that. You have no proof."

I held up the bottle. "The proof is in here."

"Which you're going to throw to me." He pulled out a gun. "Now."

This was a conundrum. The bottle might be my only leverage to keep him from killing me, but also there was a chance he was going to shoot me either way. I glanced over my shoulder. The woods behind me could provide some protection, but the deeper I went into the forest, the harder it would be for Cole and Bianchi to find me.

"Now." He punctuated his order with a shot over my head.

It echoed through the woods. Would anyone hear it? More importantly, would anyone care? We were in the boonies, where people shot on their own property all the time.

One thing was clear. Jack wasn't bluffing. He really would shoot me, and it would be as easy as shooting fish in a barrel.

I tossed up the bottle and he caught it with ease.

He was a born athlete.

Like his father.

I wanted to ask where he got the gun, but there was a more important question. "How did you crash the car without being in it?"

"Oh, so we're doing this, are we? I suppose that's how it goes with these things. I give you the satisfaction of your questions being answered before you die."

"If you shoot me, no one's gonna think it's an accident."

He shrugged. "I've set Conner up perfectly. You were onto him; he killed you. I'll be sure to plant this gun somewhere connected to him where the police will find it."

Had he envisioned this scenario? Or was he really that diabolically fast on his feet?

"So, was the good kid thing all an act?"

His laugh was bitter. "Out of everything you could possibly ask me, that's what you want to know?" He shook his head. "Wasn't it Shakespeare that said *All the world's a stage, and all the men and women merely players?*"

A Shakespeare-quoting teen killer. Didn't have that on my bingo card.

"Who knows when we all step into our roles—it's probably different for everyone—but for me, it was pretty early. I can't remember a time when I didn't feel the pressure from my mom to be a superstar. Did you know she tried to call me Jaguar, so I'd be more like Tiger Woods?" He scoffed.

"I did hear that, yes."

"All I knew was my dad's a loser, at least according to my mom, she's in debt up to her eyeballs trying to look like we've got money, and her hopes are all riding on me. I couldn't let her down. She can be pretty intense, you know."

"Oh, I'm aware."

"I want my parents to be proud of me."

"Understandable. Every kid wants that."

"You don't get it! My mom can't afford college if I don't get a scholarship. And I *have* to get on the tour. I have to take care of her before she can't—"

"Before she can't what? Take care of herself? Jack, is your mom sick?"

His expression was stunned. "How did you…did she tell you?"

"I've been noticing she hasn't been herself lately. She hasn't been keeping up her hair and nails like she usually does, and there have been other signs. Dizziness, balance issues, hand tremors."

His expression was heavy with grief.

"Is it MS?"

He nodded, his mouth pulling at the corners.

"I'm so sorry. That must be so scary for you. Is that why you started taking steroids? Because you were worried that if you didn't become a pro golfer, you wouldn't be able to take care of her?" If I could keep him talking until Cole and Bianchi arrived, I'd have a chance of getting out of this ditch alive.

"Who else will do it if I can't? Not my dad. Ike approached me. I'd been dealing with golfer's elbow, and it had fu-uh, sorry, it had messed up my tournament play over the weekend."

Even while holding a gun on me, the kid wouldn't allow himself to curse in front of an adult.

"He says to me, *dude, I see you struggling. I got something for that.* I told him no way. I needed to stay clean because they do random tests. Not so much at the high school events, but I've been doing some Q-Schools to qualify for pro tournaments. Obviously, once I get to college, they test all the time. But Ike said he had this new stuff, kinda like the Clear, but no one is testing for this one yet. It's called Pellucid."

"Clever. Pellucid basically means clear."

His brow raised. "Right. I forgot you're a writer. You probably have a pretty good vocabulary."

"I can tell you do as well. You're a smart kid and a gifted athlete. Why are you throwing it all away?"

He reared his head back. "I'm protecting my future, and my mom's future, not throwing it away."

"What about Laveda?"

He rubbed the back of his neck with the hand that wasn't holding the gun. His expression was conflicted. "I didn't know what to do. I really did care about Lee, but she was gonna rat me out to Coach Barrett. I'd lose my chance at a scholarship, at the tour. She'd already told him that she thought our school had a juicing problem, but she promised if I quit, she wouldn't tell him I was one of the guys doing it."

"What happened that night, Jack?"

His face clouded over as he reflected. "We'd been arguing about it for a few days. I told her I'd quit taking it, but she'd already hinted something to Coach, so he was paying attention. I figured I was on his radar. He pulled her aside that night at 3F, and she supposedly tried to deflect the attention away from me. Told him there are plenty of guys doing it."

"Like Austin?"

He tilted his head. "You really are a pretty good investigator, ya know that? Yeah, so Austin was one of Ike's biggest customers. I don't think she named him specifically, but she gave him enough breadcrumbs to follow. I didn't know that, though. I thought she'd told him about me."

"So you gave her spiked Gatorade. What was in it? Rohypnol? I know Ike doesn't just sell PEDs, he also traffics in date rape drugs."

His face reddened. "I didn't lace her drink to…do that. No matter what you think of me, I would never do that."

Strange. The murderer, horrified at being called a rapist.

"Also, it wasn't Rohypnol. GHB is less likely to show up in standard tests. I just needed to buy myself some time. Anyway, we get in the car, and she's upset, because he wants her to give him names. He's doing the full court press, kind of threatening her future on the team if she doesn't tell him what he wants to know. That's when I realize she hasn't told him about me. But as we're driving and arguing, my glove box pops open. It's been doing that lately. I guess I need to replace the latch. She sees a bottle of Pellucid and goes nuts. Pulls out her phone and texts Coach that she's ready to name names. I grab her phone because he starts blowing it up, calling and texting. But by then, the sleepy-time drink has started to kick in. She couldn't keep her eyes open. I pulled off to the side of the road back there." He points over his shoulder. "I sat there and tried to figure out what to do. First thing, I smashed her phone and tossed it over the edge."

I looked around. In the dim light, it was difficult to see anything, much less a phone.

"If you find it, you can go ahead and toss that up to me as well."

Not a chance.

"Did you plan to kill her all along?"

"Of course not. I heard that GHB can affect your memory. I thought it might help me convince her she dreamed it or something."

"What changed? Why did you kill her?"

Where were Cole and Bianchi? They should have arrived already. Obviously, they didn't know I was being held at gunpoint at the bottom of a gully, but I had told Bianchi to hurry.

His expression was troubled. "I never meant to kill her. I just needed to stop her. After she was unconscious, Coach was still blowing up her phone, so I thought if I crashed the car, it would be a distraction. Everyone would be so focused on the accident; no one would be worried about the other thing. Including Coach. I had the idea to cut the steering lines and blame it on him, that way if he made any accusations against me, he'd have no credibility." His scowl deepened. "I didn't think the ditch was that deep, and I didn't realize she'd unbuckled her seatbelt. I thought she'd be banged up, but okay. I think I…I think I put too much stuff in her drink, too."

I believed him that he didn't mean to kill her. There was a grief behind his gaze that revealed itself for a moment every time he reflected back on that night. But something bothered me.

"If you didn't think the crash would kill her, why not stay in the car with her? More believable that way."

"Well, I couldn't stay in the car and risk serious injury. I have a tournament coming up, and lots of tour scouts will be there. How did you figure out I wasn't in the car, anyway?"

"It took me a bit to put it together. Today, as a matter of fact. The night of the accident I noticed you had what looked like road rash on your left arm. At first I chalked it up to maybe scrapes from the shrubs and branches. On some level, though, it had always bugged me that you had barely a scratch while Laveda died. Then I examined the skid marks more closely. They weren't braking skids. They were from acceleration."

"Hmm. Yeah. Didn't think about that. I stepped on the brake and the gas at the same time to get the tires going, and then I took my foot off the brake and hit the gas. I hadn't shut my door completely, so when we hit the edge, I rolled out onto the asphalt. It hurt worse than I'd expected."

Poor baby got a scrape. Meanwhile, he'd sent his girlfriend careening over an embankment and bashed his coach over the head with a golf club.

He nervously glanced over his shoulder. Was that the cavalry coming to save me?

"Enough talking," he said. "You got your answers." He waved the gun at me. "I need to get going. I have stuff going on today."

My murder was just an item on his to-do list.

I held my hands in front of my face, as if that would protect my head from a bullet. "Wait, what about Wylie?"

"What about him?"

"Why did you have to kill him? You'd already accused him of having an inappropriate relationship with Laveda, and he was the prime suspect in the accident." I hesitated. "Wylie wasn't really pursuing Laveda, was he?"

Once again, Jack glanced over his shoulder. "I'll give you the thirty-second version, but then we really need to get this over with."

"I'll take it." Hopefully, that thirty seconds would be the difference between life and death...on the side of life.

"First, no, Coach was straight as an arrow, but it was a believable story, and it was a good diversion. But that lawyer, Onyx Carpenter, hired was gonna get him off. I was sure of it. He wasn't going to jail for any of it, so eventually people would start looking in my direction, like you did. Coach texted me that afternoon, said he'd just received some startling information pertaining to me, and he wanted to meet someplace private. Of course, I knew what it was. He'd figured out somehow that I've been taking Pellucid. And if he'd figured that out, it wouldn't take him long to figure out why I was trying to set him up for Lee's death. He never saw it coming."

A chill ran down my arms, and I shivered. "I don't think that's the information he wanted to speak to you about."

He dipped his chin and gave me a skeptical look. "What do you mean?"

"Wylie learned something else about you that afternoon that had nothing to do with steroids or Laveda's death."

"Which was?"

"You're his son."

Chapter Thirty

Jack blinked several times. "Wh-what are you talking about? Wylie was my coach. Hank Dodd is my father."

"Hank Dodd raised you. Mostly. Wylie Barrett was your biological father."

He shook his head. "No. I don't believe you. My mom never dated my Coach. She was dating my dad back in high school and college. She would have never cheated on him, especially not with Coach."

"Uh, well, that's true. I don't believe Miranda ever slept with Wylie."

"Well, then what the hell are you talking about? You're not making any sense."

"I'm pretty sure your biological parents aren't Miranda and Hank Dodd. I believe you are the son of Onyx Carpenter and Wylie Barrett."

His laugh was unhinged. "Now you're just making stuff up."

"Son?" Hank appeared behind Jack.

Jack whirled to face the man he'd always believed was his father. "Dad? What are you doing here?" He hid the gun behind his back.

Hank peered down at me. "You okay down there, Audrey?"

"I've been better. Thanks for asking."

Hank turned to Jack. "Son, what are you doing? Put the gun down. Let this poor woman go. Think of your future."

"My future?" Jack's voice rose three octaves until it cracked. "My girlfriend is dead, my scholarship is in jeopardy, and now this bitch is spreading rumors that my entire life is a lie. Do you know what she said? She said you and Mom aren't my real parents. She said—get this—Onyx Carpenter and Coach

Barrett are my real parents." He scoffed.

Hank's expression was pinched with sadness. "She's telling the truth."

"You're lying!" Jack looked between us with wild eyes. "Why are you lying?"

Hank took a step toward Jack, who backed away and pulled the gun out from behind his back.

"Don't come near me. Why are you saying these things? You're my dad. I never believed Mom when she called you a loser. Why are you doing this to me?"

Hank slowly shook his head. "I'm not trying to hurt you, son. I'm trying to make things right."

Jack waved the gun at Hank. "Stop calling me son! You don't want to claim me, then fine! But don't call me son if you don't want to be my dad."

Hank held up his hands. "I will always be your dad. I was there when you took your first step. I was there when you said your first word. I was there when you took your first swing."

"And you were there when I was born, right? Right?!"

Once again, Hank shook his head. "Your mother was down in San Diego, going to school when you were born. She came home with you in May, claiming she'd been pregnant when she left, but she didn't know until she was already at school. The timing was right. It never occurred to me that you might not be mine. Might not be *Ours*."

"When did you figure it out?" I asked.

Both of them jerked their heads in my direction, like they'd forgotten I was even there.

Hank returned his attention to Jack. "Remember when your appendix ruptured when you were like seven or eight?"

"Of course. You and I were on that fishing trip in Montana with Gramps. We had to drive over an hour to find a hospital, and I remember every bump felt like my insides were exploding."

"Right. They did your blood type before they did the surgery. The nurse came back and said you're AB negative, one of the rarest blood types. I told her that couldn't be right. Both your mother—uh, Miranda—and I have type O positive blood. I said they had the wrong person's blood test. I was freaking out because I was convinced they'd made a mistake. I nearly checked you out of that hospital because I thought they were incompetent. The nurse just gave me a look of pity and said she'd have them run it again. Same result."

Jack stared at Hank. "So mom cheated on you after all. Maybe you're not my father, but she's still my mother."

For a third time, Hank shook his head. "I thought the same thing, so I googled it. There's no way for a mother with O-positive blood to have a baby with AB-negative blood type. I confronted her when she got to the hospital that night. She refused to answer. When we got home a few days later, I sat her down and she finally told me the whole story. She made me promise I'd take the secret to the grave. It was an easy promise to make. I didn't want to lose you."

I held my breath, awaiting the full revelation of how everything had come to pass. I'd begun to suspect the truth about Jack's parentage shortly after the news broke online about Onyx and Wylie's love child. Onyx had left in late August for Los Angeles, which would have meant her child likely would have been born sometime during the following spring. Jack was born in early May. His tan skin was closer in tone to Onyx than either Hank or Miranda. He was significantly taller than them, too, taking after Wylie.

"What did she say?" Jack's voice was barely above a whisper.

"She said that Onyx had shown up down at SDSU for a Halloween party and was puking before they'd even started drinking. Your, uh, Miranda confronted her about it, and she admitted she was about twelve weeks pregnant. Onyx didn't know what to do. She didn't want to come back to Chattertowne; she had big dreams. She also didn't want to...end the pregnancy. She'd decided she was going to give the baby—"

"Me. The baby is me." Jack practically growled the words.

"Yes. Onyx was going to give you up for adoption, but Miranda dreamed up a scheme to solve both of their problems. She wanted to get me back, and Onyx wanted to have a fresh start in L.A."

"How does that even work?" I asked. "There had to have been a birth certificate issued at the hospital where he was born."

"There was. That must be how the press found out. They bribed an admin person at the hospital to create a fake birth certificate listing Miranda as the birth mother with me as the father. I guess she still filed the legitimate certificate with the state that listed Wylie as your father and Onyx as your mother. It must have been her way of protecting herself from fraud claims. She could say Miranda falsified the documents, and she had filed the correct one."

Jack's shoulders slumped, and once again, I was able to muster some empathy for him. He wasn't a monster, even though he'd behaved like one recently. He was a kid who'd been lied to his whole life by those who were supposed to be his protectors from the ugliness of the world. A kid who never felt like he was enough, no matter how hard he tried. That didn't absolve him of his crimes. But I did feel sorry for him.

I'd have felt sorrier for him if he hadn't been holding a gun on me.

"So, it's true? Onyx is my...mother?"

"Your mother is the woman who has been there for you every day of your life. Not the selfish one who sacrificed her chance to take care of you so she could pursue fame and fortune."

"And coach." Horror washed across Jack's face. He'd killed his own father.

He dropped to his knees, still holding the gun at his side.

Panic arose within me. "Jack, please don't."

He tipped his head to look at me. His demeanor was cold. Lifeless. "Don't what?"

I didn't want to say anything that might put the thought of harming himself into his mind if he hadn't been thinking of it already. "Don't make things worse than they already are."

"How can they be any worse?"

He had a point. It was a terrible situation. He didn't have the cognitive development or life experience to know things could get worse or they could get better. When I was his age, I had trouble seeing past the moment I was in. The heartbreaks always felt permanent. Despair clouded the future to the point I couldn't imagine getting on the other side of it.

"Jack, no matter what, I'm your father and I love you."

Jack closed his eyes and hung his head. Shame radiated off of him in waves. "You don't know what I've done."

"I know about what Ike's been giving you."

Jack's eyes flew open, and he jerked his head to look at Hank. "You know about that?"

"Of course I do. You're my son."

"But…I'm not. Why do you care?"

"Jack, look at me."

Jack seemed unable to raise his gaze.

"Jack. Seriously. Look at me."

Slowly, Jack raised his head to look at Hank.

"You are my son, no matter what a DNA test says, no matter what blood type courses through your body. I haven't done much in my life that I'm proud of, but I have always been proud of being your dad. Now listen to me carefully. My job is to know what's going on with you. I noticed you haven't been the same lately. Short-tempered, poor impulse control. Out of character. I started looking for explanations. Drugs was my first concern. I followed you to see what you were up to, who you were meeting. It took me some time to figure out Ike was your supplier, and then once I did, what it was he was giving you."

I wanted to know how he figured it out, but the less attention I drew to myself, the better. As long as Jack was focused on what Hank was telling him, the less likely he was to start shooting at me.

Jack's voice was small. "He said it was safe. No side effects. Wouldn't show up in testing. I really need to do well in this next tournament."

"I figured as much. Back when I was in high school, there was a guy on the football team—Jason—who was dealing roids to a bunch of us. I got super ripped, started tearing it up on the field. But then I noticed I wasn't managing my emotions very well. I punched my bedroom wall. One time, your mom made me so mad I nearly…well, that was my wakeup call. I quit cold turkey."

Was Hank's steroid use the reason why he and Miranda never had any more children? Had the drugs rendered him infertile? I'd heard that was a possible side effect.

"Was that you following Onyx and me the other night after we saw you at Louden's?" I asked.

"Yeah," said Hank. "I've been stressed ever since I heard Onyx was coming back to town." He gave Jack a pleading look. "I was afraid that now that you're eighteen and on the come up as a golfer, that she'd tried to worm her way back into your life. It's been hard enough having Wylie as your coach. Sometimes you look just like him, and I was worried he'd see it in you. If he suspected, he never said anything to me or your mother. Although, how could he? He didn't know Onyx had been pregnant, and he believed you were Miranda's kid. He'd never slept with her, so how could he be her kid's father?"

"Still, why were you following us?" I pressed.

Hank bristled like he was a little perturbed about my line of questioning. "What difference does it make?"

I scowled at him.

"Answer her question." Jack's tone was dull. "She deserves to know the truth. Everyone deserves to know the truth." Jack appeared to be catatonic at this point. I was becoming less concerned about him shooting me and much more concerned about him shooting himself.

"Fine. After I saw Onyx in the bar with you and your sister, I decided I needed to know what she was up to. I was trying to get close enough to the two of you to hear your conversation, but when I did get close, Onyx sensed I was there. I heard her say she felt like you were being watched—which you were—but then she just talked about her husband and the hall of fame ceremony, so I figured she must not be here to stir things up."

"But you continued to follow me."

"I had to get back to the bar." He shrugged.

"Maybe, but you also ended up in Holden's back yard."

"True. I guess curiosity got the better of me."

At least I knew I wasn't simply imagining that I was hearing someone following me that night. "And the rock through my window. That was you as well?"

"Yes, the rock was me. I wanted you to leave Jack alone. He'd already been through so much, and you were harassing him and his mother."

There was no point in arguing with him. I glanced at Jack. He was still frozen in place. Was he having a psychological break with all of this new information dumped on him at once?

The gun began to slide from Jack's hand. Hank reached down and grabbed it from him.

A wave of relief washed over me, but that quickly returned to dread when Hank pointed the gun at me.

"What are you doing?" But the sinking feeling in my gut told me exactly what he was doing. He was a father protecting his son.

Hank ignored me and addressed Jack. "Get out of here. I'll take care of this."

Jack looked up at Hank, squinting. "What?"

"Go on. I've got this."

Jack glanced at me. "She knows everything."

"Don't you worry about that. No one needs to know you were ever here. I've got nothing to lose. You've got your whole life ahead of you. Your dad's gonna take care of everything."

I didn't like that. "The police are on their way, Hank."

"Sure they are."

Jack scrambled to his feet. "Dad, no."

Hank turned to face him. "You're my boy, and I would do anything for you. This is my chance to make up for all the ways I've failed you."

Jack started crying. "I love you, Dad."

Hank pulled him in for a hug, the gun still in his hand. "I love you more than you could ever know."

As touching as the scene was, I took the opportunity to slowly ease myself into a squatting position so I could grab a rock the size of a softball from the ground. Just to the left of it was a cell phone with a cracked screen. I left that where it was.

As I rose back to a standing position, Hank released Jack from the hug.

I held the rock behind me in my left hand. Not my dominant hand, but it would have to do. I couldn't risk switching hands without bringing attention to it.

A surprise attack was my best option.

"You did it on purpose." The words came out before I even thought about them.

Both Hank and Jack turned to look at me.

"What are you yapping about?" asked Hank.

"Jack, you purposely used a left-handed club against Wylie to divert attention toward Meacham, didn't you?"

Jack shrugged and wiped his eyes. "We're still doing this? Okay. Yeah. It helped that there were videos all over social media of him punching Coach with his left fist at the Hall of Fame thing. Gave me the idea."

"Enough. Jack's answered enough questions." Hank turned toward his son. "I mean it. Get out of here."

As Hank turned to face Jack, the gun rotated just enough so that it wasn't aimed directly at me. I took a deep inhale and prayed to the goddess of good aim and good luck (Tyche in Greek mythology or Fortuna in Roman myth, if memory served) and flung the rock in the direction of the gun.

Unfortunately—pun definitely intended—Fortuna did *not* smile upon me, and instead of knocking the gun out of Hank's hand, it grazed his kneecap. However, it was enough of a distraction for me to jump behind a tree.

Hank took a shot and a chunk out of the bark. Thankfully, he missed my upper arm by about three inches.

"Dad, stop! I don't want you to go to jail."

Hank responded to Jack's plea by taking another shot. This one whizzed past my head.

I heard grunting, as if there were a struggle. I peeked around the tree trunk and saw Jack wrestling with Hank over the gun.

Another shot rang out.

Then, silence.

Chapter Thirty-One

Despite the quiet, there was no way I was going to peek my head around the tree I was hiding behind again. Jack and Hank had fought over the gun, and I was pretty sure one of them had gotten shot in the process.

Since they both intended to shoot me, it didn't really matter which one was still standing.

Tires screeched and car doors slammed.

"Hands on your head! Now!"

I recognized Bianchi's voice, and relief flooded through me.

Still, I wasn't ready to reveal my position. Not until I was certain the situation was fully in hand.

Once again, Bianchi's voice boomed. "I need emergency services out at Devil's Elbow, near Harley Road. Two gunshot victims."

Two? With a single bullet?

"Hold that pressure right there," said Bianchi.

Someone groaned.

"Audrey?" It was Cole.

"I'm here. Behind a tree. Is it safe to come out?"

"It's safe."

I leaned just enough to catch a glimpse of him. He was crouched over someone with both hands pressing downward.

"You sure?"

"I'm sure." His expression was grim. He glanced at the figure beneath him." Can you tell me what happened? How did they both get shot?"

"Honestly, I have no idea. They were struggling, I think. I was hiding behind the tree. I only heard one single shot, other than the ones that he aimed at me."

"Jack?"

"Hank. Although Jack was the first one to pull a gun on me."

"Looks like Jack got the worst of it in the struggle. Gunshot to the abdomen." He jerked his head backward. "Hank was hit in the thigh."

"Any chance you can help me out of this pit? I'm feeling like the girl at the bottom of the hole in *The Silence of the Lambs*."

"I wish I could, but I need to keep pressure on Jack's wound. Bianchi's working on Hank."

The damsel in distress was going to have to rescue herself. I looked around for a tree root that seemed sturdy enough to hold my weight.

"Oh, wait. I think Laveda's phone is down here."

I scoured the area until I located the broken phone. Even though the screen was cracked, her screen saver lit up as soon as I pressed the side button. Impressive that it still had 6% battery left.

Although it looked more like a Picasso than an actual photo, I was able to make out that it was of a smiling Laveda and Jack.

Heartbreaking. So much unnecessary pain and loss. So much potential squandered.

Jack hadn't been able to see past the moment he was in to consider the consequences of his actions. Perhaps it was a side effect of the illicit steroids. His lawyer would certainly argue that…if he survived.

The pointless sadness of it all weighed heavy on my chest.

Distant sirens began to wail.

I slipped the phone in the back pocket of my jeans and gripped the tree root. Mud dug in under my fingernails. So much for my wedding manicure.

I positioned my right foot on the hillside. I glanced at Cole, who was watching me. "I'd prefer not to have an audience for this. There's a fifty percent chance I'm going to fall, and a hundred percent chance that even if I make it all the way up, it's gonna be ugly."

Cole's mouth held the hint of a smile as he turned away from me. "You can do this. I have faith in you."

I paused before making the climb. "That might be one of the nicest things you've ever said to me. Even if you don't mean it, thank you for saying it."

He looked at me again. "You think I don't mean it?"

No matter how much I scanned his face, it held not an ounce of mocking or sarcasm. He actually appeared to be hurt by my assertion, and it had me flummoxed.

I twirled my fingers to indicate for him to turn back around. "No watching."

He looked away once more.

While I wouldn't have called my ascent agile, even under the most generous of descriptions, I did make it to the top in one piece. A huge accomplishment.

Two ambulances, a fire truck, and three sheriff's cars arrived moments later.

Cole stepped away as the paramedics quickly began work on Jack, the more injured of the two. He turned toward me and immediately pulled me into a tight embrace. We stood that way for what felt like forever until he finally released me with one final squeeze of my arm.

"You okay?"

"Physically, yes."

He walked over to speak with a grief-stricken Hank, laid out on a gurney, as he observed the EMTs working on his son.

Hank had come there to rescue Jack, and instead, Jack had ended up on a gurney, fighting for his life.

Did Jack deserve it? That wasn't for me to say.

What motivated people to harm others wasn't always simple. I wished it were. I preferred to have a clear picture of the good guys and the bad guys. White hats and black hats.

Shades of gray had always left me feeling unsettled.

Like with the wedding I was about to be late for.

I still had complicated feelings about Vivienne marrying Lacey. Because my sister's happiness was important to me—probably more important than a good therapist would be comfortable with—I'd done my best to set aside those feelings.

Lacey had killed a man I had once cared deeply for. She'd had her reasons, but the why didn't matter to his widow and children. Their loss wasn't mitigated by excuses.

Jack had his reasons, but what difference did that make to Laveda's grieving parents, sibling, and grandmother?

Did those reasons justify taking two lives? Nearly a third, if I was included?

Cole walked over to me. "Hey."

"Hey."

"You seem to have a lot on your mind."

I gave a bitter laugh. "It's my face. It telegraphs everything."

"It tells me that you're troubled, but not particularly why."

I indicated the two men being loaded into ambulances. "Isn't that enough?"

He crossed his arms and rocked back on his heels. "It would be, sure, but I don't think that's all."

"Would it surprise you to know I'm contemplating the ideas of justice, forgiveness, and redemption?"

He gave a soft chuckle. "Not in the least. Your mind always seems to be processing something intense."

"Frankly, it's exhausting. I want to be the type of person who just goes with the flow."

His brow shot up. "Do you? Why?"

His question caught me off guard. "Because it seems easier."

He mulled that for a moment. "Maybe. Or maybe it's giving up. What would happen to salmon if they stopped swimming upstream? They'd go extinct."

"I suppose you're right."

"I am."

I slapped my back pocket. "Laveda's phone!" I pulled out the cracked phone and handed it to Cole. "Hopefully, this holds some of the answers to our questions."

He took the phone. "Good work. Now, don't you have a wedding to attend? I'd be happy to drive you."

"Don't I need to give my statement about what happened?"

"Eventually. Doesn't have to be this exact minute." He gestured toward two county deputies. "The sheriff is going to handle the investigation. Technically, we're in unincorporated Snohomish County, so this isn't my jurisdiction, but the two departments will work together on the case."

I gasped. "Ike! Someone needs to get Ike. He's been dealing drugs, everything from a designer performance enhancer to date rape drugs."

"I know. You told me in your voicemail. Officer Burton detained the suspect about twenty minutes ago."

"Ah, good ol' Billiam."

Cole shook his head. "Are you delaying your arrival at the country club for any particular reason?"

I sighed and made fish lips. "Maybe?"

"How about we talk about it on the way there?"

"Fine. I need to grab my phone and my dress from my car. Oh, my car. Maybe I should just follow you."

"I'll bring you back to get it later." He whistled at Bianchi. "We're headed to the wedding. You coming?"

Bianchi checked his watch, said something to one of the deputies standing near him, and jogged over to us. "We'd better get a move on. It's nearly three."

I grabbed my phone from the front seat, my dress from the back seat, and locked my car. I had more missed calls and texts than I'd ever had in my life—mostly from my mother and my sister—and I didn't want to return a single one.

As Cole raced into town, lights flashing, I sat in the back seat trying to mitigate the uproar that missing my hair appointment had caused. I sent a group text to the bridal party letting everyone know we were on our way. I didn't bother texting my father, who had a flip phone. Holden had texted me, asking if I was okay. I responded that I was alive. He sent back a thumbs-up emoji, which I took as a sign he was unhappy with me.

Bianchi turned in his seat to face me. "You know we're all in deep doodoo, right?"

"She'll get over it."

"Which one, Viv or Lacey?" he asked.

"Oh, definitely, Lacey, my sister can hold a grudge with the best of them. She may forgive me around the time they celebrate their twenty-fifth anniversary."

Bianchi chuckled as he turned forward-facing. "For a little thing, that sister of yours is quite a force to be reckoned wit'."

"I'm aware."

It was one of the things I admired most about her. And while she could hold a grudge, no doubt, she was also one of the most gracious people I'd ever known. She'd been trying for years to get me to stop beating myself up for her near-drowning incident as a toddler. She'd forgiven Lacey, even after Lacey had attempted to kidnap her and sail off into the sunset, rather than go to prison for murder. Vivienne had also waited for Lacey for nearly two years as she served her reduced sentence in lady jail.

If she was able to forgive Lacey, was it fair to hold on to my own grudge?

Ultimately, did it even matter what I thought, if Lacey made my sister happy?

Cole squealed into the parking lot of the country club like he was playing Grand Theft Auto.

"We're here."

"Let's get married." The words had flown out of my mouth before I realized how they sounded.

His reflection in the rearview mirror registered a combination of alarm and bemusement. "What?"

I slapped my hand to my lips and shook my head. "Not what I meant."

His eyes sparkled. "We can talk about that later."

And then he winked. He actually winked.

Bianchi grumbled something, exited the car, and ambled toward the entrance of the reception area.

I scrambled out of the car and slung my dress bag over my shoulder.

Cole looked me up and down. "Shoes?"

"Bottom of the bag."

CHAPTER THIRTY-ONE

"Clever." He clapped his hands. "Better get in there."

I took a step forward, and he placed a hand on my arm. I looked up at him.

"Everything okay?" I asked.

He narrowed his gaze. He opened his mouth and closed it again.

"What is it? You seem troubled."

He shook his head. "Save me a dance, will you?"

My breath caught in my chest. "Uh, yeah. Okay."

He gave me a curt nod. "Good luck. I'll see you in there."

I looked down at my arm, and his gaze followed.

Instead of jerking his hand away, he stared at it for a moment. And then he leveled his gaze at me and gave me a smile that made my knees nearly buckle.

Chapter Thirty-Two

The moment I walked into the dressing room, Vivienne burst into tears. "I know I should be mad at you right now, but mostly I'm just so relieved." She was still in her robe, but her hair and makeup had been meticulously styled.

I hugged her, careful to not muss her hair. "I'm so sorry. Don't cry. Your makeup looks so pretty."

"I know, right?"

I laughed. "Where's mom?"

"Probably writing you out of her will." She touched my hair. "Geez, Audrey, you could have at least washed it. Is that a pine needle?"

I felt for the needle and pulled it out. "I thought it would get done at the salon."

Rachel waved at me. "Come sit down. I have dry shampoo and a ton of hairspray. We'll get you fixed up in no time."

"Is Onyx not coming?"

Viv grimaced. "She and Meacham are headed to the airport. She decided her presence was too much of a distraction. She wanted this day to be all about Lacey and me."

It was surprisingly self-aware of her. And considerate. "You okay with that?"

"Absolutely. After everything that's happened, the only thing that is important to me right now is marrying Lacey. Now, if you hadn't been here, that would have been devastating."

"Hey, I climbed out of a ravine using tree roots like Tarzan. There was no way I was going to miss this ceremony."

Vivienne scrunched her nose. "We have a lot to talk about. Later. For now, let's get you camera-ready. There may still be a stray paparazzi lurking around."

* * *

Thirty-five minutes later, the next Masters champion had donned his prized green jacket, and Vivienne got into position next to my father.

The power had returned ten minutes earlier, allowing the frazzled wedding coordinator time to queue "Jesu, Joy of Man's Desiring" for the attendants' march down the aisle.

Understandably, there was no sign of Miranda. I assumed she was at the hospital with Jack.

The minister stood beneath the arch, covered in greenery and yellow roses. To his left stood a nervous Lacey. She wore a white tuxedo and kept yanking at the collar of her shirt.

First to walk the aisle were Rachel and Yellin. Rachel wheeled gracefully toward the makeshift altar with Yellin at her side. As they reached the arch, they went their separate ways.

I moved into position, and Holden slid next to me. He smelled like soap and sweet tobacco. His hair was still slightly damp, and his dark curls glistened. He took my arm, and a strange thing happened.

Or rather, didn't happen.

Nearly every other time he'd touched me, I'd felt a zap. A spark. A zing passing between us.

Not this time. Instead, it felt comforting and safe, but not electric.

I looked up at him. There was a sadness in his eyes that indicated he sensed it as well. Whatever chemistry we'd shared, it was no longer there.

"We're friends, right?" he whispered in my ear.

I smiled at him. "Always."

I looked forward and we began to walk. My mother watched us intently, probably both out of irritation over my tardiness, and also concern I might trip up the aisle. Not an unreasonable fear.

In the third row on the right side of the aisle, Cole had rotated to look at me.

His gaze shot straight through me, and I shivered.

Holden whispered, "If you're cold, you can borrow my jacket."

"No, I'm okay. Thanks, though."

"He's a good guy."

Startled by Holden's statement, I glanced up at him.

"It's okay," he said. "We're okay."

I returned my attention to Cole. He gave me an uncertain smile, and there it was. Zip, Spark. Zing.

I felt a smile spread across my face. I couldn't help it.

I was happy. For the first time in a long time, I was excited about my future.

A future I suspected might hold a kiss on the dance floor.

I tried to focus my attention straight ahead, but sensed Cole watching me from my periphery the whole way down.

When Holden and I separated, I took my place next to Rachel and waited for Vivienne to appear.

And when she did, the whole room gasped.

She was the most radiant bride any of us had ever seen. I'd known she would be, but she was even more spectacular than I'd imagined.

Draped in an ethereal ivory organza dress, with her champagne blonde pixie cut swathed in a wreath of baby's breath, she looked like an actual angel. Her high cheekbones were tinged pink with excitement, and her gold eyes sparkled with sheer joy.

The guests rose as Pachelbel's "Canon in D" began to play.

A whimper came from my left. I peered around the minister.

Lacey had tears streaming down her face, her body shuddering with quiet sobs as Vivienne made her way toward her.

The tough cop who'd been raised by another tough cop to stuff her feelings, the woman who'd seen the underbelly of society, both on the streets and behind bars, the cool, calm, and collected Lacey Kimball was so overcome by love for my sister and the magnitude of the moment that she was openly weeping.

Lacey didn't avert her gaze for even a second, and neither did Vivienne. It was as if all the rest of us were invisible.

It was one of the most beautiful and sacred moments I'd ever witnessed.

I wanted a love like that.

I didn't want convenient romance or leftover love.

I wanted the *everything else melts away as long as we're together* kind of love.

And I realized in that moment I was no longer willing to settle for anything less.

My father took Vivienne's right hand and placed it on top of Lacey's left. Then he squeezed them both.

My mother made a gurgling sound. She was a full-blown blubbering mess. My father sat next to her and put his arm around her. She leaned her head on his shoulder, and he kissed her forehead.

"Ladies and gentlemen," began the minister. "We have come here today to celebrate the union of Vivienne O'Connell and Lacey Kimball in marriage. The brides would like to thank everyone for coming, especially on such short notice, and particularly under the circumstances of the events that have transpired over the past week."

The audience murmured.

"Vivienne and Lacey would also like to acknowledge the absence of Wylie Barrett, who was supposed to be here with us today. We all grieve his loss and pray for his family and friends to find peace following his passing."

Another murmur. Yellin made the sign of the cross, followed by a double tap of her fingers on her lips, and then raised her hand in the air.

"They have written their own vows. Lacey, you're up first."

Vivienne turned to me and handed me her bouquet. She was smiling, but her eyes were filled with tears. I gave her my most reassuring smile in return. She turned to face Lacey, and they grasped each other's hands.

"Viv, from the moment I heard you sing at Nautilus, I knew you were someone I wanted in my life. The way you touched my soul with your voice and the emotion behind it, I was transfixed. But my life was complicated.

And I made a lot of mistakes. I'm so grateful to you for your forgiveness, for your love, for your willingness to stand by me and wait for me to come back to you. I never believed I deserved someone like you in my life. Every day from now on, I will strive to be a woman you are proud to call wife."

Vivienne brushed a tear from her cheek. "Lacey, you are the gift I never knew I wanted in my life. I certainly didn't see you coming." She laughed.

Lacey smiled, and the audience chuckled.

"With you, I never feel the need to pretend or perform. With you, I can always be myself. You make me feel seen and known in a way I'd never experienced before, and didn't even know was possible. You give grace when I fu-uh, when I mess up." She quickly glanced at our parents and giggled. "Sorry, Mom." She cleared her throat. "Lacey, I feel safe and secure with you, not just because you can bench press more than most men I know, but because you are always looking out for me. We've already weathered some of the most difficult times in our lives. There's nothing we can't survive as long as we are in it together."

Yellin let out a sob.

I didn't blame her. My face was wet with tears.

They exchanged rings, and the minister announced that they were married.

Lacey and Vivienne shared a beautiful kiss, and as I handed Viv her bouquet, I gave her a quick hug.

"I am so happy for you," I whispered.

She smiled through her tears. "Thanks. I am so happy for me too."

"Lacey and Vivienne would love for you to join them next door for the reception. I'm told there will be dancing!"

The opening trumpet fanfare strains of Mendelssohn's "Wedding March" began to play. Vivienne and Lacey looked at each other and smiled, and then turned back to the audience. Suddenly, Rick Astley's "Never Gonna Give You Up" blared through the speakers.

"You've just been rickrolled!" Vivienne pointed at the crowd.

Most laughed. My mother looked horrified. My father smiled as he shook his head.

The happy couple danced their way back up the aisle.

Holden looked at me and gave a quick nod. I stepped toward him and looped my arm in his. We shimmied and bebopped after Lacey and Vivienne.

When we got to the end of the aisle, Holden gave my arm a squeeze. "Be happy."

I laughed. "I'm gonna try. And I want you to be happy as well."

"I'm going to be just fine." He flashed his beautiful smile.

And once again, my heart didn't skip a beat.

* * *

The reception turned out to be one of the most fun I'd ever attended. Perhaps it was the relief from knowing a killer had been caught. Perhaps it was that the preceding week had been so stressful, the party allowed us all to let off a little steam.

Even straightlaced Tony Bianchi was having a good time spinning his wife Pia around the dance floor. They'd left the kids at home with a babysitter.

After about twenty minutes of photos, the brides had arrived at the reception for their first dance as a married couple.

When the song began, a couple people snickered—it was Nickelback, after all—but soon we were all mesmerized by their dance and the aura of love surrounding them. For the first time, the lyrics penetrated my heart, and I understood why they chose it. "Never Gonna Be Alone" was a song about making up for lost time, valuing each moment because the next isn't promised, but pledging that whatever comes next, whatever hardships, whatever challenges, they would be faced together.

Halfway through the song, Cole approached me. He held out his hand and I took it. He drew me to him. It felt both surreal and exactly right to be in his arms. I was also so nervous I had trouble looking him in the eye.

"I don't bite," he said.

That got my attention. "What?"

He smiled. "I was just trying to see if I could get you to look at me."

"It's hard to see you under that cowboy hat."

He took off his hat and placed it on my head.

"What do you think? Can I pull it off?"

A smile tugged at his straight mouth. "Not really, no."

"I didn't think so."

He looked down at me. "Actually, it's pretty cute. I just think you need a little practice wearing it."

"You gonna buy me own hat?"

"Maybe. I was thinking maybe you need some in-field training."

"What does that even mean?"

He looked at me for a moment. "I'm headed to Jackson Hole to see my parents next month. Wanna come with me?"

I gasped. "You…you want me to meet your parents?"

"Think you can behave?"

"Probably not."

"Good." And then he tipped the hat back just enough so that he could lean in and kiss me.

It was a sweet kiss, quick, but it held a world of possibilities.

I looked around to see if anyone had noticed.

Of course, they had. Perennially unlucky in love, Audrey O'Connell was in the middle of the dance floor kissing Chattertowne's police chief. An outsider, no less.

Bianchi gave an approving head nod. The brides wore broad smiles. Vivienne raised both her eyebrows suggestively, and I shook my head, laughing.

I didn't see Holden. Later, I learned he'd slipped out shortly after the ceremony.

By the time Vivienne had thrown her bouquet, and Lacey had thrown her corsage, Cole and I had danced everything from the Macarena to the Electric Slide and then some. All that time that he'd played it cool, he had a fun side waiting to reveal itself.

The last song of the night was "At Last" by Etta James, the first song Lacey had seen Vivienne perform at Nautilus. As the bridge began to play, Cole led me outside to the back patio overlooking the floating 18th green. The moon reflected off the water feature. We stood close, his arm around my shoulders.

"Are you cold?" He rubbed my upper arm.

"No, it's refreshing out here. That room is starting to get muggy."

"Your sister is married."

"She is."

"How do you feel about that?"

"Happy. And a little relieved."

"Maybe now you can focus on your own life."

Defensiveness rose within me, but fell just as quickly. It was true. I'd allowed my guilt over her near drowning to keep me from moving on. Vivienne had begged me to let it go, probably because I'd been a bit smothering in my protection of her over the years. She was a wild stallion, and I was the cattleman trying to rein her in.

I laughed.

"Did I say something funny?" he asked.

"No, I was just thinking about Viv, and somehow I managed to picture myself as a rancher trying to corral a bucking bronco. Your cowboy ways seem to have rubbed off on me."

"I can't wait to take you home. I think you're going to love it there."

"You know, I think you might be right."

"I believe that's the first time you've ever uttered those words."

"Don't get used to it."

He interrupted my laughter with another kiss.

Chapter Thirty-Three

Chattertowne Coastal Current
**Onyx Carpenter Bombshell Testimony at Dodd Trial, Case
is With the Jury**
By Audrey O'Connell

Snohomish County prosecutors credit Onyx Carpenter's testimony with providing valuable insight into the case against eighteen-year-old Jack Dodd for the murders of his girlfriend, sixteen year old Laveda Volkova, a native of Ukraine who immigrated to the area a few years earlier, and his golf coach, thirty-four year old Wiley Barrett of Chattertowne, WA.

Carpenter, a former resident of Chattertowne, now resides in Los Angeles with her husband, musician Meacham Fields. She testified that Dodd is her biological son, given up at birth and raised by Miranda Gadling Dodd and Hank Dodd. Carpenter didn't dispute the facts as presented by the prosecution but pleaded for leniency for the young man.

Carpenter, who had fled to an ashram in Calabasas with her husband following the murders, also testified that Barrett, one of the victims, was the defendant's biological father. Barrett was unaware of the connection until the day of his death. Dodd was unaware of his parentage at the time of the murders, discovering those facts just prior to his arrest.

Hank Dodd was charged with brandishing a firearm, unlawful use of a firearm, and false imprisonment in a related incident that ended with the shooting of both himself and his son. He will stand trial next month.

The case has made headlines throughout the world due to its celebrity connections and tragic story. Also testifying on behalf of the D.A.'s office was Laveda Volkova's mother, who aided police in unlocking her daughter's phone, a key piece of evidence elucidating Volkova's concerns that Jack Dodd was consuming off-market and illegal performance-enhancing drugs (PEDs) in pursuit of a professional golf career. Texts revealed she'd discussed the topic at length with Dodd, and had also mentioned it to Barrett, although she hadn't named Dodd in her correspondence with Barrett. Ike Askew, an employee of the Chattertowne Golf and Country Club, was arrested in April on charges of felony possession and distribution of class C drugs, including Pellucid and GHB.

According to prosecutors, Jack Dodd intentionally cut the power braking lines of his own vehicle to stage an accident at Devil's Elbow, a notoriously sharp curve on the outskirts of Chattertowne. The defendant allegedly drugged Volkova with GHB and then accelerated before jumping out at the last moment as the vehicle drove off the road and into the gully below with the victim inside. He then allegedly climbed back into the vehicle to give the appearance he'd been injured in the crash. Volkova died at the scene, having been ejected from the car on impact.

In order to cover up his crimes, Dodd then allegedly bludgeoned Barrett with a 9-iron golf club with the intention of framing Meacham Fields for the murder. It had been widely reported earlier that day that Barrett and Carpenter had been high school sweethearts, and a birth certificate obtained by a tabloid revealed they'd had a previously unknown son together. The day prior to Barrett's murder, Fields had assaulted Barrett at the Chattertowne

High School Hall of Fame induction ceremony for Carpenter.

Attorneys for Jack Dodd argued that side effects from taking Pellucid, a new synthetic PED, impaired the defendant's judgment. They also claimed Dodd believed Barrett was "grooming" Volkova for an inappropriate relationship, an allegation prosecutors called malicious and without foundation or substantiation.

Chattertowne's chief of police, Cole Loveland—who recently announced his candidacy for Snohomish County sheriff—and Sergeant Tony Bianchi are credited with solving the murders and arresting the defendant.

The case went to the jury at the end of the court session today and will resume first thing in the morning. Be sure to subscribe to the Coastal Current online for updates on this evolving story and other breaking news.

Acknowledgments

Thank you to all my friends and family who have supported me on the wild journey.

Special Shoutout to Shawn and Deb at Level Best Books.

Thank you to Dawn Dowdle for helping to make this series a reality. You are greatly missed.

Thank you to the readers and reviewers who have spent time with Audrey and friends.

About the Author

Kate B Jackson is an Agatha Award winner, an Anthony Award finalist, and a 2x Silver Falchion Award nominated author of mysteries for kids and grownups. When she's not writing about murder and Sasquatch, she enjoys unearthing family scandals under the guise of ancestry research. She lives in the Puget Sound region. Her husband and four grown children provide a constant source of laughter.

AUTHOR WEBSITE:
   https://kbjackson.com

SOCIAL MEDIA HANDLES:
   https://www.instagram.com/kbjacksonauthor/
   https://www.facebook.com/KBJacksonAuthor

Also by K.B. Jackson

Chattertowne Secrets Mysteries:
Secrets Don't Sink (2023)
Secrets in Pink (2024)

Cruising Sisters Mysteries (Tule):
Until Depths Do Us Part (2024)
A Matter of Life and Depths (2024)
Frightened to Depths (2025)

Sasquatch Hunters (Reycraft):
The Sasquatch of Hawthorne Elementary (2023)
The Sasquatch of Harriman Lake (2024)
The Big Grey Man of Ben MacDhui (2024)